I0548829

EDGING THROUGH THE DARKNESS

Sequel to *Crossing into the Mystic*

By DL KOONTZ

Brimstone Fiction

PRAISE FOR *EDGING THROUGH THE DARKNESS*

Edging through the Darkness by D.L.Koontz steadily builds the continuing story of Grace McKenna as she seeks the mystery of The Crossings. Just when I thought I knew where this story was leading, the author took a very, unexpected turn. The twists will surprise you much as the uncoiling of a snake, leaving you wondering just where the next move will head. You will hold your breath as the finale is revealed and leave you waiting anxiously for the next installment of this trilogy from an awesome author.

~ **D.L.Holliday**
Author of the "Farra Morgan" mystery series

Being a fan of Peretti and Dekker for years now, I am always on the lookout for Faith-based fiction that pushes beyond traditional genres into the realm of mystery, suspense and the supernatural. From the first page of *Crossing into the Mystic* I felt myself drawn into Grace McKenna's sometimes dark world of "subtle vision" and I was hooked! The first book left me fretting over the plight of our heroine so when the opportunity arose, I practically jumped at the chance to be one of the first to read *Edging through the Darkness*. Having waited almost a year for the next book in the series, I am pleased to say that D.L. Koontz does not disappoint with the sequel! I found *Edging through the Darkness* as much of an absorbing and fast-paced read as its predecessor. I was pulled even deeper into Grace's world of ghosts, angels and demons. Some of my questions were answered, a few more presented themselves along the way and I find myself salivating for the next in the series! Great Job D.L Koontz! *Edging through the Darkness* is everything you want in a good book: page turning suspense, a brave and stubborn heroine and a plot line that leaves you guessing until the end then wanting more! Do yourself a favor: snuggle up with this book on a cold night but make sure all the lights are on!

~ **L. Thornhill Crane**
Author of *Come to Me Like Rain* and *Tied to the Draw*

Edging through the Darkness has once again pulled me deep into Grace McKenna's world. As the story opens, Grace finds herself once again alone and drawn back into the spirit world. Without Will to guide her, she is still learning to use her subtle vision to help the souls she meets. *Edging through the Darkness* is a wonderful story of love, loss, and faith. The only downfall to this book is that it left me wanting the next book in the trilogy right now.

~ **Tamara D. Fickas**
Writer and blogger at Girls Night In,
the blog for single, over-40 women

How does D.L. Koontz weave a tale rife with souls who've left this earth that leads me to desire a deeper connection with the living souls I encounter every day? I don't know but she does. In reading this novel about resolving the issues of the dead, I found myself more committed to reconciliation and peace with the living. Oh, and I enjoyed escaping into an engaging story.

~ **Lori Stanley Roeleveld**
Author of *Running from a Crazy Man*
(and other adventures traveling with Jesus)

EDGING THROUGH THE DARKNESS BY DL KOONTZ
Published by Brimstone Fiction
1440 W. Taylor Street, Suite 449
Chicago, IL 60607

ISBN 978-1-946758-04-0

Copyright © 2017 by DL Koontz
Cover design by Goran Tomic
Cover image by LPC Media Group as licensed by Footage Firm, Inc.
Interior design by Karthick Srinivasan

Available in print from your local bookstore, online, or from the publisher at:
www.brimstonefiction.com

For more information on this book and the author visit: www.dlkoontz.com.

All rights reserved. Non-commercial interests may reproduce portions of this book without the express written permission of Brimstone Fiction, provided the text does not exceed 500 words. When reproducing text from this book, include the following credit line: "*Edging through the Darkness* by DL Koontz, published by Brimstone Fiction. Used by permission."

Commercial interests: No part of this publication may be reproduced in any form, stored in a retrieval system, or transmitted in any form by any means—electronic, photocopy, recording, or otherwise—without prior written permission of the publisher, except as provided by the United States of America copyright law.

This is a work of fiction. Names, characters, and incidents are all products of the author's imagination or are used for fictional purposes. Any mentioned brand names, places, and trademarks remain the property of their respective owners, bear no association with the author or the publisher, and are used for fictional purposes only. Brimstone Fiction may include ghosts, werewolves, witches, the undead, soothsayers, mythological creatures, theoretical science, fictional technology, and material which, though mentioned in Scripture, may be of a controversial nature within some religious circles.

All scripture quotations, unless otherwise indicated, are taken from the Holy Bible, New International Version®, NIV®. Copyright ©1973, 1978, 1984, 2011 by Biblica, Inc.TM Used by permission of Zondervan. All rights reserved worldwide. www.zondervan.com The "NIV" and "New International Version" are trademarks registered in the United States Patent and Trademark Office by Biblica, Inc.TM.

Brought to you by the creative team at Lighthouse Publishing of the Carolinas and Brimstone Fiction:
Rowena Kuo, Eddie Jones, Meaghan Burnett, and Brian Cross

Library of Congress Cataloging-in-Publication Data
Koontz, DL.
Edging through the Darkness/DL Koontz 1st ed.

Printed in the United States of America

Acknowledgments

The path from typing a story's first word to holding the finished book in hand can be both joyful and arduous, so I'm especially grateful for a host of amazing people who've provided love, encouragement, and prayer, many of whom make up the circle of my everyday.

To Joe and Matt for being my home.

To Megan whom I wish I could see more of, but I know that London is calling.

To Johanna for loving me, even though it began by loving my son.

To Danny for your enthusiasm and encouragement (and also for buying more copies of book #1 for friends and neighbors than anyone else!).

To several incredible friends and professional acquaintances who have the strongest and widest shoulders I've ever known: Leslie C., Cynthia P., Cynthia S., Beth C., Cheryl B., Todd B., Kathy G., Crissie P., Alden C., Meaghan B., and Michele H.

To my three "sisters": Brenda, Darlene, and Mandy.

To my family in The Light Brigade who share with me the ups and downs of this writing world.

To the staff at Lighthouse Publishing of the Carolinas and Brimstone Fiction: Rowena Kuo, Meaghan Burnett, Brian Cross, and Eddie Jones for their vision, expertise, and spot-on guidance.

Finally, and most assuredly, to God be the glory. John 7:18.

Dedication

To the men in my life: my husband, Joseph O. Roberson, and son, Matthew Koontz Traverso, for loving me and always believing in me.

Nothing makes a writer happier than learning that her work resonated with readers and, in many cases, stayed with them long after the book was closed. So this is for those hundreds of people who shared their personal accounts of the supernatural with me after reading the first book in this trilogy, *Crossing into the Mystic*. First, thank you for recognizing these books are works of pure fiction, nothing more. Second, my hats off to each of you brave enough to acknowledge both the limitations of our human understanding and the vastness of the unknown that exists beyond this physical world where God has temporarily placed us. Finally, thanks for your prodding that I "hurry up and finish book two.

We at Brimstone Fiction are pleased to bring you *Escaping from the Abyss*, the third book in The Crossing Series. In case you missed Book #1, *Crossing into the Mystic*, we offer the following overview of the key characters for your reading pleasure.

Grace MacKenna – Main character. Now 17 years old. Escaped an overbearing aunt in Boston to move into a remote mountainous West Virginia estate, *Crossings*, she inherited from her step-father Jack who, along with her mother and sister, were killed in a freak accident four years earlier. Due to her fragile emotions and heightened sensitivity to death, Grace develops "subtle vision" and is able to see and talk to the ghost of a Civil War hero (William Kavanaugh).

William Kavanaugh – Ghost at Crossings. Convinces Grace to solve his murder from 150+ years ago. Of course, he's suave, dashing, charming, and oh-so-mysterious.

Clay Baxter – Incredibly handsome guy from the local town of Williamsport. Four years older than Grace, good friend of Adriana, and former soldier in Afghanistan who suffered a war injury while saving others from an IED. Sparks fly between Grace and Clay, but —thanks to Grace's Aunt Tish—they may never be together.

Seth Rendale – Another handsome guy from Williamsport. Grace's age. He's adopted, a local sports star, and a diamond in the rough. Seth is determined to win Grace's heart away from Clay Baxter.

Adriana Barrone – Grace's friend in the local town of Williamsport. A music major in college, she dreams of becoming a concert flutist. Adriana is four years older than Grace. She wants nothing to do with ghosts. Michael catches her eye at the end of Book #1.

Michael Rosenburg – Grace's fun and jovial cousin from Boston. Eight years her senior. Son of Phil and Tish Rosenburg. He works as an engineer. Loves travel. Moves in with Grace at the end of Book #1. Is smitten with Adriana the moment they meet.

Braxton Hood, Asa Garrett, Jubal McClain and Fergus Lowe – Ghosts. All four were friends of William Kavanaugh during the 1860s and fought in the Civil War together. In Book #1, Grace promises Braxton's ghost to resolve his murder, but discovers that the evil ghost of Fergus may still dwell in her home. Meanwhile, Jubal—an ancestor to Grace's deceased step-father Jack—died a natural death years after the war. Asa helps Grace in her attempts to solve William's murder. But to do so, Grace had to spend a terrifying night on the Antietam Battlefield.

Cassie Baxter – Clay's mother and owner of the café, the *Time Out*. Cassie is single and never quite got over the abandonment of her husband (Clay's father), Mason. Cassie also has a daughter Reaghan, married to Sydney, and they have twin boys.

Holland Greer – Local historian with whom Grace has some rather uncomfortable encounters. He harbors secrets and is a little too interested in Grace, Crossings, and a gold coin in Grace's possession.

Gwendolyn Bealle – Local librarian and busybody. Has a brother, Benny, and an odd connection to shady character, Holland Greer.

Nidhi Michelson – Local bank manager. Has been kind to Grace.

Henry and Greasy Jim – Two nasty home invaders who break into Crossings, demanding to be shown where the gold allegedly is hidden. Will reveals himself for the first time in an effort to protect her.

Prologue

In my experience, death is never final, and good-bye is not forever.

The dead can return to life and occupy the same space as living beings, just on different planes. Sometimes inexplicable circumstances come together and open a door between the worlds, allowing living beings and the souls of the dead to interact.

But perhaps I'm getting ahead of myself. I should explain that not *all* souls remain behind; just those whose demise is unexpected, perhaps violent, as in a horrific fire or an accident.

Or, in my experience, *murder.*

I witnessed it first-hand. When I escaped Boston to move, alone, into *Crossings*, the house I inherited from my stepfather, I befriended the soul of William Kavanaugh, a handsome soldier from the Civil War. By the time my "subtle vision" matured, I could see Will just as he looked more than a hundred and fifty years ago when he walked the earth as a living being.

What's more astonishing is that I conversed with him. We spent many evenings discussing life, friends, pleasures …

… and murder.

You see, when there is enough energy to warrant it, ghosts can seem as solid as anyone. That can be good or bad news, depending upon the ghost—or "soul" as Will taught me to say—you encounter.

Okay, I must confess that I cared more for Will than mere friendship. Fact is, I loved him. At least, I loved him enough to let him go and isn't that the real test of unconditional love?

If so, then consider me twice blessed because I also fell in love with a living man, Clay Baxter. However, thanks to my obsession with helping Will, the tide of tolerance turned against me, and I had to let go of Clay, too.

But all this belongs to another memoir. What I want to share here are the tragic events that transpired in the weeks after Will and Clay left my life.

It was a time of incredible revelations as my subtle vision continued to mature. Chief among those revelations? That mankind lives in a physical, tangible, material world, but it is influenced by an invisible, intangible, spiritual world.

A pastor I befriended suggested that the ghosts I see may be angels and demons in disguise. As you can imagine, it's the demons that are concerning. They know where we are, but only a few of us with vision can discern where they are.

Sadly, those forthcoming weeks also became a time of mourning for us—"us" being my cousin and friends from the local town of Williamsport—because one of us all too soon would suffer a tragedy within the confines of *Crossings*.

But again, I'm ahead of myself. Let me first return to where I left off in my earlier account, the moment when my whole essence veered off course.

CHAPTER 1

"**M**s. MacKenna? Are you alright?"

From the ground where I'd fallen—a forested ravine near the C&O Canal towpath and the Potomac River—I stared at the soul talking to me. This *dead* man, whom I'd befriended, had just revealed that he was Clay's father.

Clay. *My* Clay. The man I loved!

This was his *dead* father. Standing there, not even two yards from me.

Clay thought his dad was alive. *Somewhere.* That he had abandoned his family years ago. Yet, here stood Mason ... no, wait, hadn't this man just reconfirmed his name was Jarrod? Heretofore, I'd only ever known him by the latter name.

I must be confused. Maybe dreaming.

But the hot August sun reached through the lacy leaves overhead, scorching my face, and I heaved in gasps of air made pungent by the scent of soil and leaves from the earth beneath me. My skin burned and my nostrils filled, helping me process my whereabouts and the reality of the figure that stood before me.

My head pounded. How could it hurt as though I'd been slammed with something monstrous and solid, when really I'd only been hit with new information?

"What ..." my voice sounded hoarse, so I tried again, "...what did you say?"

The soul—this ghost of a man that once was—tilted his head and furrowed his brow. *So humanlike.* "I asked if you were alright."

"Before that. Your name. You said your name." Was that irritation I heard in my voice? Or pleading? Perhaps both.

"Jarrod Baxter."

I shook my head and slapped the ground, agitation washing over me. "You said Jarrod Mason Baxter. Isn't that what you said?"

He leaned back. "Oh, I see. Yes, that's my full name. Does that matter?"

Does it matter? Does! It! Matter!

Yes, it matters. That name just caused my internal landscape to shift like an earthquake, a seismic wave rupturing geological faults as platelets of elation and shock crashed together. At its epicenter, pounded my heart.

"I take it you've heard of me as Mason Baxter? Around Williamsport, perhaps?"

When I offered no response, he continued.

"I was known by my middle name. My wife is Cassie and my children—"

"I've heard of you." I didn't want to hear him say Clay's name. Not yet.

Pushing to my hands and knees, I swayed upright and, feeling unsteady, backed up a step to press against the tree behind me, welcoming its solidness.

I breathed in more gulps of air like someone who struggled against drowning. *Get yourself together and get out of here.*

"That must be where I heard about you. Around Williamsport, I mean." My words came out rushed. Intense. I didn't sound convincing. At least, I wouldn't have believed me. I had to leave before I said something I'd regret. I needed time to think, to process this. To form a plan.

Then again, did I have time? Maybe if Clay knew this truth, he'd return, defy that restraining order between us. Come back to me, where I hoped he too wanted to be.

"Mr. Baxter, I'm sorry. I'm not feeling well. It's … it's not you. I've just gotta go."

I must have sounded like I was babbling, but it didn't matter because it got me out of there, and I found myself racing along the trail, tears blurring my way and thwarting every assurance that I was firmly on the trail, the threat of a plunge to the river below very real at spots.

A vision came to mind of me dangling from a cliff. Mason had both pushed me over the precipice *and* served as my life hold. Beneath me, in the canyon below, dangerously far down, stood Clay with open arms, unaware of what or who held me, yet encouraging me to let go and drop to him. But if I did, would he see his father's face and his reach for me falter?

★ ★ ★

When my entire family perished in a car accident years ago, I learned memory can dwell on what once was. I always thought that to be the most hurtful thing about loss.

Then I loved and lost Clay, and I learned that memory also can obsess on what might have been.

The week after Will moved on and Clay left town was the worst since my parents' death. I wandered around in a daze, feeling hollowed out, devoid of hope. Learning Mason's true identity should have given me hope and focus, but instead it further confused me. How should I handle such caustic information?

Fortunately, Michael moved into *Crossings* and kept me distracted. I also held a couple evening coffee klatches with Adriana and Clay's mother, Cassie, who owned the *Time Out,* a cafe in Williamsport, Maryland, the town just across the Potomac River from *Crossings* in Marlowe, West Virginia. Despite our age differences—I, still a teen, Adriana, now twenty-one, Cassie in her mid-forties—we bonded like best friends. Sure, we linked through our relationships with Clay, but the three of us just fit together too, like books in a library, shelved together by common subject but still individual and uniquely different from the other.

When Clay left the area under threat by my Aunt Tish of moving me back to Boston if he came near me, he'd settled in Lexington, Virginia, about three hours away, to attend law school. He may as well have moved to the South Pole because he let me know he loved me enough to *not* do anything to jeopardize my stay at *Crossings*, which meant not coming home, not writing, not texting, and not calling. Further, he told me to move on with my life. But how do you move forward when you're dwelling on something behind you?

When Michael moved in, he voiced interest in exploring the old house. I wasn't surprised. There's something magnetic about old buildings that draw people to them. What's more, at eight years my senior, he was a trained engineer with a Master's degree and planned to take his professional engineering exam soon. The logistician in him marveled several times that, age and creep factor aside, the house stood rock-solid despite being a century and a half old.

I bit my lip, wondering how to tell him that *Crossings* had not weathered and decayed because a ghost—*maybe two!*—had been living here for the past hundred and fifty years; that death kept the house intact. But he cut me off at the first mention of paranormal activity.

He pulsed a stopping hand. "Sis,"—that's what he called me despite us being cousins—"I don't need to know, and I don't want to know. I think I'll be a happier man if I just mind my own business on this ghoul stuff. As long as Dracula doesn't live here, I'll be fine."

Three days later, I arrived home to find him in the parlor of the old house, the room first entered when passing from the attached apartment. He'd pushed the antique piano aside and had set up a cot.

"But there's no electricity or air conditioning in there," I said while making dinner. I enjoyed cooking, and I loved my cousin, so the time we shared at dinner was special. I also delighted at having Michael with me after Clay and Will left, so I wanted him to feel as though he'd found a home here, too. "We can figure out sleeping arrangements in here. We just need to reconfigure the space."

"There's only one bedroom," he said while snacking on chicken bits he'd picked off the fajita pizza, "and we both need privacy. Besides, there's something intriguing about that old house. I want to get to know its bones."

A week later, he revealed a keen interest in going into the house's cellar. I grew concerned and insisted he stay on the main floor. "The place is too old," I argued. "You shouldn't go down into its foundation until experts investigate and deem it safe."

But he ignored my concern, and with each insistence, grew more adamant in his refusal. I combatted his obstinacy by calling in a carpenter to assess the house and get renovations underway.

After another week, I noticed a keen change in him. I can't pinpoint how or when it started, but it became more obvious as the days progressed. He was less able to relax and to focus as if he couldn't resolve some niggling thought on his mind. Even when we reclined by the television, I'd see his leg jiggle, his neck twitch, his hands shake.

At about that time, the carpenter left one day and never returned. My calls went unanswered, and I was left to wonder if something—or *someone*—spooked him. However, I plowed forward and procured a second carpenter.

Meanwhile, Michael began to display flu-like symptoms, and Seth—who spent more and more time with me these days—and I watched him suffer chills and severe headaches. He excused himself in the midst of at least two meals so he could retch.

My concerns kicked into overdrive when he took on an air of suspicion about everything and everyone, as if the trust he earlier offered so easily was gone. One evening, I came home from grocery shopping and heard him talking. Another voice responded. It was slow, raspy. I swear, the house was so secluded, you could hear hummingbird wings. I deposited the groceries on the counter and walked toward the door that adjoined the apartment to the house, expecting to see my cousin in conversation with one of the carpentry crew.

Michael fell silent as I entered the parlor. I was startled to find him alone, an open book about the Civil War on the desk in front of him. He didn't lift his head but darted his eyes up to level an intense glare at me and pulled his brows together, as if he suspected that I'd listened outside the door before entering.

In that moment, with no explanation in sight to account for the unfamiliar voice, a suspicion surfaced—one I'd forced into the farthest recesses of my mind: that we shared *Crossings* with a maniacal ghost and therefore, if what Adriana's pastor said proved true, a demon. A clever, diabolical demon named Fergus Lowe. The man who had killed Will more than a hundred and fifty years ago. The murderer whose soul I'd seen in the house once and had mistakenly thought it was Will in another form.

I steadied myself by holding the door and forced a casual tone in my voice. "You interested in the Civil War now, too?" When he didn't respond, I added, "I want to concentrate on that for my history degree."

He continued to stare.

"Did you know that both the Union and Confederate armies moved through this area many times? They might have set up camp around here. In fact, Winchester is only a half-hour away, and they changed sides seventy-six times during the war."

He remained still. Quiet. His stare pinned me to where I stood. After a few heartbeats, I took a deep breath and excused myself with some nonsense about having several tasks to do.

In between these bouts of odd behavior, Michael acted "normal" with us, particularly around the carpenters, and with Adriana who received most of his free time, from concerts at the Kennedy Center, to a Medieval Fair near Baltimore, to long drives through the Skyline Drive in the Blue Ridge Mountains.

The thing is, aside from my suspicions about Fergus, I didn't know what to think about Michael because such disturbing and erratic behavior wasn't new to me. I'd experienced a milder version of it for several years with his mother, my Aunt Tish. I believed sickness to be the cause of her mood swings, and now here I was again, watching and waiting in the same manner. Michael seemed to be changing before my eyes. I say, "seemed" because it wasn't consistent. Just when my worry would peak, he'd return to being the same Michael I had always known: carefree, joking, filled with laughter.

So I began to live with his volatile behavior, just as I had Aunt Tish.

★ ★ ★

One night, after I'd already grown concerned about Michael, I had a nightmare. I stood in a dark forest in a swirling mist. Huge black turkey buzzards hovered and swirled overhead.

In every direction, I saw dead, barren trees, with steaming goop draping like moss from their gnarled branches. Here and there, the same goop lay in patches beneath the trees and a creek bed, boiled and vaporized as it inched toward me. Somehow, I sensed I would be devoured if it touched me.

All around, in the trees, and reaching to the mountains in the horizon, roved an army of malformed demons. Thousands of them, some small, like dwarves and gargoyles, with humps and horns and claws; others much larger than humans, with misshapen, twisted, deformed bones.

Closer and off to my right hung a large bell. To its left, stood Will's murderer, Fergus. He looked down at Clay kneeling several yards away, bound and gagged, head angled upon a chopping block. A few feet away stood Seth, Will, and Will's wife, Naomi.

Fergus announced a vote as to whether Clay should live or die. If the bell rang, he would die.

Somehow in my panic, I counted on my vote, combined with those of Seth, Michael, and Will, outnumbering those of Fergus and Naomi. Clay would live!

But then, the voting started, and Michael voted for Clay to die. I looked at Seth, imploring him to cast a positive vote, but Fergus laughed and said Seth's vote no longer counted.

The bell started ringing incessantly.

I jolted awake like a frightened child, struggling to breathe, and realized that my phone was ringing. As I reached for it, I glanced for the familiar slice of light that glowed beneath the bathroom door, the comfort light I never turned off at night.

The call came from my childhood friend, Kate, who was involved in a student exchange program in France. She complained about that country. I listened: She hated how rude they were there to Americans, she was coming back to the states and not returning to college this fall, she was exploring careers and might join the military to follow in her father's footsteps, she misses him so much and can't believe he died in Iraq. And on and on.

Meanwhile, even though I thought I was awake, my mind visualized that hatchet dropping …

… and Kate's face misting into Clay's, and back and forth until I wasn't sure if the hatchet had fallen, or onto whom.

I never did go back to sleep that night.

★ ★ ★

Clay's departure several weeks earlier rendered the door wide open for Seth, and he happily walked through it. At first, I thought this would bode problems, so I made it clear how I felt about Clay.

Seth nodded and said, "I understand."

He continued asking me out, and I explained that I didn't want to mislead him.

He took my hand and said, "Let *me* worry about *my* feelings."

When he suggested a bike ride, I rolled my eyes. "Seth, you know my answer to that."

He frowned. "If you'd rather stay home alone than go out with a friend, then I respect that."

With that logic, I relented.

So, late one Saturday morning, Seth and I sat on the porch at *Crossings*, facing the long, rolling green lawn that sloped down to the Potomac River, lemonade in hand, our bike ride on the C & O Canal complete.

"You still miss him, don't you?"

Him? I must have appeared a million miles away because Seth's question startled me in its double precision about Will and Clay. I stopped the glider and studied him. There's no way he could know I spent countless nights sitting on this porch with Will discussing life, death, and all things in between, and that my thoughts had been there just now. I assumed he was referring to Clay. I searched his face for signs of rivalry, but instead saw concern, curiosity.

It hit me full-force how different Seth had become. Understanding. Kind. Patient. Wise. *Incredibly* wise. I looked at him across the four feet of distance between us and, instead of seeing the spoiled boy athlete I had come to know, I saw a mellow, big-hearted, young man.

I nodded, letting him conclude what he wished. "But, I'm enjoying this. Right here. Right now."

"Good deal." He gazed back toward the river. "It's especially beautiful today, eh?"

See what I mean? He could have jumped on my comment as being all about him, about us. But, instead, he opted to keep it casual, easy, attributing my comment to the overall nature of the day. The new Seth gave so generously and asked for little in return.

I leaned back, closed my eyes, and surrendered to the steady sound of the glider rocking on the wood porch. A few minutes passed before my stomach growled, and I invited Seth to eat lunch with me.

"Sounds good." He stood and offered me a hand. "I'm hungry, and it's kinda' tense at my house anyway, so the more I stay away, the better."

He'd alluded to this discomfort once before, but I'd been so lost in my own self-pity that I hadn't inquired further. It was time I reciprocated concern. "Come on. Let's talk about that while I make sandwiches."

Twenty minutes later, we finished our lunch, but not our conversation about his family. As it turns out, not everyone appreciated Seth's transformation in the past few weeks. In particular, his future plans were at issue with his father.

"Dad's angry I want to study medicine. He's demanding I major in athletics." Seth picked up our glasses and carried them to the dishwasher. "He said he won't pay for college if I choose medicine."

"You're serious?" I turned from the sink to see his face, to read his sincerity. I'd always thought most parents wanted their children to study medicine as opposed to *any* other major. "Why is it so important that you study athletics? He's a doctor, isn't he? I'd think he would want you to continue the family profession."

Seth nodded. "An anesthesiologist. But he loves pro football. He wants me to become a coach for a professional team someday. Make big bucks. Get free tickets for him. Rub elbows with stars. Stuff like that. He said then he'd be proud of me."

"I'm sorry." I wrestled with how to offer comfort without it sounding like pity. "I'm sure he'll be proud no matter what you do."

"It's not just that." He removed our plates from the table and stacked them on the bottom shelf of the dishwasher. A lock of sandy hair tumbled forward as he worked. "I told you I'm adopted, right? 'Course, Mom and Dad don't know that I know. I overheard my dad say so once … on the phone. That was kinda' weird."

"I bet."

"Anyway, it makes sense. I look different than my four sisters … they're all short with brown hair."

"Don't they remember how you came into the family?"

"They've never said anything. Besides, when I was born, they were only ages two through four. The twins were three, so I doubt they'd remember much about my arrival anyway."

He closed the dishwasher door, walked back to the table, parked in a chair, and stretched out his legs. "I've always been spoiled. I admit it. I've always gotten anything I wanted, thanks to my mom. I had an aunt that doted on me too when I was little, but she moved away, and we didn't hear from her anymore. Now my dad, that's a different story. He treats me differently than my sisters."

"How so?"

"He dotes on them. But he always puts conditions on me. As long as I do sports, and whatever he says, then I'm treated just fine, too." His tone held no sign of anger or complaint; rather, he sounded like he was sharing the results of an objective observation.

He stretched his arms and let his hands come to rest behind his head as though to support it. He looked so relaxed, as though the Red Sox dominated our conversation rather than the drama surrounding his birth. "You'd think that if someone went to all the trouble to adopt a child that they'd love him no matter what, wouldn't you?"

"Maybe fathers are just harder on their sons." I shrugged as I wiped the table. "You know, to make them stronger. Tougher."

"Maybe, but I don't think so." He sat forward, parked his elbows on his knees and dropped his chin onto his fists. He then struck me as restless, more agitated by the situation than what he admitted. "It's okay. I'll figure it out. Maybe I can get scholarships or grants."

"Maybe you could do both. Major in sports medicine or Phys Ed but take lots of biology so you could still get into medical school," I said, reminding myself of the always-chipper Adriana. "Maybe if you pursue both, your dad will help."

Seth shook his head. "I need to focus. I'm serious about medicine. When I was sick in the hospital and you put that gold coin on me, I knew something weird happened. It's almost like it fought some kind of demon inside." He tapped his chest once, his gaze locking onto my eyes. When he spoke again, his voice grew lower, his tone, serious. "That's what happened, isn't it? That coin had a spirit or a power in it that exorcised something out of me … didn't it?"

Before I could answer, he nodded and continued, as though he already grasped the answer. "How could I ever go through all that and not want to learn more? I want to study the effects of faith and miracles on healing. What role does divine intervention play? I want to learn as much as I can."

I didn't know what to say.

"And, I want to hear more about your ability to communicate with … the beyond. Grace, I won't give up on this until you share everything with me."

I nodded. It hit me that his interest in paranormal phenomenon was not born out of petty curiosity, but—like mine—out of hope. And that I needed more hope too. I was tired of being alone and on my own. Tired of keeping things to myself. Tired of living and breathing behind veils of secrecy.

If I wanted to change things, to stop feeling so alone, to figure all this out, I needed to let someone in.

I reached into the hip pocket of my biking shorts and pulled out the gold coin he'd referred to. "Okay," I said. I took his hand and placed the coin in his palm. "You hold this while I change into jeans. We'll walk Tramp to the river and talk about it."

His eyes grew wide as he cradled and studied the coin, as though it were a talisman to all the secrets of life.

★ ★ ★

You don't have to see things to believe them.

Take love, for example. Or the wind. You can't see it or touch it or hold it in your hand, yet most people have experienced it and know it is real.

Or faith. People with a faith in God can't grasp onto something to show their skeptical friends, yet they know their hearts have grasped onto something real and life-changing.

On the other hand, can you always believe what you see?

That's the question I wrestled with as I walked with Seth. The souls I'd encountered were real: Will, his wife Naomi, his friends Braxton and Asa, even Clay's father, Mason, and countless figures I'd seen, but never met, in the backdrop of my life. Yet I expected Seth to question my sanity.

We walked in silence, Tramp several yards ahead, vacuuming the ground with his nose. As we headed northeast toward the river, the Shenandoah Valley stretched south behind us. The land around *Crossings* looked like a rumpled sheet back-dropped by pillowed mountains, and I appreciated, yet again, how the rolling terrain and towering trees served to cocoon the property, making it feel private, even hidden away.

Seth remained quiet as we walked, as though he sensed that I wrestled to find the simplest words to explain a complicated topic.

I threw my hands up, frustrated. "It's going to take a while to explain this."

He smiled, undeterred. "I'm not going anywhere."

"You're going to think I'm crazy, or some nutty channeler of the dead."

"Try me." He turned to walk sideways a few paces, wiggling his fingers as though to encourage me to just get on with it.

"But it's so ... bizarre."

"I get that. Our own *Nightmare on Elm Street*. No problem."

I exhaled, and my shoulders slumped. "I can see and talk with the souls of the dead. You know, ghosts."

He stopped, so I did too. We had made it about halfway to the river, and we stood alone on the long, sloping stretch of lawn.

His eyes searched my face as though he expected me to say "gotcha."

The probing of his stare discomforted me, so I continued. "I befriended William Kavanaugh, a soul ... a ghost ... that lived in *Crossings,* and he dwelled in the coin when I placed it on you in the hospital. When you found me in Sharpsburg with Clay, your anger made you vulnerable to a demonic soul, and it entered and possessed your body. Do you remember—"

"Are you kidding? I remember feeling like I'd never be able to breathe again. Like something clawed at me from inside. And that was just the beginning of the weirdness."

I watched his face as he spoke. He looked calm, accepting, so I continued. "At the hospital, Will came out of the coin and removed the demonic soul from you."

I paused, figuring I better answer the dozens of doubtful questions he was sure to have before continuing. Instead, Seth surprised me.

"I knew it!" He jumped off the ground and swiped his fist through the air. "I knew it!" He ran his hands across his face, which by now sported the biggest grin I ever saw on him. He laughed, full, rich, and heady, then smacked his hands together and turned around, making me think that he'd done a similar routine on the football field when he scored a touchdown. "This is so awesome."

He grabbed my arms long enough to say, "Tell me more. No! Tell me everything. Wait! Let's sit by the river and talk. I want to hear every detail."

★ ★ ★

Perched beside Seth on rocks on the steep bank of the West Virginia side of the Potomac River, and looking across its wide expanse at Williamsport, Maryland on the opposite side, I explained my subtle vision and the many events that transpired after moving to *Crossings,* even describing how Will had ejected two home invaders, Henry and

Greasy Jim, who'd broken in and threatened me.

When I finished, I turned to him. "Wild, eh?"

He nodded, pulled the coin from his pocket, and focused his gaze on it. "Wild. Incredible. Amazing. Pick your adjective."

He stretched back on the rock, placed his left hand behind his head, and studied the coin in his right hand, the picture of a man relaxed, but full of contemplation. "I suspected most of what you said. I've been researching ghosts and energy, but most of it reads like nonsense."

"I read that stuff too. None of it sounds like what I've experienced."

"One theory that might explain what you see is matrixing. Our brains are wired to recognize shapes and patterns. It gives us the ability to create a familiar image or sound that would otherwise be unrecognizable or overwhelming. It helps us make sense of the unknown. We subconsciously do matrixing by attempting to find things we recognize in the things we see."

I thought about that a moment. "But, I didn't just see and hear. I interacted with souls too. How does matrixing account for that?"

He frowned. "You're right. It doesn't. We're predisposed to think that if there isn't scientific proof of something, then it doesn't exist. But I'm learning that science isn't always precise. Some things just can't be proven in a lab or explained away with a theory like matrixing."

"Adriana's pastor would agree," I said and watched him lean forward, a look of expectation on his face. "He suggested that if I encountered ghosts, they might be angels and demons in disguise." I kept my tone even, giving no sign of what the words summoned up in me. I still hadn't come to terms with the notion that the souls I saw could be demons. "He said he doesn't believe that the spirits of people who have died remain here. That if I saw a ghost, it was probably an angel or a demon, despite the form it took."

Seth uttered a sound that suggested this was heady information. "Pastor Dale said that? I like him. He's a sharp guy. Intuitive, ya' know? I'd take him at his word."

My mouth dropped open. "Sharp? How do you know? I thought you only went to church for the free meals."

He shrugged. "That was then. This is now."

"But I've never seen you there."

"That's because you don't go to the sunrise service. It's no big deal."

"It is a big deal." I hesitated, trying to choose the right words. "You've changed, Seth."

He nodded and looked away, as though embarrassed. "A nice way of saying I'm no longer a pompous jerk."

"I didn't mean—"

"It's okay." He smiled and made eye contact again. "I admit it. I was full of myself. I thought I could make a pit stop at college, grab a degree, and conquer the world. My self-importance was wrapped around what I planned to be, rather than what I was. Then, when I had that odd experience in the hospital, I saw what I really was." He closed his eyes and shook his head. "Look, we got sidetracked. You were talking about demons."

"Just that Pastor Dale said demons are evil spirit beings who were once angels but fell from righteousness when they became Satan's accomplices. He said they can be deceptive. Cunning. Masquerade themselves as whomever or whatever they wish. Scary stuff."

Seth puffed his cheeks out as he exhaled, and his forehead wrinkled, as though deep in thought. "So this coin, then, proved pivotal in protecting us both, assuming the pastor is right and that these ghosts are demons. I mean, if what you say is correct, then William Kavanaugh used it as a vessel to carry his energy, right?"

I nodded.

"But if demons can be cunning, how did you know you could trust him?"

I shrugged, feeling a little foolish and defensive for the trust I'd so naively bestowed to Will. "He guided me on a lot of things. Helped me understand. And he rescued you. What further proof did I need?"

"But, couldn't that be part of a deception, too?"

His question made me uncomfortable, and my stomach knotted. "Seth, what does it matter now? He's gone. He left without hurting me. There's our answer."

He studied me a moment, as though trying to determine how sure I actually was, then dropped his gaze to the coin. "Yeah, you're probably right. So be careful you keep this safe."

"For more reasons than one." I chuckled, but it sounded fake, nervous. "Holland Greer saw the coin once. In the *Time Out*. It was weird. He seemed familiar with it. And far too interested in me having possession of it."

"I've met him. At the library. He can be a little overbearing. What did he say to you?"

"He said fourteen-hundred and sixty of these coins were minted in Georgia. In 1856. They were uncirculated. Seven hundred and fifty of them disappeared soon after being minted. They've never resurfaced. That coin," I pointed to it, "is one of them. It's worth about $13,000."

He exhaled a whistle. "Times seven hundred forty-nine? That's what? More than ten million dollars out there somewhere."

"That's what Holland implied."

Seth studied the coin again then looked up. "What are these little grooves on the side?"

"Jack and Grandma Sadie had it attached to a chain. A small bracket gripped the sides to hold it."

"Doesn't sound very secure," he said. "You should have a hole drilled into it. Then string it on a chain. Wear it around your neck. You don't want to chance losing it."

"I'd like to secure it better, but I don't want to change it. Jack gave it to Grandma Sadie, and she gave it to me this way."

He frowned. "I get that. But she's gone now. It would hurt you more if you lost it." His voice softened, but his tone ripened with conviction as he continued. "Look forward, Grace, not back. Do it your way. Make it work for you. Protect it so you never lose it."

"But how? Where? I don't want to alert anyone around here to the fact that I have it. Any jeweler is going to recognize it as real gold ... a *lot* of real gold."

"Hmmm ... true." Seth twitched his jaw and looked back at the coin, his mind searching for an answer. "I've got it. A pawn shop. They buy and sell gold. We'll get out of this area. Head south to Martinsburg. I know a place. Went there years ago. It's a dive, but most pawn shops are familiar with stuff like this. And they don't ask many questions unless you're trying to get cash for an item. They'll probably be able to drill a hole in it without damaging it."

★ ★ ★

The *Risky Business Pawn Shop* sat on the fringe of Martinsburg's city limits. The wood houses and shops in this part of town looked shabbier than the brick and stucco buildings we passed downtown. Metal bars covered most of the dirty windows of the businesses; others were boarded over completely. The huge, sagging porches of the row houses hosted everything from rusty appliances to stained couches, to assorted spillover that didn't fit inside. Trash littered the street. Graffiti suggested a few things I'm too embarrassed to mention, and dogs snarled warnings from behind metal fences. I shot Seth a look that asked, "Are you serious?"

He shrugged. "I don't remember the area being this bad. There's the place."

He pointed to a shop on the opposite side of the street and steered his Mini Cooper into a tight U-turn, stopping near the front door. For the first time in my life, I wished a cop had witnessed that illegal activity; at least then I'd have rested a little easier about being in that neighborhood.

"Tell you what," Seth said, eyeing the shop and obviously finding it lacking. "Why don't you wait here with the doors locked while I go in and make sure the place is still open?"

"Open, or *safe*?" I admit—my tone had a bit of a smart aleck to it.

He grinned and patted my hand. "Let me scope it out to make sure it's safe for you to come in."

I nodded and handed him the coin.

Five minutes later, I grew tired of being the visual target of a grimy man across the street. He perched on a tattered chair, one I deduced to be the height of design in the '60s and filled his mouth with tobacco from one of those little round cans. I tolerated his first two spits into an orange bucket on the corner of the porch, but when he followed the third spit with a croaking cough that retched up something he wiped onto his ripped T-shirt, I gave up and decided I'd take my chances with the pawn shop. I climbed out of the car and hurried into the *Risky Business.*

The gloom and disarray of the street carried into the store. Bowed shelves lined the walls, supported by deteriorated dark paneling. Where there was no paneling, the molded drywall had warped away, revealing pipes and wiring.

Several glass cases, all smudged and dusty of course, housed items as disparate as watches, guns, and CDs. Logic and organization proved to be in short supply considering the presentation of the merchandise. The floors bore layers of grime, and a stained linen curtain blocked patrons' views from looking into the back. The aroma of cigarettes and cheap aftershave hung in the air.

Seth stood at a counter with his back to me. Across from him, a man leaned down, eyeing the coin with a tiny jeweler's magnifying glass. I took note of stringy, greasy hair.

Seth turned when he heard the door. "Tired of waiting?"

I'd almost reached him when the man behind the counter slowly straightened to see who entered.

That's when my heart stopped. I'm not sure when it started again. I'm sure it wasn't until after his eyes shot wide as walnuts and his cheek twitched, because when I saw awareness light his eyes, the fear hit me even harder.

I remembered this man all too well: those crooked sideburns, the yellow teeth that propped up a grin as he attacked Tramp with pepper spray, those weathered hands that held a knife to my throat and slapped me so hard I would have fallen if not for his grimy partner gripping my hands behind my back.

Greasy Jim! One of the two men who had invaded *Crossings* right after I moved in. Will had tossed him and his no-good partner over the porch railing in a violent rage.

"You okay?" Seth said, stepping toward me. "You look really pale."

This exchange must have given the man time to compose himself because he nodded his head toward the back room and said, "I'll git ma' tools." He licked his yellow teeth and glared at me a second longer, as though waiting for me to contradict his plans. Then he turned and bumped into a pile of boxes behind the counter before hurrying behind the curtain.

Seth snickered. "What's his problem?"

The question was rhetorical, but I had an answer.

"Seth!" I grabbed his arm. In a fearful whisper, I said, "Do you remember the story I told you about the two crooks who invaded my house the night I first saw Will?"

I could tell Seth sensed my urgency. His eyes searched my face for understanding. "Why?"

I jabbed my index finger toward the back room.

His eyes widened in sudden understanding.

"No way!" he said much too loudly, so I shushed him.

He gripped me by the shoulders and, in a hushed voice, said, "You're kidding, right? Okay, it's cool. Don't worry. You're fine. You're with me now." He talked to me but looked like he was plotting a million exit strategies in his head because his gaze searched wildly around the shop and outside the window, even as he continued to hold me in place.

Remember, just a few minutes earlier, I wondered, "Where's a cop when you need one?" Well, guess who walked through the door at that instant?

I swear my plea had come to life, accompanied by a comforting thought not to be afraid that whisked through my head. The uniformed officer looked just the way you'd want a cop to look when trouble found you—mid-thirties, built like a stalky, muscular bull, and exposing a gun strapped at his belt.

Before turning to peruse the items in the counter behind us, he grinned and shot me the oddest look, like he knew he'd entered the right place at the right time. He tipped his hat and said, "Afternoon." I glimpsed curly black hair, yellowish-brown eyes, and dimples.

Seth had let go of me when the cop walked through the door, but now he furrowed his brow, leaned closer, and whispered. "Do you know him?"

I shook my head.

If Greasy Jim looked uncomfortable before, he looked downright panicked when he emerged from behind the curtain and saw the cop. He hesitated, as though he hoped to figure out how to extricate himself from the premises. Obviously seeing no options, he continued. "Here." It came out like a squeak. He swallowed, and his Adam's apple bobbed, all the while darting his gaze between me and the cop. "Here," he said in a deeper voice and licked his teeth again.

His hands betrayed a slight tremor as he put the coin on the counter. A perfect hole had been drilled and polished near its top edge and a small gold O ring had been fished through to accommodate a chain. "That do it?"

Seth smiled and picked it up, looking as though he enjoyed Greasy Jim's discomfort. "That's great. What do we owe you?"

Greasy Jim stared at the back of the cop. "What? Oh. Nothin'. Just take it and go. And here." He leaned over to another counter and grabbed a gold chain off the top. "Take this." Then, despite the presence of the cop, he burrowed his gaze directly into my eyes and broke into a small crooked grin. "Wouldn't want ya' to lose it. Never know *where* you'd find another."

I registered the threat, his reminder that he believed more gold could be found at *Crossings*. Right before Will had removed him from my house, I swore to him I knew nothing about gold. That was true at the time. Now, here I stood in his shop, verifying that indeed I did have gold in my possession.

We left. As I climbed in the car, I breathed a sigh of relief but wondered if I'd maneuvered around a huge hurdle, just to hurry down a one-way street.

CHAPTER 2

Two weeks later

"That's it! I'm outta here!"

The voice sounded as much panicked as it did final, like it belonged to a man who'd found himself being attacked in the dark and could not see his assailants.

I hurried from the attached apartment into the foyer of the old estate in time to watch the burly carpenter unhook his tool belt and sling it over his shoulder. Michael stood nearby, a frown furrowing his brow.

The carpenter continued grousing as he lumbered about, collecting his things. "I can work 'round snakes. And Dobermans. And asbestos. Even smart-aleck homeowners. But not spooks. Or voodoo. Or whatever you got in this house!"

As he bent his substantial frame to snatch his toolbox, a screwdriver fell from his tool belt. He made no move to pick it up. "And if y'all had a lick of sense," he said as he hastened to the front door, "you'd leave too."

"What? No." Michael trailed behind him, hands outstretched, posturing the stance of reason. "The place is a hundred and sixty years old. It creaks. It's huge. It's—"

"Evil," the carpenter snapped as he whirled to face Michael. He stomped back two steps and tapped his index finger into my cousin's chest, the paunch of the carpenter's belly jiggling with each jab. "This house has evil in it. Mark my words. There's somethin' here. I can feel it." He paused long enough to swish his gaze from left to right, around the room, then looked back at Michael and jabbed two more times as he finished, "I'm leavin', and I ain't comin' back!"

He bolted to the door like a man retreating from battle.

With that, the third carpenter in more than a month of renovations hastened out of our lives.

The door slammed behind him and silence permeated the room. Even Seth and Adriana, who'd followed me into the spacious foyer, remained still. These two had witnessed the mounting problems regarding the renovation and our revolving door of carpenters. I wondered if the word "evil" reverberated through their minds like it did mine.

It was Labor Day weekend, and the four of us had returned to *Crossings* from an afternoon park festival. Michael had strolled into the old house to check on the carpenter while the three of us remained in the apartment to prepare snacks and queue the movie, preparing to share an afternoon of fun.

Instead, as we now stood in awkward silence, all we shared was tension.

Michael and I exchanged knowing glances, the unspoken message, twofold: (1) here we go again, and (2) do *not* say anything in front of Adriana.

Michael didn't have "subtle vision" or my insight into life after death, but he'd seen enough carpenters come and go to understand that *something* in the house frightened them away.

I hadn't yet figured out how to tell him my suspicions that we shared *Crossings* with Fergus Lowe. Besides, in Michael's volatile and temperamental state, I wasn't sure it would be wise to do so.

"So much for that," I said, picking up the abandoned screwdriver. "Maybe we need to rethink this whole renovation."

I walked to the front door and retrieved the skeleton key that had fallen off the wall when the door slammed shut. After rehanging the key, I turned to face the others.

As I opened my mouth, the wall behind them shimmered as if a burst of energy rippled through it. My words caught in my throat, and I swallowed them.

Fortunately, the others did not see it. There's no way I dared explain to them that I suspected paranormal activity.

Then again, it was *only* a shimmer, whereas ghosts manifested to me in full human form, and thanks to subtle vision, I could *see* them. Perhaps my eyes played tricks on me now. Either way, I must have looked confounded because a frowning Adriana stepped to my side.

"Don't stop," she said, rubbing a comforting circle between my shoulder blades. "You just need a carpenter who appreciates old houses. When you find the right one, he'll turn this place into a gorgeous mansion. Come on, let's go back to the apartment and continue celebrating your birthday. You've been seventeen for four days. That cake's long overdue."

Adriana, my dear friend, always made lemonade out of lemons.

"I agree with Ade," Seth said, stepping to my other side and squeezing my forearm. "We'll look online again. Find other carpenters in the area. Come on."

Despite my concern, I smiled at his comment. After being possessed by a ghost that summer, he'd become an avid student of healing and spirituality, and researching the answers to anything that perplexed him.

"You're right," I said, hoping to deflect the focus from me. Besides, I didn't want to stop the renovation. That and prepping for my homeschooling lessons kept my mind off Clay and Will and what to do about Mason. "We'll just keep searching." I looked at Michael for reassurance.

Instead, I glanced in time to see him shiver as though a cold draft wafted over him.

"You know, it's none of my business," Adriana said, stepping back and putting her hands on her hips as though she just got an idea, "but—"

"You're right." His tone harsh, Michael turned to face her, any sign of his easy-going demeanor replaced with an unyielding hardness. "It *is* none of your business."

Adriana stiffened as if hands gripped her shoulders from behind.

"Michael!" I admonished. This time, the knowing glances bounced between Seth and me. We'd discussed Michael's erratic behavior but continued to attribute it to all sorts of things: fatigue, stress, boredom, mold and mildew, flu.

Michael shifted to plant his legs wide, clenched his jaw, and puffed his chest with, I suspect, equal parts air and attitude. His eyes looked cold, hard, flinty.

A flush raced across Adriana's cheeks, and her chin dipped down. "It's okay, Grace," she said in a meek voice. "I should go anyway." Still, she glanced at Michael and hesitated.

The three of us didn't say a word as we waited for the tense moment to end, grasping at hope that he might ask her to stay.

That quickly, he quivered again and rubbed his forehead, his expression softening before our eyes. "No ... no, babe, stay. I'm ... sorry. I feel another one of those headaches coming on again." With his free hand, he reached for Adriana.

I exhaled, glad that he offered her the chance to restore the shreds of her dignity and any hopes for their blooming relationship.

But my concern for my cousin ripened anew.

★ ★ ★

An hour after the carpenter departed, the four of us relaxed with kale chips, cake, and a movie. Judging by the stilted exchange of mundane comments, I think it was safe to say that everyone plowed through the motions of *trying* to enjoy the afternoon, rather than actually succeeding.

If I were a betting person, I'd wager that Michael's thoughts involved a mix of renovation plans and what might be making him sick, that Seth scavenged his brain for a solution to securing a reliable carpenter, and that Adriana still licked her wound from the hurt that Michael inflicted. When I saw her reach for a second piece of cake, I confirmed my suspicion. Adriana's food cravings increased in parallel with Michael's moodiness.

"We have to get Internet out here," Seth said, interrupting my thoughts.

I cringed. Even after a month of hanging out together, I remained uncomfortable with his casual use of "we" needing to do anything, particularly at *Crossings*. I'd made it clear to him several times that we were not a *we*. Still, he chose to keep company with me, patiently waiting for me to discover, as he'd once said, how "perfect" he was for me.

Before I could respond to Seth, Michael laughed, his jovial demeanor restored. "Try convincing Grace of that. She's turned into a Civil War guru. They didn't have Internet in those days, so there's no need for it now." He leaned over and tousled my hair. "Isn't that right, Sis?"

I slapped him with my napkin and feigned a chuckle. "That's not true. I just want to follow the logical order of steps in fixing up this place. Besides, you have Internet at work, Michael. Why do we need it here?"

"So … you … can find … more … good recipes," Adriana said, licking her fork between words. "This cake is delicious."

I forced a smile. "I guess that's reason enough."

As Michael and Adriana launched a side conversation about particular dishes I'd made, I glanced at Seth to offer him a look that I hoped said, "It's okay, forget it." I could tell he regretted his comment the instant he had said it; with good cause too, given he already knew why I did not want more technology at the house.

The reason: Will had told me that technology could alter his source of energy. Seth *knew about*, but he didn't *comprehend* the deep loss I harbored from Will's departure. I had told him about my ability to communicate with ghosts, and that I didn't want technology to impair any potential contact with *good* souls. What's more, I didn't want technology to assist in stirring up any situations with *bad* souls.

Seth reached over and squeezed my hand. "Do it your way."

I nodded but looked back at my cousin, wondering if my concern about thwarting interaction with bad souls was already too late.

CHAPTER 3

After our movie ended, the group disbanded. Seth left to report for his volunteer assignment at the hospital. I felt like a third-wheel with Michael and Adriana, and I figured they needed time alone, so I walked Tramp, brushed Chubbs, and set out to visit Cassie at the *Time Out*. I intended to learn as much as I could about her husband, Mason, whom everyone believed had deserted his family years ago.

As I crossed over the Potomac River via the Cushwa Basin Bridge, my mind shifted from Mason to Braxton, Will's friend. I had promised Braxton that I would resolve his murder too, but I flinched at the thought of visiting him at the Antietam Battlefield again. To resolve his death would involve *watching* his murder, he said. The thought tied my stomach in knots.

No, Braxton would have to wait. By far, Mason merited first priority. I wanted ... no, *needed* to resolve his death, to set Clay free from the feelings of abandonment he'd assumed all these years. He needed to know that his father would never have left him willingly.

First, I had to prove it.

With this determination, I steered my car off the long bridge and into Williamsport. I'd grown attached to the town. Quaint and simple in a Norman Rockwell kind of way, its citizenry proved eclectic, from hard-scrapple farmers living on the outskirts, to commuting professionals from Washington, D.C. who wanted their investments in housing to buy them a little bit more.

Williamsport was large enough to have its own tourist attractions—the C&O Canal and several Civil War memorials—but small enough for rumors to cross the town in nanoseconds. And here I was, heading straight into the rumor mill. From what I'd experienced, both coffee *and* gossip brewed at the *Time Out.*

I hadn't seen Cassie or been in her café for a while, so finding it crammed with patrons startled me. Not only did people fill most of the tables and booths, but many stood in line at the counter as well. Despite the size of the town, the café looked as though most of the patrons could have been plunked into the shop fresh off a street in Manhattan. Several businessmen, ties loosened and jackets slung on their chairs, talked sports at a round table in front. A businesswoman, two booths away with sleeves rolled to her elbows, clacked hurriedly on her laptop. A young man and woman off to my left, sporting the bright-colored spandex of serious long-distance bikers, studied a map. A ponytailed teenager in the corner highlighted her textbook; Russian literature, I noted from the cover.

My mind conjured up the contrast of an empty café, as it was on the last day I spent with Clay. It was romantic. And beautiful. And perfect. Now, looking at the busyness, memories seemed to mock me of what once had been.

I scanned the place but didn't see Cassie. Behind the counter, stood a man I did not know, and Zebecca, Cassie's newest part-time employee and the daughter of one of her friends. A few weeks earlier, I met her at the music store where Adriana worked. Zebecca was fifteen years old but acted twelve, loving flamboyance, celebrities and *E!* television.

As I headed in her direction, two rail-thin guys in tight riding gear blocked my path. They studied the menu boards overhead.

"This place is pretty busy for being in Mayberry RFD," one biker said, laughing at his own joke. I detected a New York accent.

The other one nodded. "Do ya' think they know what espresso is here in the boonies?"

I smiled. These two were likely from the long line of hikers and bikers visiting from someplace more urban, generally strangers fresh off the Canal riding trail, determined to stretch and mainline caffeine, and filled with the pretentious notion that they had a deeper understanding of what made the world go 'round.

Skirting around them, I reached the counter in time to see both

Zebecca's pink-tinged ponytail and her massive hoop earrings bobble to and fro as she lugged a tray of dirty mugs through the swinging door in the back. I figured the cups were destined for the dishwasher and that she'd be right back, so I leaned against the counter to wait.

"What's your pleasure, young lady?"

The voice came from the man behind the counter. Handsome, late forties, with salt-and-pepper hair cut down to a buzz, he stood with both hands on the counter, arms flexed, as he waited for my response. That's when I noticed his muscular physique.

"Nothing, thanks. I'm looking for Cassie. I'm a friend."

"Aren't we all?" He laughed and dropped to rest his thick, hairy forearms on the counter. "She's out running right now. Getting ready for a 10K. Back in about an hour. I'm Lawrence Whitman," he said, standing again and thrusting a hand forward. "But call me Whit."

He had a firm grip. "Nice to meet you, Whit," I said and meant it. The guy appeared to enjoy himself behind the counter, and I thought his exuberance should be bottled. "I'm Grace MacKenna."

"Well, Grace MacKenna, you may as well drink something while you wait. How about a pumpkin-spiced latte? First of the season."

★ ★ ★

Five minutes later, I drank my latte while perched on a stool at the counter. Zebecca had returned, and between serving customers, she and Whit relayed his life story.

He retired from the Marines after spending years overseas—Germany and Italy—met Clay at Walter Reed Hospital during Clay's recuperation, and that led to a part-time job at Cassie's café. Until he could move into his own place, he rented the apartment over Cassie's garage.

"Clay used to live there, you know," Zebecca said as though she delivered new information to Whit, "until he had to leave because of—" She stopped mid-sentence as though it dawned on her who was listening.

Whit, who'd been busy filling sugar bowls as we talked, hadn't seen

Zebecca's panicked look.

"Because of what?" he urged. "You mean that romance that went south? Yeah, I heard about that. Poor kid. Deserved better. I guess we all get involved with the wrong person from time to time, eh?" He looked up at Zebecca, and I moved my gaze to my cup. She must have looked stricken because Whit said, "What? What'd I miss?"

"Nothing," I said, gazing back at Zebecca's flushed face and then to Whit. "It's okay. I'm the romance that went south."

"Oh. Well, color me red. Hey, sorry, little lady. Still learning the lay of the land here and who the players are."

I couldn't speak, so I nodded and offered a quarter-moon smile.

"Maybe you'll get back together, ya' know?" He shrugged. "You two are young. You never know—"

"Whit, isn't that your daughter?" Zebecca said, almost gushing, awkwardness forgotten.

Whit and I followed Zebecca's gaze to see a dark-haired young woman walk through the café door and proceed toward the counter. Even if she hadn't paraded the distance to us like a confident runway model, I think every man in the place still would have turned to stare at her.

Zebecca leaned in to whisper. "Isn't she amazing? She has the most incredible wardrobe, too. So cosmopolitan."

When the young woman reached the counter, she said, "Papà, zee shopping in dees area is ghastly. It's … è orribile …" She continued her complaint in Italian and brushed back long dark locks of thick hair as she spoke. I had to agree with Zebecca. The woman's olive complexion and her features all came together to produce one of the most attractive women I'd ever seen in person.

"Francesca, baby, you already know Zebecca," Whit said, ignoring her rant. He'd come out from behind the counter, put his arm around his daughter and turned her toward the two of us. "And this is Grace MacKenna, a friend of Cassie and Clay."

"Grace MacKenna," she repeated. A spark of recognition glittered in her eyes, and I wondered how she knew my name. Okay, I wondered *who* had mentioned my name to her—Cassie or Clay. She looked me over from head to toe, then back to head again, as though she rated me on some mysterious scale I wasn't familiar with. When she cocked her head and smiled one of those insincere social smiles we all try to master, I deduced that I scored rather low on her scale.

"Pleasure to meet you." I opted to be polite and climbed off my stool to offer eye contact. I had nothing against this woman. Perhaps my feelings of inadequacy were my own. I thought of Eleanor Roosevelt's famous quote: "No one can make you feel inferior without your permission." I decided I wouldn't give her permission.

Rather than return my greeting, she turned her back and grabbed her father's arm. "Papà! I need to speak with you. I need ze car, eh modo che io possa Visist l'..." From there she steered her father to the opposite end of the counter, all the while talking in Italian, so we watched them go. Whit shot back a look as though to say, "Sorry."

Zebecca waved her hands toward him. "It's fine! I've got it covered." Then she turned to me, eyebrows raised. "Wow, huh?"

I gave her a flat smile. "Yeah, wow."

"She just arrived in town last week."

"How long is she staying?"

Zebecca frowned. "Whit's not sure. He said she blows in with the wind. I'm not sure what that means, but I think he meant she kind of does whatever she wants."

"I would think that's probably what he meant."

"She lives in Rome. *Rome!* With her mother. Whit's ex. They met there, you know."

"No, I didn't know." I didn't know how to tell Zebecca I didn't care either.

Fortunately, a customer distracted her who also didn't care. He just wanted to place his order.

I sat back on my stool and checked my watch. Cassie wasn't due for another twenty-five minutes. I questioned my wisdom of waiting for her.

But what else could go wrong?

I had my answer in seconds when Clay's sister, Reaghan, walked through the door.

★ ★ ★

Huge from pregnancy, Reaghan walked straight to the counter, followed by her husband, Sidney, and her twin boys, Ethan and Elias. She held several files in the crook of her arm, and I remembered she worked as a bookkeeper and accountant by profession.

As this was the first time I'd seen Reaghan since Clay left the area, I braced myself for her anger, certain she would place blame on me.

Instead, she plopped the files on the counter and turned her gaze in Francesca's direction. "Look at her," she said to no one in particular. "She has more curves than a coiled snake. She makes Kim Kardashian look like a tomboy."

Zebecca, now behind the counter, looked up and beamed. "I know. Isn't she great?"

Reaghan looked at Zebecca with a frown. "Don't you have some work to do? I tend the books for Mom, so I know she's paying you to do something."

"Reaghan." Sidney admonished her in a gentle tone. I'd always liked him. He struck me as her polar opposite: calm to her storm, water to her fire. "Chill, hon. She's just visiting her father—"

"Who *also* should be working." Reaghan huffed and rolled her eyes.

Two of the stools beside me were now vacant, so Sidney helped the boys climb onto them. As he placed his order with Zebecca, Reaghan looked at me.

"Where's Mom?"

I suppose I should have been insulted that she didn't even say hello, but instead I relaxed, glad that I wasn't the target of her ire. "Mr. Whitman ... Whit ... said she's running."

Reaghan shook her head and looked up at the ceiling. "Of course, she is. She's always out running. She builds a kingdom here and then turns it over to teenie-boppers and a former jock. Amazing. If she'd pay more attention to this business, we could all retire happy."

Just when I thought she'd finished her rant, she turned her ire on me. "And you, Grace ... you and my brother better get things straightened out before that one," she said bobbing her head toward Francesca, "gets him into her clutches. She's a real piece of work."

I choked on my latte. Was she giving me an endorsement? Encouraging me to continue a relationship with her brother? The last time she and I talked, she dissuaded me from *ever* seeing him again. She as much as said I was the wrong kind of woman for him. Now I was the *right* kind?

"There's nothing I can do," I stammered. "The police ... my aunt Tish ... they—"

She exhaled an exasperated breath, shook her head, and dismissed me by turning to Sidney. "I'm taking these files back to the office. I'll be about ten minutes."

Sidney nodded his head. "We're good, honey. Take your time."

I doubted that Reaghan even heard his response. She turned and walked to the back, and I noticed patrons parting to give her a wide path. I wondered if her size made them move or the scowl on her face.

I looked back at Sidney with raised eyebrows, and he grinned and said, "Never a dull moment, eh? So how are you doing, Grace?"

Still reeling from Reaghan's conniption, I asked, "Is she okay?"

"Who? Reaghan?" He laughed. "Why do you ask?"

I shrugged. "Well, I haven't seen her since Clay left town. I figured she'd be mad. That she'd blame me. Now it turns out she's mad I'm *not* in his life."

"She did blame you for his leaving. But then the Italian bombshell stormed into town, and now she's grateful to you that he's gone. Reaghan could tell Francesca seemed interested in Clay and—"

"Clay met her? He was here?"

"Oh, yeah. Sorry about that." Sidney frowned. "He came back last week to move things out of his apartment. Whit's living there now. I'm sure if things were different he'd have—"

I made a dismissive gesture. "It's okay. I know." Despite Sidney's imposing physique—about six-five in height, broad shoulders, premature baldness—he oozed pure gentleness, so I recognized that he meant well.

"Anyway, Reaghan is concerned about Clay. She imagines him getting distracted by Francesca and moving to Italy … ah, maybe I should just shut up right now."

"Sidney, really, it's okay. How … how is he doing?"

"Good. Busy. Law school is a lot of work."

I nodded.

"How about you? You're homeschooling this year, right?" Sidney worked as a career counselor at the local community college, so his question didn't surprise me.

"I'll start sometime in the next two weeks. I can set my own schedule. I have all the books and course materials I need. It'll be a light load since I already finished most of my high school requirements back in Boston."

"That's good. I guess you'll use Internet for the lessons? If you need any of the resources at the college, let me know. I can arrange for a pass."

"Thanks. My cousin, Michael, is with me now, and he can sign the paperwork. If I need Internet, I'll use the WiFi here or the library or at the church. Pastor Dale said I could work in a quiet room there since the church is never locked." I shrugged and offered a weak smile. "I think he's kind of taken pity on me. We talk occasionally."

"Yeah, he's a good guy. I was going to offer my help, but it sounds like you've got everything lined up and ready to go.

"Well, there is one thing," I said, feeling awkward. "Michael isn't too reliable these days … you know, because of work. So, if I need an adult to sign off on anything…?"

"Just call me," he said. "I'd be happy to help. Besides, you'd be helping me. Reaghan is thinking about homeschooling the boys. Working with you would help me understand the process."

Elias looked up from his bagel. "I go to school," he said with a mouthful of food.

"Pre-school," Sidney clarified. "Half days."

"You do?" I couldn't help but grin at Elias's pride. "You must be a big boy now."

Ethan must have felt the pressure to garner equal attention because he chimed in too. "We're having twins."

I didn't want to hurt his feelings, but I wasn't sure what he meant. "You mean you *are* twins?"

He looked at his dad for help.

"No, he means we're *having* twins … *again*," Sidney said. "I guess you hadn't heard. Found out day before yesterday."

"You're having another set of twins?"

He smiled, nodding.

I missed a beat while that information sank in. "Are we happy about this?"

"We're not sure yet. I tend to take the attitude that it is what it is and that we'll figure it out as we go along. I do feel blessed. I mean, we're all healthy. Reaghan, on the other hand, is already panicking about how we'll pay for college. That's why she's so concerned about this place."

I looked around the café. "I bet she's glad Whit works here now. The place is busier than I've ever seen it."

"It is." He nodded. "But it's not because of him. Cassie's the creative genius. Despite paying no attention to the place, she's made it an inadvertent success."

★ ★ ★

Fifteen minutes later when Cassie arrived, I looked at her with new eyes—eyes that took in not just my friend, but also a sharp businesswoman.

Sidney spent that time explaining Cassie's "inadvertent success" with the *Time Out*. When Interstate 81 closed due to construction a few weeks earlier, traffic had been detoured onto Route 11, which ran right in front of the shop. Cassie stationed Zebecca along the road to distribute coupons to backed-up traffic. Meanwhile, Cassie escaped to the gym.

At another time, when Whit ordered what he thought were six donuts from a charity and they turned out to be six dozen, he called defeat, seeing no interest from the patrons. Cassie, on her way out to run, told him to cut them into quarters and scribbled a sign that read, "A quarter for a quarter." They sold out within the hour. Turns out, people wanted one tasty bite, but not an entire donut. Now the café made a profit on the effort each day.

Still another time, Cassie distributed "cupcake coupons" to children at nearby vacation camps. The next week, those same kids brought dozens of new parents into the café.

Finally, when the Chamber of Commerce held a training day, Cassie had Whit deliver free muffins and coffee, while she went running. The Chamber booked her for two other events.

"She was severely distraught when Mason left," Sidney said, sounding much like a trained counselor. "She's trying so hard to prove to herself that she can be attractive. Desirable to men again. That she can do something big with these marathons. Ironic thing is, she's already done something big with *this* business." He gestured around the café and shrugged before adding, "I guess it's human nature to sometimes pursue the wrong dream."

I suppose it's also human nature to read into people's remarks, because I wondered if Sidney hoped I would recognize Clay as a dream that I shouldn't pursue. Before I could sulk about it, Cassie appeared at my side, sporting a fresh apron.

★ ★ ★

I felt better for about five minutes—the time it took for her to hug her grandsons, determine that Whit and Zebecca had things covered and lead me to an empty table.

The savvy, focused businesswoman that Sidney had just described was anything but. As we moved through the crowd, she barely acknowledged patrons' greetings, ignored tables that needed to be bussed, and made it clear she didn't want to talk about Whit or Zebecca.

"Grace," she said as we tucked into our chairs, "I hear you and Seth are seein' a lot of each other these days."

So that's what bothered her. Her son had left the area because of me, and she had the impression that I already moved on to Seth?

"We're just friends. And Clay promised he'd come back. Is that what you're concerned about?"

She sighed and brushed a couple crumbs from the table. "I s'pose. I just can't stand anyone else leavin'. His bein' gone has just stirred up all those old feelings again. Of Mason leavin'. Guess I thought that when Clay came home from the service, he would stay here for good."

"Cassie, I begged him not to go."

"I know, hon. But he said one of you had to leave. Why does everyone think that leavin' is the answer?" She smacked her hand on the table before running it over her forehead.

I recognized frustration when I saw it. This was as much about her husband's supposed abandonment as it was about Clay. She needed to believe that Clay had a passion for the area that would always bring him home. I'd never thought you could see a broken heart, but here it sat before my eyes. I recognized it from my own experience of having lost my family. I was more determined than ever to resolve Mason's murder, but I needed to get some answers from her first.

"I don't know what else I can do about Clay. But, I want to ask you about—"

"Grace!"

I turned to see Adriana head toward me, her eyes swollen and red. She held her side as though it pained her. Before she said another word, I suspected, from the look on her face, that this involved Michael. With a sinking feeling, I wondered if things were now irreparably broken between them.

"What's the matter? What happened?" Cassie and I asked together as we parked her in a chair then sat beside her.

"Michael," she sobbed, "he's a crazy man. So violent! There was an intruder ... Michael beat him up ... and then we argued ... he was so mean. He pushed me! I don't *ever* want to see him again as long as I live."

Later, I would look back at that as the pivotal moment when everything in my life shifted. Resolving Mason's death moved from first to second place.

My plans, my priorities, my focus all changed because I stopped being afraid *for* my cousin and instead, like Adriana, became afraid *of* him.

CHAPTER 4

Adriana said that after I left *Crossings*, she and Michael watched another movie, a period film, set in the 1800s. When one of the characters lugged an old jug to a well, it reminded Michael of one he'd seen elsewhere in the house. He left to fetch it.

My pulse raced as I thought of where he'd seen the jug. "Did he go into the cellar?"

Both she and Cassie gave me a look that suggested my question smacked of being both ill-timed and unnecessary.

I mumbled, "Just wondered."

"Yes, he did, and he was gone a long time." Adriana sniffled and hiccupped. "I got concerned and headed into the old house, toward the cellar to find him. When I got halfway down the steps, I heard two voices. *Two*! Neither of them sounded like Michael. I got scared. I was afraid to move. Afraid they'd hear me. So I crouched down, and that's when I saw them through a partition. One *was* Michael! But it wasn't his voice. He sounded like someone else. It was so creepy! Everything he said came out like a snarl. I was so scared." She choked and grabbed a napkin from the metal dispenser and wiped her eyes.

"It's okay, hon," Cassie said, her voice soothing, but she hoisted her eyebrows and shot me a look that suggested she was taken aback by Adriana's story. "Just slow down. Take a deep breath."

Adriana continued. "The other guy must have broken into the house because Michael said something about trespassing and that he couldn't believe the guy was stupid enough to try again."

"Try again?" I said. "You mean to enter the house?"

Adriana shrugged. "I guess. Michael argued with the guy as though they knew each other. Even asked him where his sidekick Harry ... no,

Henry was. That's the word he used, sidekick.

I could feel the color drain from my face. My hands grew clammy. "What did this guy look like?"

Cassie scowled as though to say, "What does it matter?" but I ignored it. Truth is, I was almost undone by Adriana's pain and her tears, but more urgent matters trumped her hurt at the moment. "Ade, can you describe him?"

She sniffed. "I dunno ... mid-thirties, maybe. Tall. Real skinny. Ugly yellow teeth, grimy clothes. The oiliest hair I've ever seen. I remember because the light hit it and his red knife when he turned from Michael."

Oily hair. Red knife. Grungy. Skinny. A sidekick named Henry. *It had to be Greasy Jim!*

"Ade." I scooted to the edge of my seat, dropped my voice, and spoke in slow, purposeful delivery. "What did they say? Exactly? Can you tell me?"

"I don't know. It happened so quickly, and I was so scared. I think the guy said Harry ... no, Henry ... yeah, Henry was in prison. Then Michael's voice got even more ... horrible. I remember he hissed—"

"Hissed?" My breath caught on that word.

"Well yeah, cause that's what it sounded like. He said that if this other guy thought he would get a share of the bounty, he was sadly mistaken. The guy got mad and lunged at Michael with the knife. I think I screamed, and Michael jumped on top of him. He was so fast. I saw a snake move like that once at the National Zoo. It gave me nightmares afterward, and—"

"Ade," I said, in as calm a voice as I could muster, "what happened after Michael jumped on the guy?"

"He walloped him. Knocked him to the ground. I mean, he was like a wild man. No, more like an animal. I swear it was like he had claws or something. Then he started hitting the guy ... in the face again and again ... just kept pounding away. I was afraid he was going to kill the skinny guy, so I ran down the steps and tried to pull Michael off. That's when he cursed and shoved me. And I mean hard. I lost my balance and fell onto some wooden storage crates, then to the floor. And yet, when he saw me lying there hurt, I swear I saw remorse in his eyes. But something else too. He looked ... manic, furious. Like he was filled with rage but was trying to fight it." She broke off then, as if reliving the memory.

I took a deep breath. "What happened to the guy?"

"In that second when Michael looked at me, the guy moaned and tried to move. Michael stood and picked him up by his shoulders. I'd never seen anything like it. Like he had super-human strength. He threw the guy up the steps. All in one toss! The whole way up. Then he went up too. I scrambled after them. I was afraid Michael would kill the guy."

My shoulders threw back. "I don't think he would—"

"Grace." Cassie's icy, one-word admonishment shut me up.

Adriana sniffled and continued. "At the top of the steps, the guy tried to fight again and knocked Michael's glasses to the floor. Michael grabbed him, dragged him to the front door, put his foot against the guy's back and pushed. The guy flew through the air. I mean, he flew! At least as far as this place is long. Michael slammed the door shut and turned around to look at me. I was scared to death. He reminded me of a crazed person. But then he softened. Just like that." She snapped her fingers and hiccupped again. "He looked so pale and tired. Said his hand hurt and didn't know why! Can you believe that? He'd just beat some guy senseless, and he didn't even remember doing it. He said he was having trouble breathing. Like something scratched at him from the inside."

"What'd ya' do?" Cassie asked.

Adriana frowned, tilted her head, and wiped her eyes again. "I told him to stay away from me. That I never wanted to see him again. That we were through. Then I left as quickly as I could."

We watched Adriana calm and mellow as she finished her story. Cassie motioned toward the counter. Whit arrived and placed a glass of water and a piece of blueberry pie in front of Adriana. From the frown Cassie cast Whit, I could tell she'd meant for him to bring water and nothing else. She turned her focus back to our trio and patted Adriana's knee.

I felt like an odd-man-out, seated apart from their togetherness. Cassie was already upset with me, and now my best friend had been hurt because of my cousin.

"I'm sure he didn't mean to hurt you, Ade," I said. "You know he's normally a gentle person. He hasn't been himself lately. Come on, I'll go back with you and we'll—"

Cassie shot me a stern look, but Adriana's face downright chilled me. She looked so hurt, it hit me that forgiving Michael was way off in the distance if she ever cared enough to even try.

"No way," she said, wiping her eyes with one hand and shoveling a huge bite of pie into her mouth with the other. "I'm done with him. I told him I didn't want to see or hear from him anymore. No calls. No emails. No texts." She paused to stuff another bite into her mouth. "And Grace, if you have a lick of sense, you'll either kick him out or get him some help."

"What? I told you he's—"

"The point is, he's volatile," Cassie interrupted, her gaze burrowing into me. "Listen to what Adriana's saying. Watch your back. I have an extra room if you need it."

I opened my mouth to say that I thought Adriana was exaggerating, but I knew that wouldn't be well-received, so I said nothing.

Adriana continued, and I couldn't tell if she was talking to herself or us. "I should be in New York practicing for my concerts, and instead I drove the whole way home this weekend just to see him. I'm not sacrificing my dream for any man," she said with sudden chutzpah. Then, she turned to Cassie. "May I have another piece of pie?"

She was right of course. Not about the pie because it was obvious she used food for comfort, but rather about focusing on her career. She was finishing her senior year in music performance at the Conservatory of Music in Brooklyn and hoped to be a flutist for the National Symphony Orchestra in Washington D.C. Now wasn't the time to excuse herself from opportunities at college. Besides, she'd started dating Michael the same week that her former boyfriend, Darius, broke up with her. Cassie and I had been concerned that she had rebounded too quickly.

"You broke up with him? He heard and understands that?" For some reason, I needed that clarification again.

"Yep. We're done," she said. Her eyes looked cold and flinty one moment, but filled with tears the next. "He was so wonderful at first. I really started to care for him." She stuffed in the last piece of pie and said around a mouthful, "I'm going back to New York. Cassie, I'll call you. Grace, I'm sorry, but I don't want to see you or talk to you for a while. It would be too awkward since Michael lives with you."

I opened my mouth to argue, but Cassie spoke first.

"That's fine, hon. I'm sure Grace'll respect that." She threw me a look that said I had better respect it. "You just go on back to school now and heal. Move on. Focus on that flute. And Grace, watch your back."

An awkward silence fell, as if all the bonds that connected us had been severed.

Whit arrived with a second slice of pie and placed it in front of Adriana. Oblivious to the somberness of our table, he grinned and said with a wink, "Adriana, you sure can pack it away. Careful those jeans don't get too tight."

Adriana stood in a huff and tossed us a gruff, "Good-bye, I'm going back to school," and walked out. Cassie shot Whit one of those *did-you-really-just-say-that?* looks, shook her head and left the table. I slouched back in my chair.

Whit looked flummoxed. "What? What did I say?"

★ ★ ★

I remained at the table, alone, lost in thought. I'm not sure how long I sat there, but Cassie stayed busy behind the counter so long, I began to wonder if she was avoiding further conversation.

I nursed my latte and wondered what to do next. If what Adriana said was true, the way Michael had extricated Greasy Jim from *Crossings* sounded otherworldly and similar to the strength Will had displayed when he hurled the same man over the porch railing. What's more, the similarities between Adriana's descriptions and Seth's experience of being possessed by a demonic soul were too uncanny to ignore. No, their heads weren't spinning, and they didn't hurl green liquids like in the movie, *The Exorcist*. And their cars didn't soar through the air in a burst of flames like in *Carrie*. That was Hollywood's version of otherworldly weirdness;

this was real. Seth and Michael both voiced fear that they'd never be able to breathe again. Seth had used the words, "clawed at me from inside," and Adriana said that Michael complained that something "scratched at him from the inside." The phrasing struck me as too similar to deny.

My thoughts shifted to Mason. I wanted to help him because that might bring Clay back, but now I had no choice. I had to help Michael first. This meant accepting that he might be inhabited by a demonic soul.

Braxton had suggested that Fergus may be in the labyrinth of tunnels that lead from the cellar of the house to the root cellar on the other side of the hill. He said Fergus could be dangerous but would probably limit his movements to the underground area. I needed to know more about Fergus and those tunnels. But, how could I solicit answers from Braxton without helping him in return?

What's more, I'd have to visit Braxton as soon as possible. With a sigh, I shifted my gaze to my left where a mirror hung. Feeling tired and defeated, I expected to see myself looking 117 years old, rather than the 17 I'd just become.

Instead, I saw Will's face.

Right there, staring back at me. My heart raced, despite recognizing the moment as a daydream. As I stared, his face morphed into Kate's. Was I tired, or losing my mind? My thoughts wandered back to the nightmare in which Michael voted against Clay, assuring his death. Kate had called then, waking me from that dream.

With a start, I heard my cell phone ring. I looked at the incoming number. It couldn't be ... could it?

"Kate," I said. "It's great to hear from you again."

"Grace! I'm in the states. It took longer than I thought because I came back on a cruise ship rather than flying. It was awesome. Happy birthday! I can't wait to see you! I'll be there in a day or two."

"You ... you're coming here? But what about your mom? And school?"

"Silly," she laughed, and I could almost see her shaking her head at me. "We talked about this a couple weeks ago. Honestly, Grace, weren't you listening? I'm not going back to Boston. After Europe, who could return to that boring high school? Ick."

"But what about your education?"

"I'm either going to start late at a private school near my sister in Richmond or get my GED and start college in January. Don't you remember me telling you?"

Too embarrassed to admit that I did not, I ignored her question. "You're always welcome. You know that."

"Great. I have your address, so I'll find you. Gotta' go. I'm so tired. See you soon."

I stared at my phone a moment after clicking off the call, wondering if I dare call her back to reschedule. Then again, perhaps her peppiness would provide some relief. Kate was carefree and happy-go-lucky in ways that I never could be. Besides, she'd understand if I had to excuse myself to tend to personal matters. Best to let her visit. Maybe she could be a good influence on Michael.

With my mind back on my cousin, I decided to talk to Holland Greer to learn more about the tunnels. I knew of no one else who might have knowledge of their specifics. But where to find him?

The phone book, of course. His address and phone number might be listed.

That's how it came to be, minutes later that I found myself staring at Clay's name and address. When I asked Cassie to borrow her phone book, she pointed me to the café office. At her desk, I reached for a tablet on which I planned to write the address. And there it was. Right on top: Clay's name, penned in Cassie's writing. Beneath it, an address in Lexington. 17201 White Street. The address etched into my brain.

As it turns out, Holland's name was unlisted. So, I used the search engine on my cell phone. The result: no address or phone number, just a P.O box for professional work. I decided to check at the library. He often lectured there. The library employees would have to know how to contact him. However, the library was closed on Sundays. I'd have to wait until morning.

I ran my fingers over Clay's address one more time—17201 White Street—and left the office.

CHAPTER 5

The next morning, everything seemed peaceful. I awoke to a cloudless sky and discovered Michael had already gone to work. He'd been asleep when I returned home the night before, so I was spared from discussing the last afternoon's events. In the calm of the morning, I almost allowed myself to be fooled into believing that all boded well in *Crossings*, but I knew otherwise, so I walked Tramp, showered, and headed to the library.

Williamsport sits on a series of rolling hills that rise from the Potomac River and flatten out as the land stretches north and east. The library, likewise, perched on a hill, making it look like more of a low-slung structure than a two-story building. With a red brick, flat institutional dullness, it didn't seem to fit in the quaint downtown.

During my drive, I kept hoping Ms. Bealle, the head librarian, would not be at work. She had a way of making me feel out of sorts like I'd wrecked and washed up on the wrong shore. Would it be too much to ask that Emil or Denita, whom I'd also met in the past few weeks, be on duty at the front desk?

Apparently it was too much to ask.

As soon as I stepped inside, I encountered Ms. Bealle, a short wisp of a woman in her 60s, with pinched features and gold-rimmed spectacles perched halfway down her nose. When I say I "encountered" her, I mean that I heard her before I saw her. Her trademark clackity layer of bracelets announced her location. I often pictured her as smugly exerting her control over library patrons with those orbs around her wrist; she would tolerate no loud talking, even honored it herself but relished the clanging of her own jewelry.

As I approached the desk, I decided to be direct.

"Ms. Bealle, I'd like to get in touch with Holland Greer. Can you help me find his phone number?"

She sat behind a large stack of books that, from their location on the lengthy counter, suggested they had been returned but not yet logged in. From the way she studied each book, then made notes on a ledger to her right, I surmised she worked to change their status by hand, ignoring the barcode scanner that sat to her left.

I wasn't surprised that she would *not* give me priority over her task, but I was surprised that she didn't even raise her head to talk with me. Instead, her brows arched, and she inched her gaze up to meet mine, peering at me over the tops of her glasses. Her eyes bore a cold brilliance that made me feel like a suspect under interrogation.

"What is this about?"

Her brazen question startled me, and I considered responding that it wasn't any of her business, but I figured that would get me nowhere. Plus, there was no point in me being rude, too. The first time I'd met Gwendolyn Bealle, I developed the impression she was enamored with Holland Greer. Her behavior now—the curiosity, the protectiveness— further confirmed my hunch.

"I have questions about the history of the area. I thought he might know the answers."

She finished logging the book in her hand, set it aside, and lifted her head to meet my gaze. "He does not take phone calls from teenagers, nor does he receive visitors. He is an intensely private man." She said the last three words with added emphasis. Reaching for another book, she continued, "If you have a little school project, I suggest you just leave it for him. He's here a few times a week conducting research. I'll be sure he gets the message."

I considered that a moment. Clearly I would not get his number from her although she surely had it for coordinating library events. And, I didn't want to hang out at the library, waiting for him to show up. The only option left involved going to his house. I loathed the thought of paying him a personal visit, but I had no choice. I needed his help. *Now.*

I removed a pen and paper from my backpack and, in a more chipper voice, said, "You know what? I'll just drop the questions in the mail. As head librarian, you have his address, right?"

She froze, and the color drained from her face. I sensed she knew I'd caught her. Not to share his address would reveal too strong of a personal interest or protectiveness of the man.

"Yes, fine," she said with a sigh as she straightened her back and added a dose of superiority to her tone. "It's 4125 Scratch Gravel Road, Williamsport."

I held back a snicker, but I'm sure she saw my lips form a smile before I could squelch it. I found it amusing that she recalled his address so easily, but she must have thought I was reacting to the oddity of it.

"The name of the road has nothing to do with the man, Ms. MacKenna," she said, a lecturing tone in her voice. "The road is west of town, near the quarry, so there is gravel everywhere ..." she continued, flailing her hand randomly, "... down his lane, around his shed, even right up to his front door. It's quite annoying and sticks to my shoes when—"

She hitched her breath as though catching herself for saying too much.

I'd gotten what I wanted, so I pretended not to notice.

"Thank you, Ms. Bealle. I need to check my email now," I said and headed toward the computer room in the basement.

As I walked away, I focused on two bits of knowledge I'd just gleaned: one, Holland Greer may not accept visitors, but Gwendolyn Bealle had sure been to his place before, and two, Ms. Bealle used my name. As far as I recalled, my name had been placed before her only once, about six weeks ago, when I'd checked out two books about the Civil War.

Was her memory that good?

Or, had Holland discussed me?

★ ★ ★

The computer room sat at the end of the hallway in the library's lower level. To the left and right off the wide corridor sat small meeting rooms, a lecture hall, and a unisex bathroom.

I checked a few emails in rapid succession. I was such a poor communicator on the web lately that I guess friends back in Boston gave up on me. I didn't bother looking at Facebook or Twitter. Social networking didn't interest me these days. Besides, what I needed to know, I could read easily enough on my cell phone.

I logged into a map site and downloaded directions to Holland Greer's house. It would take less than ten minutes to drive there.

Then, because I couldn't stop myself, I typed Clay's address into the search engine. The results said he lived three hours and twelve minutes away. With a shaky hand, I hit the print button on those directions too. I'm not sure why. I wouldn't be welcome there. But just knowing how to get to his place made me feel closer to him.

I stuffed the papers into my backpack and stood to go, but my body began to shake and dropped back into the seat. The tingling spread across my shoulders then traveled down my arms, producing tiny goose pimples. Tucking my shaking hands under my elbows, I waited until the sensation ended. It felt so familiar. Clearly, it was hunger striking because I hadn't eaten in a while. I decided to get a burger at a fast food restaurant on my way to Holland's house.

The hallway was quiet as I headed toward the stairway. It flashed through my mind that Ms. Bealle would be happy about that.

As I neared the last room on the right, the door drifted open, as though someone controlled its movement. I looked inside, as anyone would, given that there was nothing else to see in the expanse of hallway. I saw pale green walls and a faded tapestry hanging over a table where two people worked. One of the two, a boy of about thirteen or fourteen with shoulder-length hair and clad in black leather, sat strumming at a guitar. Behind him stood an older brown-skinned, ponytailed gentleman, dressed in an out-of-style oversized shirt. He reached over the young man's shoulder as though helping to place the latter's fingers on the correct strings.

They gazed at me, then at the door, a questioning look on their faces. *Did they think I had opened the door?* At the same time, I wondered if my face mirrored theirs because no one else was in the room but those two. The boy and I exchanged a smile as though to say, "How odd; you never know about these old buildings."

Then, the full force of what I saw hit me: The ponytailed figure was a ghost.

Startled, I stepped past the doorway several paces but found that my legs would take me no farther. I leaned back against the wall and took a few deep breaths.

Just then, the boy stepped out of the room, turned left without seeing me, and headed toward the restroom.

My body reacted faster than my mind could decide what I should do. I turned and stepped into the room. My heart raced, but not from fear because the ghost, the soul, had been helping the young man.

The soul leaned over the table, studying the young man's paperwork. He looked up, and our gazes locked. Will had explained that souls tended to assume they could *not* be seen. It was rare for them to encounter someone like me with subtle vision.

I nodded. "Yes, I can see you."

The right corner of his lip twisted. He smiled and straightened to full height. "Highly unusual," he said in an accent I didn't recognize.

I wasn't surprised by his humanlike movements. Will had explained the phenomenon, that when souls physically manifested themselves, they most often take on the physical form of the "host" body that they had in life as this is how a soul "remembers" itself looking. It comes from conditioning. The physical traits, the psychological traits, the habits, the movements—they continue with the manifestation.

I stepped closer. "My name is Grace. And you are …?"

"Aryeh Calfcort, at your service."

I assumed the boy would be back soon, so I spoke in a rush. "I have subtle vision. It's a long story. May I ask what you are doing here?"

He chuckled, seeming to understand my need for speedy answers.

He pointed to the tapestry behind him. It depicted a building, a few plank crosses on a hill and some sort of labyrinth beneath. "I prefer this room because of this art. I find such comfort in it."

"I don't mean this room. I mean, what are you doing here? *Still* here. On Earth. If you don't mind me asking."

"Ahhh," he nodded in understanding and rubbed his chin. "I was a musician. My dream, to write a song that would change the hearts and minds of men ... and women, of course. A song that would inspire change, or draw young lovers together."

He sat down on the edge of the table, one foot still on the floor. "Unfortunately, I died forty-four years ago in an auto accident, on the bottom step of this library. The driver fell asleep. Veered off the road. Drove right into me." He looked down at the sheet music on the table. "I never finished writing that song, so now I'm helping this young man write it."

"You're helping him write *your* song? That won't bother you? That he'll get the credit?"

"On the contrary. It's not my song. In fact, the song is already written."

I must have looked confused because he continued.

"Creativity and inspiration are divinely bestowed. Artists are simply being blessed when it is gifted onto us. We merely reproduce *here* what is bestowed *there*," he said arching his hand over his head.

"So, when you're done …?"

He sighed. "In my experience, most people give up when it gets tough. But assuming he finishes the song, then I will pass on."

A door opened down the hallway.

"Are you an angel?" I whispered quickly, hoping he'd detect my urgent need to know.

Aryeh affected a quarter-moon grin but said nothing, and I sensed the boy getting close to the room. I desperately wanted an answer to my question before I left, but instead he said Godspeed."

The boy returned and stopped inside the door, shooting me a quizzical look.

"Nice tapestry." I shrugged and left the room.

I wasn't sure what to think of what just happened, but I decided I didn't have time to figure it out. I needed to help Michael.

CHAPTER 6

Within minutes, I stood at Holland's front door, summoning the nerve to knock.

Ms. Bealle had not exaggerated about the drive or the gravel. I'd followed a narrow asphalt road for about a mile out of town as it coiled through the hillside until I reached Scratch Gravel Road. I couldn't see the quarry from Holland's property, but I could see the gravel.

Everywhere.

His house—a two-story frame structure—and a few outbuildings rose out of the pebbles and stones like an island. The house looked unthreatening, tidy, with enough architectural features at the door and windows to appear respectable.

I climbed the small front porch, knocked, and waited. I studied the heavily draped windows beside the door, wanting to know if Holland would peek to who rapped at his door. He never did.

After a few seconds, I heard metal on metal at the door, like a half-dozen locks being undone, unbolted, and unhooked.

When he cracked the door, I think we were startled in equal measure; him by my visit, me by his appearance. Gone were his signature dress pants and sports coat, and in their place he wore soiled, baggy trousers and a black T-shirt, ripped at the left armhole, and spotted with stains. He smelled of tobacco and body odor and looked curiously uncomfortable and exposed, like someone who'd been caught raiding a cookie jar.

Memories of our earlier encounters raced through my mind: Him showing too much interest in *Crossings*, me overhearing his half-truths as he filmed a documentary at Antietam, Adriana describing his departure from the lane that led to my house when he knew I wasn't there, him revealing a level of familiarity with my gold coin that startled me.

"Ms. MacKenna. I expected a delivery man." His voice sounded flat, annoyed. Even though I hadn't yet said a word, he looked as if he expected me to demand something he had already determined to refuse. "Are you lost?"

"Mr. Greer, may I have a moment of your time?"

He frowned and wrinkled his brow.

"Please. I won't stay long."

With thumb and index finger, he began to stroke his goatee, an effort that dislodged a crumb from somewhere in those white hairs and sent it spiraling toward the floor. He didn't notice. Was he nervous? Apprehensive? Just buying time?

"What is this all about?" he asked.

"My house. Actually, the tunnels underneath the house. You know about them, don't you?"

Interest flickered in his eyes. "Of course, I do."

Still, he hesitated, and I sensed that he wrestled with hearing me out or shutting the door in my face, no doubt able to do either with equal indifference.

"You said you specialize in the Civil War era. My house pre-dates that a few years, but I hoped to ask you a few questions about it anyway."

He moved back to let me enter. "A minute. I'm quite busy."

As I stepped through the door, I felt like I stepped inside the man. The exterior shifted from acceptable, conforming, to an insipid interior, devoid of comfort. The house registered cold in a way that had nothing to do with temperature, and a chill raced down my spine. I smelled mold and a litter box long overdue for a change.

I was never in a house as unadorned as Holland's. He'd done nothing to distinguish the place. Nothing graced the flat surfaces, no family photographs, novelty items or magazines to distinguish his taste. It was as if the room had been left unpolished so as to leave guests with no opinions or hunches whatsoever.

Tattered, blasé-brown furniture sat atop filthy, worn shag green carpet, the combination reminding me of rectangles of freshly turned graves in a grassed cemetery. Water-stained wallpaper peeled from the north wall like snakeskin. Curtain rods sagged, and beneath them masking tape held a cracked window together.

Claustrophobia crept in on me, and I noticed that doors, not open archways, secluded the room from others. I don't know what I expected. Certainly not to find the house warm and inviting. However, I thought I might see personal items that would help me put one more piece of the confusing Holland Greer puzzle in its place.

"I don't waste money on frivolous things," he said, as though attempting to explain that he had more wealth than what he could show in this house, a greater reserve of valuables elsewhere. He struck me as a man who considered himself as alien from the world in which other people lived.

He didn't ask me to sit, and he cut right to the point.

"What do you want to know?" He shut the door and stepped around me, placing me, thankfully, closest to the door. *Was he concerned I'd move farther into the house?*

"Everything. How many tunnels? Where do they go? How big are they? What were they used for?" I shrugged. "Stuff like that."

He removed his glasses, set them on a table beside him, and crossed his arms. "There are at least eight tunnels, each about six feet wide, that connect to five rooms ... more like bunkers. Each about ten feet by ten feet. The tunnels run in several directions and connect again, almost like a maze. However, they all take you back to either the house's cellar or to the root cellar. Well, except one ... it allegedly once stretched to an old stable that's long since gone."

What surprised me even more than his instant recall and detailed familiarity with the tunnels, was the enormity of what sat beneath my house. Overwhelmed, I wished I could sit, but Holland wasn't offering that option. I stood straight, despite my shaky knees.

He continued. "They were dug in the mid-1700s, when anything west of the Potomac was considered part of the frontier. As I'm sure you are aware, your house is known as *Crossings*, but it wasn't the original

Crossings. Josiah Sawyer built the original as an inn and tavern. Settlers moving into the Shenandoah Valley tended to cross the Potomac at that spot because the river ran shallow. But the area also harbored Native Americans who weren't so happy with settlers taking over the rich hunting ground in the Valley. Before Sawyer built the tavern, he dug a series of tunnels."

"You mean, to hide?"

"Hide. Wait. Store goods. We can only conclude he thought he and his guests might have to escape to the underground if attacked. It's believed that the five bunkers each had their own doors and were stocked with supplies. Settlers could remain there for days."

I considered this. Will had said nothing about the tunnels. *Why would he hide that information? Was it possible he hadn't even known about them?*

"Were the tunnels ever used for that? To shelter settlers, I mean."

"No one knows for sure. But yes, it is believed settlers hid there." He cocked his head and gave me an intense look before continuing. "It's also believed that many settlers died there. Some mysteriously."

"Mysteriously?"

Holland nodded. "Some accounts say that Sawyer had some rather ... *peculiar* beliefs. He's been described as everything from a zealot to a heretic to a provocateur of some early form of occult. It's rumored that any man who crossed him disappeared. I have my doubts about any of that, though."

My knees began to shake again, and I tightened my leg muscles to keep from falling. "What happened to the tavern?"

"Presumably, it deteriorated away or burned down. Just like the barn, allegedly, where Sawyer died in a fire. We know that when David Kavanaugh purchased the land in the 1850s, he built *Crossings* using part of the stone foundation that remained there. Many years had gone by, so it no doubt seemed innocent enough. It's logical to assume that the workmen found the entrance to the tunnels, but no one knows for sure. Nor would anyone know whether those tunnels are still open, given its years of disuse ... unless you know otherwise?" He arched an eyebrow waiting for my response.

"No, I've not been down there." Best to leave Michael out of this conversation.

"I see. You have heard, I'm sure, that prior to your stepfather, no one has been able to gain access to *Crossings* for decades?"

I nodded, but I wasn't about to offer him any more information. Besides not wanting to discuss it, my mind headed in a different direction. I tried to figure out what to ask that might yield answers to help me understand Fergus's reason for being there. All I could conclude was that something dwelled in the underground of the house.

"If you haven't been down there, then how do you know so much about the tunnels?" I directed that thought to myself as much as I did to him. Then the answer struck me. "You have papers about it. A drawing? A map!"

The look on his face gave him away.

I stepped toward him. I'm not sure where my confidence came from. I needed to see what he had. "Mr. Greer, if you let me see the map, I'll take you into the tunnels."

I'd obviously made him an offer he couldn't refuse. He was intrigued. I could see it in the slight twitch in his cheek, the sudden hitch in his breathing. For a moment, he blinked, and I suspected that fear of sharing the secrets of his map with me warred with his greed to get inside *Crossings*.

I wondered if I'd just made a pact with a scoundrel of diabolical proportions, but I stood firm and waited for his reply.

He continued to hesitate, studying my face, before relenting. "Wait here." He turned and exited through a door to my left, firmly closing it behind him.

And I did wait there, for as long as I could, which as it turns out, wasn't all that long. I don't know if it was regret at the deal I'd just cut or the odd voice that kept saying, "go on, follow him." *From inside my head?* But, after only about a minute, I did just that. I followed him through that door.

I startled at entering a long, dark hallway, rather than another room. A naked light bulb hung from a single black wire, and it sent stark shadows into the corners. I counted four doors, each closed. Where had he gone?

"Mr. Greer?" I tried his name twice. Nothing.

Then, behind the first door on the right I heard a noise. Relieved, I proceeded to it. I knocked as I said his name but didn't wait for a response. Instead, I turned the knob and stepped inside.

I felt like I had just stepped into a Hollywood prop storage room, filled with assorted paraphernalia that would be used in a cheap horror flick.

CHAPTER 7

Scattered from wall to wall sat the strangest assortment of items I'd ever seen outside a museum. Their oddity wouldn't have registered with anyone else, but it did with me for many reasons.

First, I'd researched ghosts ad nauseam when I first became aware of Will's presence in my house. I recognized here the signs of equipment used for ghost hunting—the electromagnetic devices, the digital video cameras, the mirror galvanometer, the infrared thermometers, the recording machines.

Second, I saw shovels and boots soiled with reddish brown dirt, signs of someone digging, searching.

Third, lanterns and flashlights sat on a sagging wooden shelf off to the right. Necessary for clandestine snooping when the rest of the world slept.

Fourth, most startling of all, three souls stood by a window, lazed on a couch, and draped around an old chest. The rest of the room bulged with antiques, from buckets to chairs, to a spinning wheel, to oxen yokes. The souls must have placed their energy centers in those items when Holland moved the objects and had no choice but to come along.

Oblivious to my intrusion, the souls remained unfazed; they did not know that I could see them. Again, I recalled Will's tutelage: do *not* acknowledge strange souls because they might be dangerous.

I didn't hear Holland arrive behind me such that when he spoke, neither his words questioning why I stood in the room nor the anger in his voice registered with me at the time. I whirled with such fury that I think he thought I might hit him.

"You're not a historian. You're a ghost hunter! The whole world thinks that you're searching for historical knowledge, but you're hunting for ghosts!"

He pulled his shoulders back and took a deep breath, as though he intended to do damage control.

"Ms. MacKenna, it's true that I dabble in parapsychological and phenomenological research ... that means the science of supernatural manifestations," he said in a condescending tone.

"I know what that means."

"There's nothing wrong or shameful about the study of paranormal research. It's just that it's not a lucrative ... or *accepted* way ... to make a living." He cringed on his own words, his hands fisting. "I am equally interested in history, so I present that aspect of my work to the world instead. I'm sure you'd agree that if I took the reverse approach, I'd get much less respect from my colleagues and my viewing public."

He struck me as a man of single focus and double talk whose work proved unscientific and often scorned, so he couched it as history to secure an air of authority, maybe even respectability.

"Besides," he continued, moving into the room and randomly touching one antique after another. "Can't you feel the energy? There's something here, something about these artifacts ..."

He looked half-crazed as he talked about the tangible things, and the irony of it hit me. Here stood a ghost hunter surrounded by three ghosts that he didn't even know he'd inadvertently brought home.

"You can't see them," I said in whispered surprise.

Instantly, I regretted my words. He wheeled around and stared at me as though my comment had plumbed a needling passion that swelled in him. He pounced at me, and his words revealed he had come to a conclusion long ago and intended to snatch his chance to voice it.

"But you can, can't you, Ms. MacKenna?" He said my name the way he might say *sewer rat* and arched a confident eyebrow, challenging me to deny him. "You see something here, don't you?"

In my peripheral vision, I saw the three ghosts congregate in the far corner, their focus on me. My breath caught, but I didn't back down. My gaze locked with Holland's like sabers, each awaiting the other's move.

The map was rolled up in his hand like a baton, and he tapped it into my shoulder as he spoke, inching closer. His eyes grew dark, his voice demanding. "Go on. Tell me what you see."

Panic gripped me.

Then, the room shook, or was it just me? It happened so fast, I couldn't be sure. It started at my head and moved down my body, then through the room, growing in intensity as it spread. I reached out to steady myself with the wall. Holland fell against the shelves and onto the floor. Two flashlights tumbled down on top of him.

It ended as quickly as it started.

I didn't know what had just happened. An earthquake? A quarry blast? The souls? Whatever occurred, it worked to my advantage. Holland didn't look hurt, so I decided to get out of there. I spotted the map on the floor where he had dropped it, sitting there between us like a slab of meat between two starving dogs. I leaped forward and snatched it. "I'll return this later."

The souls didn't move as I hurried into the dreary hallway. Brazenly, I turned around and looked at Holland. "Forget the tour of *Crossings*, Mr. Greer. This," I said and held up the map, "in exchange for keeping your secret from the world. We'll call it even, and I'll—"

From the floor, rubbing his head, Holland shot me a look that shut me up. His eyes smoldered, the gaze seething in anger and intensity.

I fled down the corridor, through the graveyard-like front room, across the splintered porch, then stopped when I reached my car and gasped for air, as though I'd come up from the depths of a dark, murky lake and crashed through the surface.

CHAPTER 8

My heart still pounded by the time I reached Williamsport's city limits.

Thoughts of the angry individuals I'd pitted against me—Holland, Greasy Jim, Fergus—hovered and circled over me like vultures. I was the carcass, and they were waiting to swoop in for the banquet.

I wondered if demons stalked in that way: Do they hover in the dark shadows waiting to pounce? Laugh when you break? Celebrate when you fall?

I needed courage and solace from these threats, if even briefly, so I decided to clear my head with a walk along the canal by visiting Mason. If I couldn't be with Clay, his father would have to do.

A few weeks had passed since I'd last seen Mason, learned his full name and recognized him for the first time as Clay's father. I still wrestled with what to do with this knowledge, but my eagerness to see him now swelled so strong and swift that I forced myself not to exceed the speed limit. I'm not sure why seeing him excited me so.

Perhaps because I knew so little about his son.

Sure, I'd learned the big things, the kinds of things that you could learn from friends: where he golfed, his position on the high school football team, his major in undergraduate school. What I didn't know were the little things. The things even his friends might not know: How did he feel after losing his lower leg in Afghanistan? Who taught him how to drive, and did he pass the test the first time? If he could do anything without financial concern, what would it be? I *wanted* to know it all, but I *needed* to know at least one thing; something his friends didn't know. Something that would bind us. Something that would require us to get together again.

I needed a lifeline, and Mason had become that for me.

The parking lot was crowded at the C&O Canal visitors' area, but I pulled my SUV into the last remaining spot, hid the map under the seat, then headed to the towpath. Hikers and bikers were everywhere, some preparing for their treks on the towpath, others leaning over a tributary bridge watching the river flow by, some picnicking on the lawns.

Just a few yards into my hike, I startled at seeing a soul sitting under a tree, the first soul other than Mason I ever saw along the canal. At first, I thought he was a re-enactor because he had a bushy beard and wore the same dirty, loose clothing—redneck bandana, oversized white shirt, tannish-brown pants and wide-brimmed hat—that I had seen in the historic pictures in the visitors' center of the canal works from the 1800s. He looked bored sitting on the ground leaning against a tree and methodically whittling at a piece of wood. The only other thing I registered was that he was semi-transparent. I whisked my gaze away, lest I inadvertently make eye contact, just as I'd done with the souls at Holland's house. I was here to see Mason, and my mind had no room for another ghost right now.

I hustled along the distance to the spot where I'd spoken with Mason before, left the trail, and descended into the ravine, the river now to my back. The canopy of trees blocked the sun, and the dampness of the earth permeated the air. Despite having been here before and having met Mason, or rather his soul, I grew anxious. I had learned that, just as with certain people, some souls can turn on you quickly too. I had seen Will's wife Naomi ooze charm just minutes before she'd tried to strangle me.

"Mr. Baxter!" I called twice.

"Here, Ms. MacKenna."

His voice came from my right and sounded deep and welcoming. I turned that direction, rounded a clump of trees, and there he stood, about three yards away. Seeing him always conjured up a mix of emotions. He was so delightful and kind, that I felt flustered in his presence and guilty that I may have doubted my safety with him.

However, he was a soul and not a living man, and that saddened me. Not just because he was Clay's father and had lost his life far too young, but also because, in his jeans and polo shirt, he looked like he should still be alive today. In contrast, I thought of Will. He'd been a delight, and I loved him in many ways, but he wore the tattered clothing of a Civil War uniform, and that had always reminded me that even if his life hadn't ended prematurely, he still would have been dead more than a century before my birth.

But Mason … I should be traveling home with Clay to meet his father in the warmth of their home, not meeting the remnants of his death here in this cold, remote patch of woods.

Mason smiled. "To what do I owe this distinct honor?"

I learned at that moment that for a smile to be contagious, it doesn't have to come from a living person. He was a distinguished-looking man, dark features, late-forties. I could imagine him sweeping Cassie's heart away once upon a time.

I swallowed, hoping my voice would hold. "Just wanted to say hello."

He cocked his head. "I'm delighted you did. You look much better than you did the last time I saw you."

My cheeks warmed. On my last visit, when I recognized his name as that of Clay's father, my knees buckled, and I fell to the ground. I never did tell him that I knew his son.

But now I would.

"I feel much better, thank you." I took a deep breath. "Mr. Baxter, I—"

"Mason, please."

I shook my head, almost embarrassed. "I can't call you that."

"Buy why? You did before."

"I didn't know who you were … are."

His eyebrows arched, and he studied me. "And now you do?"

I nodded. "I … I'm friends with Cassie and Reaghan and Clay."

Mason frowned. "I see." He paused and said the next two words with such sadness that it made my heart ache. "My family."

I nodded.

"Are they well? Enjoying life?"

"I suppose," I said, wishing I could offer him more—a concrete answer, a happy story.

He moved to the left and folded onto a large rock that jutted out of the bank of the ravine, as if he'd been dealt tragic news and had to have physical support to continue. "They were everything to me."

"Then why did you leave?" I too dropped down on a rock. I imagined what I wanted him to say, what I needed to hear, but it battled in my mind with what I suspected he would say. "What happened? Did you have a disease? An accident? How did you end up here, and why didn't you say good-bye?" My questions fell rapidly over one another like toppled building blocks, so that I had to stop and take a deep breath.

"I didn't leave."

"What does that mean?"

He ran his hand through his hair and emitted a weary sigh. "I'm not sure it's in your best interest to know."

"How could it be in my worst interest? I mean, for some reason you didn't pass on. Why?" An edge crept into my tone. I just needed him to say it.

"It's been said that a murdered man won't rest until justice is done."

And there it was. That word again.

Murder.

The malicious or premeditated killing of one human being by another.

The selfish and deliberate destruction not only of a person's physical life, but also his hopes, his dreams, his purpose in the world.

Arguably, the worst crime a person could commit.

A sin in every decent religion.

A vile act that changes the life of more than just the victim.

When I heard his words, it crystallized in my brain that I'd known it all along; known that this man would never abandon his family and that an accident would have been too easy to discover.

With a groan, I dropped my head into my hands, closed my eyes, and relived a conversation with Clay. We drove in his truck, somewhere in South Carolina, on our way to southern Georgia to confront Will's wife, Naomi. One of his hands gripped the wheel and the other held one of mine. He said, "I used to hope that Dad got called away by something larger than himself. Maybe he uncovered some sinister plot and disappeared to protect his family, or he was whisked into a witness protection program and couldn't contact us for our own safety."

The vision faded from Clay to Cassie, and I imagined her sitting across from me at the café, talking to her coffee cup, as she shared her memories. She said, "I used to imagine how Mason would come back. I'd be pourin' some coffee and turn to see who had just come in the door. And there he'd be. Bundles of presents in his arms. As though to explain that he left so that he could go somewhere and make a better life for us. Or I'd open the office door and instead of the package delivery service, he'd be standin' there with roses in his arms."

The vision flashed back to Clay again, walking beside me as we took Tramp for a walk. He said, "In the military, I finally came to grips with Dad's decision. I learned you can either pity yourself or you can accept that only *you* are responsible for your own happiness. Once I took control of my future, I forgave him."

Just as quickly, the vision returned to Cassie again, and she said, "Abandonment is an illness. It'll kill ya' if ya' let it."

Cassie's lament cut through my heart, and I looked up to see the soul of her murdered husband sitting not more than twelve feet from me.

He watched me process his news; watched as it rolled over me like a derailed steam engine, taking my reaction full circle and landing where I suspected he thought I would: right back at his concern for my best interest.

Neither of us voiced the obvious: That if he was murdered, and no one knows, then the murder is unresolved. Given that it occurred in the past fifteen years, his murderer could still be at large. Still out there.

Still, perhaps, in Williamsport.

He gestured toward me. "And now you understand."

I nodded, looking at the ground.

"It doesn't matter." I whispered because I couldn't produce volume. "I will help you solve this."

"No. This is not like your William Kavanaugh's death. You solved his murder, and I applaud you. But in my case, you will not only have demonic souls to contend with, but you'll also have to add a much more formidable opponent … or opponents … of the living kind."

I stifled acerbic laughter but spewed my thoughts: "I've already been attacked by demented ghosts. One tried to strangle me. Another possessed my friend's body and almost killed him. It can't get much worse. I think one is attacking my cousin at my house even as we speak."

I threw my hands over my mouth. I hadn't meant to tell him that. I didn't want him to know how pathetic and outrageous my life had become. I wanted him, one day, to think of me as worthy of his son.

He jumped at my words. "What makes you think that?"

Seeing no recourse, I explained Michael's drastic change, his disorientation, and his aggressiveness toward Greasy Jim. "He's got this look in his eyes," I continued, "that I've seen before, but not on a human."

"What do you mean?"

"I once saw a rabid fox while hiking with Jack, my stepdad. It started wobbling right up to us, even though it otherwise would be scared of people. It had this wild look on its face, like it had no idea what it was doing. Michael reminds me of that fox."

Mason leaped up from his perch and crossed the space between us in the blink of an eye. "You must go and help him now. You need to stop this from happening."

I started to cry, all the events of the day collecting on me and washing into my tears. "I don't know how."

"You do. You *do* know how."

"But I want to help *you*. I want to—"

"We will talk about me later. I can wait. Now is the time to help your cousin. Remember, I said that a living person might be more potentially harmful than a demonic soul?"

I nodded.

"That's because a living being can move around. He has that advantage over a soul who only has power when he's near his center. So, go. Use that knowledge—that a demonic soul has limited range of movement. Go help your cousin exorcise this demon from his life. Then you can come back, and we'll talk about me. By then, you'll have more experience and be better able to tackle the mess that resulted in my murder."

I suspected that when I returned to talk about his death he'd again refuse to let me help. But we could argue about that later. He was right. I had to put Michael first.

"Do you know this demon that is trying to possess your cousin?"

"I'm rather sure it's the same man who killed Will."

Mason looked confused. "But why would Will leave before removing the murderer from your house?"

"I guess Will didn't know he hid there." I took a deep breath. "I wish Will had never left."

"I'm sure he never would have left a lady in distress had he known," he said and smiled. "Particularly one so beautiful."

I looked down, embarrassed.

"Unfortunately, what would work best," Mason said, "is to find another soul that understood the murderer well. His motives. His strengths and weaknesses. A soul you can trust. Did you meet any of Will's other friends in the course of your sleuthing?"

I nodded. "Two of them. Asa Garrett. On the battlefield. But he's passed on now. And a surgeon named Braxton Hood. He was in a dumpy little shed on the outskirts of Sharpsburg. It was converted into a makeshift field hospital after the battle. I promised him I'd come back to solve his murder."

Mason frowned and dropped his gaze to the ground. "Another murder? Oh my." He paused and looked back at me. "It sounds as though you may be able to tackle two problems in one by dealing with Braxton. Don't you think?"

"Yes," I blubbered, "but I'm afraid of him."

"Why? What scares you?"

I described his brooding manner, his dark demeanor, his cold voice, his despairing attitude. I explained how I had met him one moonlit night and how it made me feel. I even shared that Braxton was accused of murdering everyone in his field hospital the night the Antietam battle occurred, an accusation that Will had called preposterous.

"The worst part," I continued, "is that Braxton said I have to *watch* his murder in order to solve it. I mean, it's just a shed to everyone else, but when I step in, it becomes a nightmare. It's frightening and hot and smells of blood and dead bodies, and I see it all, as if it's occurring at that moment."

"Oh my. Are you sure that's your only option?"

"It is."

"And did Will trust Braxton?"

"Implicitly."

"Then you have no choice but to have faith in Will. Sometimes we're called to take action on things we don't understand. It involves faith. Trust. In the Book of Psalms, God promises to shield our lives and deliver us from the wicked. I should have leaned into that myself." He looked away for a moment before meeting my gaze again. "Besides, you must do this for Braxton, too. A man has a right to clear his name. For the truth to be told about his death."

Later, as I headed home, it struck me that Mason had been talking about himself as much as he was Braxton. Mason wasn't as interested in resolving his murder to find out who had done it, as much as he wanted it resolved so that his family would know he had not abandoned them.

★ ★ ★

As it turns out, my return home solidified my plans: I had to visit Braxton as soon as possible.

When I stepped through the doorway, I witnessed a difference in my pets, or, I should say, my cat. Tramp greeted me with typical happy-dog fever, tail wagging. Chubbs, however, blurred by me. I opened the door just as he leaped from the couch near the open doorway that adjoined the old house. He rushed to the bedroom door, turned and looked back, then crouched, back arched, fur on end. His pupils expanded; his eyes looked black. A menacing hiss snaked from his mouth then he turned and dashed into the bedroom.

Will had told me that cats could see, and even sense a soul's presence whether the soul manifested or not. As a result, Chubbs's peculiar behavior served as a barometer of activity within the house.

I took a deep breath and stepped inside, but I scooted Tramp outside so he could do his business. I'd seen Michael's car in the driveway. I called his name, but no answer. Alone in the now-quiet room, I began to relax, thinking Chubbs might be having a wild moment, the way most cats do. But then I heard a creak. Just a slight pressure on the floor could cause such a sound, but it was there and it sounded close. I waited, straining to hear, my heart pounding.

Michael appeared from behind the doorframe and walked into the apartment. He looked pale, fevered, disturbed, like he'd just had another attack and barely fought it off. The word "deranged" came to mind, but I refused to entertain that notion. I couldn't deny, however, that with his appearance came the sense of an unearthly quality that sent a chill crawling down my spine.

For the briefest moment, his half-savage eyes studied me coldly from behind his now-patched wire-rimmed glasses. He walked toward the refrigerator. I toyed with the thought of asking him about Adriana and Greasy Jim but decided it might sound confrontational. "I wasn't sure if you were here."

"What's that stupid cat's problem?" he growled. "Won't even come near me. Acts like I'm the enemy."

He pulled out a bottle of water and guzzled the entire thing in one effort, then turned and tossed the bottle into the garbage can. "I'm going back to bed. Not feeling well."

I couldn't stop myself from asking, "What happened to your glasses?"

He stopped, midstride, and tilted his head, like he was trying to remember. "I don't know." He said it with such sincerity and wonder that I believed him.

He didn't even remember how his glasses broke.

With a zombie-like stupor on his face, he returned to the old house and shut the door behind him.

I dropped into a chair as his words seared through my mind. *"The enemy."* That's what he said. The final, icy comprehension of the brewing situation hit me and burned because sometimes the truth just resonates on some level that only the truth can.

It burned into me that Chubbs had seen a soul in Michael.

That the soul was a demon.

That Michael was in trouble and didn't understand the extent of the danger.

That I had to stop this possession before it was too late. *Irreversible.*

That I had to see Braxton *that* night.

That words and worrying were no longer action enough. I had to stop sandbagging the perimeter and, instead, take steps to combat the storm that was coming.

Tonight.

CHAPTER 9

The Antietam Battlefield sits on about twelve acres of fields amidst the Appalachian foothills and is devoid of vendors and souvenir shops. In daylight, in all directions, you see rolling hills, a distant scattering of houses and farms, and narrow roads for touring, which are flanked with War-era zigzag wooden fences encouraging visitors to remain on the paved track and off hallowed grounds.

When night arrives in this vast stretch of rolling hills so far from city hustle, the darkness is thick and absolute, blanketing the valleys and sunken roads, enfolding the statues, and reducing the landscape to nothing more than degrees of darkness.

Add to this already blackened, monochromatic backdrop a covering of low-lying bloated clouds which pushed the darkness toward the earth, blocking out the moon and stars, and the result was, all things considered, *not* a good night to visit an isolated, eerie battlefield.

What's more, the remoteness and the purity of the battlefield, so devoid as it is of tourist traps, produced an eerie emptiness in the dark, and I marveled, yet again, at its frightening seclusion from the time and space and pulse of the rest of the world.

As I drove to this spot where more than twenty thousand men were wounded or killed all in one bloody day, I recalled what I read about the aftermath of the battle; that every house and barn and store and church and schoolhouse, and even corncrib and cow stable between Sharpsburg and Boonesboro gorged with wounded and dying men.

I knew my way around most of the battlefield because I'd been there a couple times. The shed where Braxton "resided"—and I use that term loosely because "haunted" would be a better descriptor—sat a stone's throw from the battlefield.

I parked as close to the shed as possible, a distance of about a hundred yards and thousands of racing heartbeats and frightening possibilities away. Stepping out of my car, I peered into the darkness, but it proved impenetrable. I'd packed a flashlight but didn't want to use it, lest I draw unwanted attention.

Trying to adjust to the darkness, I dragged my gaze back and forth, up and down the fringe of the town, toward the battlefield, and let it come to rest on the weathered shed, looking for signs of anyone, living or dead. As before, the awareness of paranormal activity and the inkling of danger—constants at Antietam—prompted an instinctive chill down my back. I couldn't shake the feeling that the edges of the shadows inched toward me, like spreading inkblots. When you're looking at dark on dark, it's hard to be certain.

The air stilled as the sounds of night upped their volume—crickets and a train—mixed with occasional sounds of battle—a cannon booming, a man screaming, a rifle shot or a sword clash. Of course, most of those sounds were limited to an audience with the ability to see and hear the dead.

All in all, I'd heard worse; I had been there closer to a full moon, a time—according to Will—when the divide between the living and the dead is at its thinnest, and, therefore, when souls are most active. On this particular night, the moon wouldn't be full for almost a week. So these occasional, distant sounds, while heart-wrenching, sounded calm compared to what I'd already experienced.

I wanted to avoid seeing anyone—living or dead—until I found Braxton. From earlier visits, I learned first-hand, that the ghosts, the souls, restlessly walked the battlegrounds, and that many of them posed danger. The problem is that in at least one pertinent respect, they resembled the living: It's hard to tell which are friend and which are foe.

I approached the shed like a hunter stalking his prey ... a few steps, then watched and listened.

A few more steps.

Watched. Listened.

More steps, staying flexible, looking around, listening, inhaling, ready to bolt if need be.

But I sensed nothing disconcerting except that of my own pounding heart.

Once beside the shed, I noted it was being overtaken by vines, its roof covered with tree debris. It gave off a forlorn sense of having been abandoned and left to rot forever. I crept next to it and cat-walked in its shadow until I could peer around to its front porch, hoping against hope that Braxton would be standing there.

No such luck.

Instead, the soul of a man I'd never seen before sat on the porch, feet dangling off the side. His shoulders hunched, and his hands rested flat on the boards at his side. He looked tired, beleaguered. Time meant nothing to souls, so I wasn't surprised to see him just sitting, endlessly waiting. Because of his location—on the porch of what had once served as a field hospital during the battle—I assumed that this soul died at or near this spot.

He blocked the entrance to the front door, so I had no choice but to confront him.

I took a deep breath, steeled my courage, and said, "Excuse me. I need to see Braxton Hood. Is he here?"

At that, the man raised his head toward me. When our gazes met, and he registered that I could see him, his nostrils flared, his eye sockets glared a reddish yellow, and his mouth metamorphosed, wolf-like, complete with fangs. Too startled to scream, I watched as his body swelled, bigger and bigger. He swooshed into a standing position on the porch over me, towering at least eight feet tall.

He reined back, and when it looked as though he intended to thrust a heaving breath of something vile at me, Braxton walked out of the shed. In one heartbeat, Braxton reached out, and I swear his arm morphed into a huge gauzy wing that hit the man, and sent him rolling to the edge of the porch roof where he hung, or hovered, I couldn't tell which. He just perched there, undulating, arms dangling, head tilted forward, looking defeated.

I was too stunned to move, but Braxton acted nonplussed. He

turned and spoke with a calm that belied what I'd just experienced. "Ms. MacKenna, don't be a fool. You must not let your guard down."

Meanwhile, gasping, steadying my breathing, willing my heart to calm—these were what concerned me, not a discussion about what I'd done wrong.

"You must not make eye contact until you know with whom you are dealing."

I clenched my jaw and tried to fasten my gaze on him, unsure how to proceed and all too aware of the frightening soul dangling from the porch eaves. As though Braxton understood my turmoil, he gestured for me to follow, descended the steps, and walked to the side of the porch where vestiges of light shone from a pole light on the next property. The dim illumination revealed a broken fence and an odd assortment of junk.

When I thought I could talk coherently, I dispensed with cordial greetings. "I need your help." I tried to sound and look normal, but my racing heart demanded that I sit, lest I collapse onto the ground. I plopped down on what looked like an abandoned hood of an antique car.

He cocked an eyebrow. "Fergus?"

I nodded. "Michael, my cousin, is living with me now. At *Crossings.* You already know that Fergus may be there. I think he's trying to take over Michael's body."

Despite the faint light, I could see Braxton flinch when I said Fergus's name.

He shifted, crossed his arms and leaned against the fence, as though settling his stance for a long conversation. "What leads you to this conclusion?"

I told him about Michael's before and after personalities, his penchant to explore the underbelly of the house and the shimmering wall.

"What I don't understand," I continued, "is why Will never mentioned him. Is it possible—"

"It's quite elementary. Fergus hid from view. Will never detected him."

"But … for a hundred and fifty years? I mean, surely in that time he'd have come out for—"

"For what? Conversation?" His tone suggested ridicule. "Nourishment? A cup of sugar?" He shook his head as though dismissing nonsensical questions. "We're dead, Ms. MacKenna. We have no need or desire for those provisions anymore. Sustenance, companionship, time … they are no longer essential factors in our make-up."

I wanted to counter that everything in *my* make-up wanted to know why he was so gruff and rude. Braxton had been murdered, and he didn't know by whom, but Will had been murdered too, and yet he managed to be kind, even gallant. Braxton, on the other hand, always demonstrated boorish, brooding behavior. If Will hadn't loved him, and if Michael didn't need him, I'd have never set foot near this soul again.

"So Fergus hid," I reasoned. "For what purpose? And what does he hope to accomplish by taking over Michael's body?"

"I don't know the answers to your questions. But you can be assured it is for a calculated, sinister reason. I believe you said Will told you about Fergus's treasonous activities during the war?"

I nodded.

"Then you know he changed immensely from the man we had gotten to know at the university. He had a nefarious intent for every action he undertook in the war. His evil deeds no doubt carried over into his death."

"Will described him as an opportunist and a spy."

Braxton scoffed at that. "Not a spy. A commander needs spies to find out the enemy's location, his capability, his strength. No, Fergus wasn't that loyal or selfless. He was a double spy, and double spies are traitors. Betraying both sides for the profit there is to be made."

I looked away, startled by the venom in Braxton's tone.

He continued. "More than that, he was a liar and a thief to his core. Now that he's no doubt facing eternal damnation, he hopes to make a tidy pact with the Devil to ease his suffering. This means he intends to carry out some diabolical deed to earn favors."

"With the … the Devil?" I gasped. "You're telling me the *Devil* is behind Fergus? *The* Devil?"

"I'm telling you that evil is powerful, Ms. MacKenna. It is indubitably real and threatening, and you must thwart it or you may see your cousin perish before your eyes. Doctors will ascribe his death to any one of several diseases, and no one will ever comprehend what the true cause is. In the interim, you or any of your friends may die or disappear at his hands too. A push down the stairs, a pillow over your face, a sudden disappearance, a—"

"Stop it!" I stood and struggled for air. I could feel the threat in his words approach me like a cloaked figure, solid and determined to inflict harm. I pumped a hand at him and lowered my voice. "I get your point."

He flinched, startled by my outburst. "Do you? Are you truly cognizant of the gravity of this situation?"

"It's just that he isn't always this way. Sometimes Michael is as normal as—" I broke off before foolishly saying "you."

"That's how evil works. Your Michael may seem quite normal to neighbors, friends, colleagues. Haven't you ever heard of someone committing atrocities and afterward people express surprise? They'll say they didn't see it coming. That he seemed like such a good person. That's how evil settles in. Slowly. Steadily. Until the vulnerable vessel, for this repulsive wickedness has been irreversibly consumed."

I made no comment, and I could tell that Braxton read the impact of his words on my face. His tone sharpened: "You need to intercede and stop him now."

"But how?"

"First, you need to know when the autumn equinox will occur. Fergus will need that for full possession to be complete."

"Equinox?"

"The moment when the sun crosses the Earth's equator from the north and moves to the southern hemisphere."

"I get that. I know what the equinox is. What I want to know is why then?"

"It is a time of perfect equilibrium. A twenty-four-hour split between light and dark. Equal measure. Time ..." he hesitated as though choosing his words with care, "...can seem to stand still. There is a decrease in the visible light spectrum due to the loss of daylight hours as the earth approaches winter. As a result, the veil between the worlds is weak. Vulnerable. Transforming."

Two weeks! That's about how long I had before autumn arrived, the third week of September. I'd learned in school that equinox is what marked the beginning of the season.

"So what do I do?"

"First, you have to figure out what Fergus's plans are." Braxton stepped away from the fence, pacing as he talked, back and forth, on an invisible line about three yards in length. He looked like a scientist intent on solving a problem, oblivious to the world around him.

"His mere presence at *Crossings* suggests that he died there, although that's not certain. What's more, he must have perished in the midst of heinous intent. My guess is that he is attempting to finish what remained undone at the time of his death. There has to be something at *Crossings* ... or something he *believes* is still at *Crossings* ... If we could identify who his enemies are or what roots him there ..."

He whirled around. "Eva! She may be able to offer insight into Fergus's plans."

"What? But she's dead."

"As am I."

"But you already told me you didn't know what happened to her. You're just saying this so that I help you find her. I already told you I would help you solve your murder ... and find Eva ... but that will have to wait. I need to help Michael now."

"Ms. MacKenna," he said, exasperation in his tone, "don't you see that to do one, you must do the other?"

I dropped back onto the rusty hood, heaved a tired sigh, and dropped my face into my hands. "How can I do all this? I don't even know where to start." I could feel tears welling up but determined not to let this cold, daunting soul see them. It was awkward enough to have cried in front of Mason, but I refused to show my weariness to this contentious soul.

"It's rudimentary. You line up your tasks and tackle them one at a time."

When I didn't respond, he sighed. "Are you familiar with lining up dominoes, just to watch them fall?"

I looked up, confused, wondering what a children's game had to do with anything.

"In dominoes you line up the pieces. None of them move until the piece just before it moves. So, you must line them strategically. First, you must figure out who killed me. Once you know that, you will have a good idea of what may have happened to Eva. Once you know Eva's whereabouts, another domino, you can talk to her to learn more about Fergus … who his enemies are, what roots him to the house. Once you've determined that, you can solve the riddle of what he is after."

"You make it sound so easy."

"No, it's not easy." He shook his head. "It's quite daunting, to be honest. And, it's not without risk. But it is your sole option."

"Maybe I should just move. That's another option. Get Michael out of there."

"That would be a huge mistake. Possession has already begun, so Michael would fight a move. You might find yourself in grave danger."

"But Michael would never hurt me."

"Perhaps not. But Fergus, in him, would."

I flinched and rubbed a hand over my forehead, remembering Braxton's dictum on an earlier visit; that *solving* his murder would involve *watching* his murder during the full moon.

"So what happens after I watch you being … killed? I just start wandering the battlefield to identify the guy to you?" I didn't mean to sound sarcastic, but I did.

He didn't notice. "No, no, no. My murderer would no doubt have stolen away from this carnage."

"But if that's true, then how can he be here that night? Doesn't he have to have died here for his energy to be here? To manifest himself, to be able to commit the murder again?"

"He will appear as a residual," he said in a tone that suggested he thought I should understand.

"A residual?"

Braxton shook his head and paced again. "A residual. He won't be here fully. You'll be able to tell the difference. It's doubtful he died here, but he did commit evil here by murdering the people in the shed that night. The remnants … the residual effects of his deeds … they remain because his acts proved so heinous." He stopped, a frustrated look on his face. "You've heard that truth always wins out?"

I nodded.

He splayed out his hands. "Proof that it's true. Truth causes residual effects. Evil cannot escape. He will appear less … present. And fortunately, for you, he will be less dangerous."

"Dangerous?" Who wouldn't pick up on that word?

"Of course. We are discussing evil of an unfathomable nature. Someone who committed murder for the personal gain of more evil. If he had died here and remained fully present, it could be extremely dangerous for you."

"But … what if he *did* die here? What if he *is* fully present? What do I do then?"

"There is nothing you can do, except act nonchalant. Act as though you don't see. Don't make eye contact. Don't appear to threaten him."

"How can I act nonchalant when I'm standing in a dark shed in the middle of the night for no apparent reason whatsoever?" I hissed the words in the loudest whisper possible and wrapped my arms tight against sudden unexpected chills.

"*See* … but don't watch. You can do that. Act as though you've just stopped here for a brief respite on your way to somewhere else. Hiking seems to be popular among your coterie. Do that."

"In the middle of the night?"

"Ms. MacKenna," he said, annoyance obvious in his voice, "the souls won't be focused on you. They are not going to take the time to determine whether it's night or day or what your schedule may be."

He turned, and his next words made it clear that discussion of residuals and danger was complete. "Now, you will have to line up even more dominoes before witnessing my death. You need to know who the key suspects are. There are two distinct possibilities. Thaddeus Fleming Calhoun and Dr. Lorentz Bohrman. You will have to research in advance. Find photographs of what they looked like and—"

"Photographs? Where am I supposed to find those? It's not like they're on the web."

"What is this web?"

"Never mind. Where can I get these pictures?"

"Use your head. Books. Archives. Museums. I've heard tourists mention a museum of Civil War medicine." He paused to smirk. "Incredible. An entire museum devoted to medical practices that occurred during four years that were nothing but a tragic stain on history. Regardless, I think it is located in Frederick. Now, if my murderer is neither of those two, then we will have to meet again to discuss other options."

"I don't understand." My mind still wrapped around the notion of danger, but I tried to follow Braxton's conversation. "How can you be so sure that one of those two men killed you?"

He stopped pacing again. "I had identified Bohrman as a charlatan. No more a surgeon than you or the people who tend to the grass on these lawns. I never reported him because we were severely short-staffed, and he was, at least, learning on the job."

"That's terrible!"

He ignored my outburst. "If Bohrman, then he must have killed himself after shooting us because his body fell to the floor beside mine. That would mean Calhoun wasn't here, and it's safe to hope that Eva may have gotten away."

He was pacing again. "Now, our second option is Calhoun. A despicable man. Eva was a slave girl, and he owned her."

I nodded. "Will told me. He said you loved her."

"Loved … yes." He stopped pacing and looked into the sky, his voice growing soft, wistful. "From the instant I met her. She was beautiful and graceful despite her wretched living conditions. She always smelled of Cherokee roses. The Calhouns required her to put sprigs of dried roses and spices in their clothing after washing them and to soak the linen handkerchiefs in the scent."

"Will said you helped her escape. That you solicited Fergus's help."

"Yes, well, what Will didn't know was that Eva and I had married. Our marriage is the pivotal reason that my father sent me away to university. He wanted to distance us. Pretend the marriage didn't exist. I returned home, when I could, to be with her. Later, when she was with child, I took action to get her away from Calhoun. My only option was to steal her away from there, which as you might know, was considered a crime at the time. Stealing a slave or aiding escape was punishable by death."

Although I found it hard to fathom that this brooding soul could feel love for someone else, the sadness of his story touched me. I thought it best if I didn't interrupt.

"Calhoun wanted her back. The man was a lecherous son of a—" He broke off, collected his composure. "Regardless, if Calhoun killed me, then that means he had followed us, in pursuit of Eva. He may have found her with Fergus, which would explain how Fergus ended up in prison. Calhoun had relatives in this area, so he may have had help arranging for Fergus to be arrested. That would be like him, to prefer that Fergus die a slow, rotting death in prison than to kill him outright. In that case, Eva may have been taken against her will back to the South."

He stopped pacing. "In either scenario, I'm sure that Eva and the gold were targets."

Gold! How did that fit into this scenario?

Braxton explained that after war broke out, word reached him that Calhoun had gone mad, beating the male slaves and abusing the women. Braxton secured a brief leave of absence and with three horses, journeyed one hot summer night to collect his wife and her brother, Moses. Calhoun discovered their plan and pursued them through the thick woods of South Carolina.

"He and his men shot at us, taking down one of the horses." His hands fisted on the words. "That left two. I began to panic, wondering what we would do. Then, in what proved to be a final gesture to the love he held for his sister, Moses yelled for me to take Eva and go. He stayed behind to create a distraction. Before I could argue, he thrust a small flour bag into my hand and ran toward our attackers. Later, we opened it and found gold."

I braced myself before asking, "What happened to Moses?"

"He was gunned down like an animal."

I didn't know what to say. I just sat there, despondent, drained of energy.

Braxton dropped to a tree stump, opposite me. "I don't know where the gold came from. I assumed Moses took it from Calhoun whom, I'm guessing, secured it through trade. Perhaps even stole it from the offices in Dahlonega. Once back in Virginia, I cashed in a few of the coins and stayed in hiding with Eva. When circumstances brought Fergus and me together again, I was desperate, so I solicited his help with Eva. I had to return to my war assignment. I had no idea at the time that by placing my wife in his care, I was making a deal with the Devil."

"But if you paid Fergus in cash, then why did you tell him about the gold?"

"I didn't," Braxton said. "I gave it to Eva to keep. To help her escape when she needed to buy or bribe assistance. I impressed upon her the importance of keeping it hidden."

"How much gold?" I imagined the seven-hundred and fifty pieces of gold that Seth and I had discussed earlier in the day. "Maybe she couldn't carry it by herself."

Braxton sniggered. "Hundreds of coins of pure gold would weigh a mere three or four pounds. Eva could have hidden it under her skirts and never make anyone the wiser. My guess is that Fergus tricked her into trusting him."

"So you just sent her off with Fergus? Just the two of them?"

Braxton shook his head. "I did not trust him that much. I also secured help from my brother and his wife. Fergus took Eva to *Crossings* and put her into their care."

"Aaron Kyd Hood … and Savilla," I whispered, pulling on a memory.

Braxton cocked his head. "How did you know my brother's name?"

"Will mentioned it once." I looked away and took a deep breath before looking back and adding, "He loved you like a brother."

Braxton stared at me for a moment, or perhaps it's more accurate to say he stared through me at a memory, then he groaned and turned his head.

Startled, I asked, "What? What is it?"

"This. The memories. They are excruciatingly painful. I can't feel new emotions, but while I remain here, I'm conditioned to forever recall that sense of loss, of parting with Will and Eva and losing all that we once dreamed could be."

"I'm sorry." My voice sounded little more than a whisper. It was all I could manage.

He looked into the sky. "These memories are like field surgery. So much pain and no analgesic for relief."

CHAPTER 10

I arrived home around 9 p.m., hoping to avoid Michael and drop in bed. My plans changed when I saw Seth's car in the driveway, parked beside an unfamiliar car which sported a rental sticker on the back.

Just outside the apartment door, I heard the crooning sounds of *Red Hot Chili Peppers*. The tune mixed with three sets of laughter. I recognized each. Despite my concern for Michael and the tiring talk with Braxton, I was thrilled to see my old friend.

"Kate!" I said, entering the apartment.

She sat on the floor, brushing Chubbs, who basked in the attention. Michael and Seth sat on the couch and chair, watching Kate. Between them, on the coffee table, sat popcorn and iced tea. Since Michael and Chubbs shared the same room, I thought the evening might be pleasant after all.

"Gracie!" Kate climbed off the floor in a flash and pulled me into a hug.

"You look great," I said, hugging her back. And she did. She'd always had the look of a model—tall, willowy, with legs that stretched on forever—but now she wore her hair cut in a bob, and it suited her. "Love the hair. When did you arrive?"

"About two hours ago. At the same time as Seth," she said flashing him a smile. "It's given me a chance to get to know him. And to get caught up with Michael. But *you* are the one who looks great. I wish I looked like you."

I ignored the comment. Kate thought the Pillsbury Doughboy looked better than her. Despite her flirtiness and a penchant for being scatterbrained, she always extended kindness and compliments to everyone.

As I moved further into the room, Tramp pounced on me, no doubt jealous of the attention Chubbs enjoyed. "Hold on, boy, I'll take you out in a minute."

"No need," Michael yelled from the couch as he reached to turn down the stereo. "I took him for a long walk right before they arrived."

Surprised, I looked at Seth. I wondered if he, too, was taken aback by Michael's kind and *normal* behavior. He shrugged and lifted his eyebrows as though to say, "I can't figure it out either."

"Thanks, Michael," I said with a little too much enthusiasm. "I really appreciate it."

He laughed. "What's the big deal? I do it all the time."

I looked at Seth again before turning my focus to Kate. I put my arm around her shoulder and pulled her back into the sitting area. "So how are you? How long will you be here?"

"Great. And, I'm not sure how long." She laughed. "You know me, Grace, I'm a free spirit, but I had to see you for your birthday ... although, I guess it's over now. Anyway, I have to get my senior year underway somewhere ... probably Richmond. That's where Roxanne lives now." She broke off to look at Seth and explain, "That's my sister," before turning back to me. "They're starting late this year due to construction on a new high school, so that might work for me."

"That's great," I enthused. "Three hours away is sure better than eight back to Boston. We'll be able to get together on weekends. Now, what have I missed?"

Kate chuckled. "I was just telling Michael and Seth that I wanted to go to school to be an anesthesiologist. But Seth said his dad is one and that it involves years of school and pressure. So I don't think that profession is for me."

"So, you gave up the military idea?"

"What? Oh, yes. Days ago. Could you see me in one of those uniforms?" She exaggerated a cringe.

Stifled by her logic, we all grew quiet.

"Well," Michael said as he climbed off the couch and carried his empty glass into the kitchen, "I'm the old man in this group, and I have a job and a long commute in the morning. Gotta get up at six, so if you'll excuse me, I'm going to call my girlfriend for a while and then turn in."

Kate chuckled. "Wow Michael, you've got it bad. This Adriana must be something."

"I'll make sure you meet before you leave. Night, Sis," he said as he passed by on his way to the old house. He pulled me into an embrace. "Hope you guys have a good evening."

Seth shot me a look again, then dropped his gaze down to his glass.

When Michael reached the door leading into the old house, he turned and looked back at us. "Oh, and Kate?" An unmistakable hint of warning had crawled into his voice. "Welcome to the Dark Side."

I caught my breath, waiting to see what he would do next, what he might say, expecting him to transform right before our eyes again. Instead, he chuckled, walked through the archway, and closed the door behind him.

Kate hesitated as though trying to process Michael's words and odd behavior. She shook it off with a laugh. "Um, yeah. Night, Michael." She stood and stretched, oblivious to the eye contact exchanged between Seth and me. "Where's the powder room, Grace?"

After she left the room, I hurried to Seth. "What's with Michael?"

"I don't know. I haven't seen him this normal in weeks. Didn't you say that Adriana broke up with him?"

"Yes!" When I heard the volume in my voice, I dropped it to a whisper before continuing. "She said she told him no communication. No calls. No texts. No emails. No nothing. He acts like he doesn't even know it."

"Or doesn't remember," Seth suggested in a concerning voice. Momentary silence fell as I thought about his words. He moved to the edge of his chair and leaned toward me. "You didn't tell me your friend Kate was visiting."

"Sorry. I just learned her plans earlier today. With Kate, things are never definite." As I spoke, I could see Seth's amusement at my comment. I smiled, knowing full well what he must be thinking. "So what do you think?"

He shook his head and raised his eyebrows. "Amazing."

I wondered how to interpret his comment. I could have taken it many ways. For some reason, I hoped he meant that he recognized how scattered and unfocused she was. So why did I feel an unexpected sting of jealousy by his single-word remark?

"Yeah, she's something," I said, pretending to brush lint off my sleeve. I didn't want to read his face, to learn what "amazing" meant. "With Kate, you never know how long she'll be around or what she'll do next. I guess I could change my schedule to—"

"I can help out. Take her to lunch. Show her around the town, or take her to a movie or the mall. Whatever. Then you won't have to change whatever you're trying to do for Michael."

I opened my mouth, but nothing came out. My brain locked in a loop, a thousand questions combating for attention. Finally, I made eye contact with him and saw a warm smile.

"Thanks." I mumbled the word. His was a generous offer, so why did I feel so bereft? Shouldn't I be glad he showed interest in someone else? Sure, I loved Seth, but I wasn't *in* love with him. His presence made my heart ripple with happiness, but Clay's made my heart thump like a bass drum. For the first time, it struck me: Perhaps the heart thumping out of control … perhaps that constituted infatuation, whereas love embodied the steadier, more comfortable beat. *I wondered …*

"Man, it's freezing in here," Kate said, returning to the room. She rubbed her hands over her arms. "I can understand the Gomez and Morticia Addams chamber where Michael sleeps being cold, but you'd think the heat would work better in here."

I caught her joke about the morbid looks of the old house, but what registered with me was that I thought the apartment plenty warm.

"Here," Seth said reaching across the sofa to collect his jacket. "Wear this."

"Seth, you sweet, sweet man," she said. "You are so gallant. But that's okay. I need to bring my bags in anyway. I packed a sweater."

Seth offered to retrieve her things, so she gave him the car keys.

When he left, Kate squealed. "Grace, your boyfriend is awesome. He's so cute and so attentive and so … so … charming."

She must have missed the confused look on my face because she continued.

"He said he volunteers at the hospital? He's just about perfect, isn't he?"

And then it hit me. "No, Seth is not my boyfriend. We're just friends."

Her jaw dropped. "You're not dating?"

I shook my head.

"Well," she said, smacking her hands together. The sign of a decision made. "Then I think he should be my boyfriend for a while."

Her comment hit me in that odd spot that Seth's comment whopped me earlier. Where did this jealous feeling come from? I had no right to feel this way.

When Seth returned, Kate extracted a beige sweater from her travel bag. "That's better," she said, pulling it tight around her. "I'm chilled all over."

"Are you feeling alright?" In its isolation, my question hovered like it came out of nowhere.

Kate must have thought so, too. She looked surprised. "Yes … I mean, I guess." She cocked her head and pondered the question. "I just started feeling funny in the past couple hours."

Alarms sounded in my head. *Michael. The house. Fergus!*

"So, you felt good all day, until now?" I tried to sound casual.

"No, not good, just okay. The ship made me wobbly. I guess I'm a landlubber. Once we reached land, I was exhausted. Maybe I got cruiselag." She laughed. "You know, instead of jetlag? Anyway, I had to pull over and take a couple naps on my way here."

Feeling fatigue from travel and experiencing chills in my house were two different issues in my mind. I couldn't shake the notion that she might be getting sick from Fergus's influence, just like Michael. But how could it happen so quickly? I decided to keep her busy in the next several days and to have her sleep in my bed, not on the couch which sat close to the old house.

"Hey, you two," I said, "I'd like to do some research on medicine during the Civil War." I shrugged. "Part of homeschooling for this fall. Seth, isn't there a museum about Civil War medicine around here somewhere?"

He nodded. "About a half-hour away."

"Want to join me?" I asked them both.

Seth flashed a look that said he understood my intent to keep Kate busy and out of the house. "Yeah, that'd be great," he said. "I'm in a work-study program in high school, so after my classes end at eleven, I'm free for the day. I usually report to the hospital, but I could go without problem. I mean, the museum is about medicine. What about you, Kate? Will you come too?"

Obviously flattered by Seth's encouragement to tag along, Kate said, "Sure. You know, I've been thinking that maybe a career in nursing might be fun. It's less stressful than anesthesiology, and you get to talk to a lot of people. I'm good at talking. I could get a feel for the work tomorrow."

"Kate," Seth said with a chuckle, "medicine in those days was different. It … never mind. You're right. It's a great idea."

Kate's words rang true: Seth was an awesome guy.

CHAPTER 11

The National Museum of Civil War Medicine is housed in a two-level structure on Patrick Street, in downtown Frederick, Maryland. It took us several hours to tour, as the museum presented thousands of relics and tidbits of information to absorb. Because Seth planned to study medicine, and Kate fancied learning more about nursing *and* Seth, they inched their way through. So I moved ahead on my own, hoping to find a picture of Dr. Bohrman on a wall placard.

The displays presented a bleak story of medical training in the late 1800s. Most medical practitioners in the war had received only two terms of six-month-long lectures, with the second term often being a repeat of the first. Surgeons had little or no clinical experience and few opportunities to practice surgical procedures. Doctors and nurses had little understanding of germ theory, antiseptic practices, and the importance of sterilizing equipment, as these discoveries would take a few more years. What's more, many of the wartime's early commissions as surgeons required no proof of medical training or ability. History proved that several charlatans professed to be doctors so they could stay behind the battle lines. Braxton had accused Bohrman of this deception.

Surgeons, one display said, earned the nickname "sawbones," because the principal surgical procedure performed during the war involved amputation, accounting for three out of four operations. Between the North and South, surgeons conducted about 50,000 amputations during the four-year war, prompting harsh criticism and earning them the reputation of being butchers.

However, as another display pointed out, if doctors delayed amputation more than forty-eight hours, the death rate doubled due to development of blood poisoning, bone infection, or gangrene. With those odds, it's not surprising that most surgeons favored immediate amputation of arms and legs.

One exhibit said that between skirmishes, men "battled the diseases of the camp," and that of the 620,000 soldiers who died during the War, "two-thirds of them died not of bullets or bayonets, but of disease."

Thoughts of Braxton's miserable life as a surgeon overwhelmed me. He must have been continually tired and overwhelmed, with no time to recover, think, pray, or breathe! No wonder he was so aloof. At one point on the second floor, I groaned and dropped my forehead into my hand. I just wanted to rub away some tension and bleakness at what I'd encountered in the museum.

"You feel it. That's good. It shouldn't be forgotten."

The voice, laden with a heavy Southern accent, had come from my right. "Yes, I can," I responded with knee-jerk politeness to whoever had sidled up beside me. I looked over to offer a quick acknowledgement, but instead my jaw dropped as I took in the disheveled soul standing at my side.

All these years since the War and he still looked as though he just stepped off the battlefield. Over his dusty, gaunt frame, he wore the ragtag jacket of a Southern uniform. His clothes were torn and filthy, grizzled hair brushed his shoulders, and he had no left arm.

It was too late to walk away. We'd made eye contact, and I'd already reacted to his words. I watched as he, in turn, registered surprise that I saw and heard him.

"You can see me."

I nodded.

He studied me like I was an alien being plopped down into his world.

I gestured to the exhibit. It included a wall mural from Antietam. "Were you there? Did you know Braxton ... Doctor Braxton Hood?"

He turned his gaze to the picture. "No, Miss, I wasn't in that battle. But I knew Doc Hood. He was a loner. Not well-liked 'cause a' his work."

"Why? Because he performed amputations?"

"Yes, Miss. Men called him Dr. Hoodwinked 'cause he'd convince ya' your life was more important than yer arm or your leg. T'wasn't 'til them was gone, that ya' learned he tricked ya'. It wasn't the same life without 'em. Not in them times."

"But that's crazy. He tried to save lives."

The soul shrugged. "Wasn't that so much as what happened down near Great Falls. You know, near Washington ... the Yankee capital."

"What do you mean?"

"Folks blamed Doc Hood for the death of Andrew Crowell. Farm kid from Mississippi. By the time the war broke out, Andy'd already lost his right hand. Sawmill took it. But he wanted to fight. Do his share. So he signed up."

"But how could he fight with just one hand?"

"He could still tote a gun. Perch it on his stump and fire with the other hand." He shook his head. "But not for long, cause he took a bullet in the left arm. Up near the shoulder. Started turnin' all shades of purple. Swelled up bigger 'n a gut-shot coon. Doc Hood took the arm off. 'Course, Hood said he had no choice. Andy went into the operation fightin'. Begged Doc not to do it. Said he'd rather die. But Hood ordered the men to hold Andy down, and he took the arm anyway."

His story sapped my energy, and I reached for the display to steady myself. I didn't know for whom to feel worse—Braxton or Andy Crowell. "But Braxton ... Doctor Hood ... had to do it. The young man ... Andy ... he would have died otherwise, right?"

"That's what they say, Miss. Still, that done made no difference to Andy. He tried life with no hands for a coupla' weeks."

"What happened?"

"Didn't work. Couldn't feed himself. Or pull up his pants. Shoot, they had to scratch his nose. Pick the lice off him. He couldn't even wipe himself without help, if you know what I mean, Miss. His life was done. He'd never even been out with a girl, and now no girl'd ever want 'im. He wanted to die. Started askin' other people to kill 'im 'cause he didn't have no hands to do it hisself."

"How awful." I tried to picture the young man in my mind. "How old was he?"

"Seventeen."

My age! "That poor kid … man. And Braxton, he must have felt awful."

"Ol' Andy, he was so out of it, he decided to end it hisself. Just walked to the cliffs at Great Falls where the rocks was highest. Everyone watched him go. They could tell he was unhinged … madder than an angry hornet. Figured he wanted to die. Finally, some o' the men started yellin' for him not to do it. Then more joined in. They come 'a runnin', yellin' for him to stop. Beggin' him to think 'bout what he was doin'."

"But he didn't stop."

"No, Miss."

"Why didn't they stop him? Tackle him? Drag him back?"

"He was too far ahead."

"But they could have run."

The soul shook his head as though to say, "You don't understand." He looked back at the mural, but I sensed he was seeing countless situations of such misery instead. "It wouldn't done no good. Andy wanted to die. Those men was strugglin' with life and death too. Wonderin' what it was all for. Thinkin' they'd never see home again. Worryin' they could be another Andy. Maybe worse. Guess they figured they'd wanna die too if they was Andy."

"But that's terrible. They just watched him die?"

"Ya' might argue none of 'em had the heart to save him, but the truth is that none of 'em had the heart to stop him. None of 'em wanted to be the one to assign Andy to a life of no hope. No chance he'd ever be able to make a livin'. Not even be able to do his business alone."

Speechless, I tried to process this story. The War had been excruciating for everyone involved. The times had been difficult, the sensibilities different. Life and hope were skewed and took on different meanings. Sometimes the hope to die surpassed the hope to live. It struck me that men's ideas of helping one another had become distorted, as well.

"The way I heard it," the soul continued, "many of 'em bolted for the cliffs, but it took a while to git down to the water. They pulled Andy out. By then it was too late. He was gone. The easiest thing to do was blame Doc Hood. Andy wouldn't a' wanted 'em to do that though."

I didn't know what to say, but I'd heard enough. The desperation and angst together wrapped around me like a heavy quilt, smothering me in its thickness, such that as I peered out from the folds, I could see it all as Andy might have seen it. Andy returning home after the war and not being able to climb off his horse, or open the front door, or shake his father's hand. Andy trying to figure out how to saw wood or milk a cow or a plow a field without hands. Andy trying to court a girl, but not being able to touch her cheek, help her with her wrap, pull out her chair. I turned to say something inane about how times had changed and that now artificial limbs restored all these abilities. That's when he turned toward me, and I saw his right arm.

It had no hand.

"You're Andrew Crowell!"

He didn't react. Didn't turn to meet my gaze. "Yes, Miss."

"But you're here. Your center ... where ..."

He turned and pointed his stump toward the glass display behind us. "That Bible over yonder. It was mine. Tossed it on the cliff before I jumped. Couldn't see no sense in destroying it, too."

"But ... if you owned that ... then why would you ... don't you think ..." I swallowed, trying to restore my composure. "I was always taught that suicide was ... you know ... wrong. That it comes with certain irreversible repercussions." I shook my head as I heard my own words. "I'm sorry, but aren't you afraid of ..."

He gazed at his boots, and his face grew somber as I watched him conjure up that moment from a hundred and fifty years earlier, a painful return, it looked to me, but one to which he appeared to have grown accustomed as though he'd lived it time and time again. "Eternal damnation?" He turned to look at me. "Yes, Miss. I was at first when I realized I'd actually died. I was made aware right away that I'd made a big mistake. I saw that there was still a lot I coulda' done here on Earth without my hands. A *lot* more."

"Like what?"

He shrugged. "I still had eyes to witness life. To see my family. A mouth to tell 'em things. To teach, to preach, to offer hope. Feet to carry messages. To take a walk with my ma and my sister. I learned we all have wounds. They're just not always as visible as mine. But by the time I learned I'd made a mistake, it was too late. Lucky for me, there are sometimes second chances. I'd been a real good man before my death, Miss. I'd lived a good life. A pious life. Maybe I have a chance to prove myself again."

I considered this a moment, wished Will or Pastor Dale were with me to verify the possibility of Andrew's story, to explain the odds of his hope coming true. "I'm glad you can still have a happy ending." My voice sounded little more than a whisper, but it was edged in doubt.

He shook his head. "Nah, it ain't that easy. And it ain't for certain either. Fact is, some might call *this* hell. The waitin'. The wonderin'. Just endlessly tryin' and wonderin' if you're doin' enough. If that will make a difference or if you'll still end up bein' punished forever by your own actions."

I looked around, taking in the boundaries of his existence now. "What are you doing to make a difference?"

"I use my stump to kinda' nudge folks to linger, to read a little more, to learn what they can. On Sundays, I go to that church next door and watch out for them little kids. Open the doors when someone is lookin' for somethin'. Hide the keys to them auto cars when I get the notion someone might be in an accident if they leave too early. Other such things, too."

"But how?" I eyed his stump. "I don't understand. I thought when we died that we were made complete again."

He looked at his stump too. "We are. I can manifest it when I need it. But this way it reminds me to help out."

I had more questions and wanted to hear more about those missing keys, but I could hear other people rounding the corner toward us.

"I have to go, Andy. If I come back sometime, will I find you here?"

"Yes, Miss. That'd be real nice."

He turned away as though to leave, but then looked back. "And

Miss? I'm guessin' you musta' met ole Doc Hood somewhere? Don't be too hard on him. I once saw him operate on a man whose upper jaw'd been blown away. Rest of us lost our stomachs just lookin' at the guy. Another time, me and a bunch of men helped Doc pull a herd of swine off a wounded guy. The man had lost both legs and couldn't move. The hogs was eatin' his flesh. Doc did what he could to save him. Them kind of experiences, and the way the men hated Doc Hood for doin' his job … well, I'm just sayin' you can't live through many of them times without it startin' to change ya. We all worked hard, but his was work that *made* ya' hard."

He turned and walked away. *Right through a wall.*

Overwhelmed, I hurried to a restroom where I backed up to a wall, slid to the floor, and sobbed.

★ ★ ★

After paying for our purchases at the bookstore, Seth, Kate, and I walked across the street to a deli. We ate, lingered, relaxed, and agreed that we should see more of Frederick one day.

"But not that museum," Kate said, dropping her sandwich to her plate. She'd only taken one bite. "I'll go anywhere but there again."

Seth grinned. "I thought you wanted to study nursing."

"Not your thing?" I asked.

"No way." She smiled. "I could never do that kind of work. But that's okay. I know you're both teasing me because I don't know what I want to do. But I'm not like you. It doesn't just come to me. Unlike you, I'll have to reach my decision through process of elimination."

Seth and I both hesitated. I could tell that Kate's insight surprised him, too. But, she wasn't done. She continued, imparting wisdom about the importance of selecting the right career, and it left us downright speechless.

"Everyone has a hunger that gnaws at their hearts, ya' know? It has nothing to do with money or status or anything external. I mean, I love my clothes and looking good, don't get me wrong. But the hunger comes from in here," she said, jabbing her finger into her chest. "We all want meaning and answers about God, love, death, good, and evil." She picked up her glass and sipped. "I want work where I can explore all that and help others find it too. I want to do work I was meant to do. With whatever talents I've been given."

See what I mean about being speechless? That this wisdom came from Kate astonished me. All I could do was blink. Well, blink *and* feel bad that I might have misjudged my friend.

"You're right," Seth said and reached his hand across the table to squeeze hers. "We all have to find what's right for us in our own way. I think that when you finally decide, you'll be spot on." I heard sincerity in his voice.

I'm sure it'd been a long time since Kate blushed, but she did now.

"Thanks, Seth," she said, her eyes sparkling.

In my discomfort at their locked gaze, I quipped, "Wow, what happened to you in France?"

Kate grinned. "Well, I went there thinking I'd like to teach the French language one day. My dad said his great uncle died there in World War II, helping to free them from the Nazis. I wanted to, you know, kinda' pick up his cause on helping the French thrive. But they never smile. And they kept telling me what was wrong with America even though we fought and died to save them. So I've scratched teaching off my list." She looked down, moved her knife away from her plate, and spun it slowly. "Truth is, what I said about the heart a moment ago, my dad wrote those words. In his last letter. I memorized them. I want to make sure I don't waste time learning them the hard way." She yawned and stretched. "Can we go now? I don't know why, but I feel so tired."

Neither Seth nor I said a word about her dad. Judging by his look of understanding, I surmised that Kate had told him her father died in Iraq.

"Have you ever thought about career counseling?" Seth inquired, standing and pulling together our empty plates and cups for the garbage. "We have a friend named Sidney Paness who could help you."

They continued their conversation about careers as we walked to our car, at which time Seth discovered his car keys missing.

Fifteen minutes later, we pulled out of the lot, having retraced our steps and finding the keys in the bookstore.

"That's so weird," Seth said as he steered onto the interstate. "I never took them out of my pocket. I don't understand how they fell out."

Kate complained about nausea and a stiff neck, and she fell asleep almost right away, so Seth turned the radio on to a low volume. Within minutes, the station reported a multi-car accident on Route 70 at South Mountain. The announcer said traffic could be backed up for hours and that travelers should take alternate Route 40.

Seth exhaled a whistle. "Geez, we'd have been caught in that if we'd left earlier."

I turned my gaze away from Seth, looked out the side window, and smiled as a vision flittered across my mind of Andy jangling Seth's keys.

★ ★ ★

If Seth and Kate ever wondered why I purchased the ugliest, and seemingly the most boring, book in the museum bookstore, they didn't ask. But I had my reasons: on page thirty-eight, I found a picture of Dr. Lorentz Bohrman, taken the week before the Antietam battle.

I intended to study his picture until I memorized it so well that I could guide a sketch artist to do a perfect rendering.

Even then, I planned to tear the page from the book and carry it with me to Antietam when I witnessed Braxton's death. His analogy about dominoes made sense, but I'd always found the game tedious and risky. If one piece is handled poorly, then the entire lot can fall from anywhere in the middle, rendering the whole effort a failure.

Before I could solve his murder, I had to line up two key dominoes: the one in my hand, a picture of Dr. Bohrman. The other, a picture of Thaddeus Fleming Calhoun. If I couldn't find that latter domino on the Internet, I'd have to make a trip to Savannah, where Braxton Hood and Calhoun had once called home.

CHAPTER 12

B efore retiring Tuesday night, Kate and I agreed we'd take Tramp for an early morning walk on the C&O Canal. The plans floundered, however because she didn't get up until 9:15 a.m. Still, we walked for about a half-mile before she begged off, saying her muscles ached, and she wanted to go back to *Crossings* to read. I suspected that she wanted to climb back in bed because she looked tired and acted disoriented.

We had traveled in separate cars, and I planned to meet Seth at the library in a few hours, so Kate offered to take Tramp back with her. After arguing that she shouldn't drive alone (she won), then securing her promise that she would stay in the apartment, I agreed.

She laughed. "Gracie, you need to chill. You're too worried." She opened her car door and folded into the driver's seat with an exhale that suggested she was bone-weary and happy to sit. Tramp barked from the back. "What's the big deal if I stay in the apartment or explore the house?"

I shut her door and studied her through the open window. What could I say that would sound plausible? "You just seem a little … weak. That's all. And the house is old. Probably unsafe. You never know about something that old."

"It *is* old, isn't it? Imagine if those walls could talk! And there's probably a lot of relics and remains, around the area, too."

"No! I mean … there's nothing exciting out there. Just an old cemetery and a lot of green lawns and trees. Huge, old trees."

Her eyes widened. "A cemetery? I bet it's ancient, like the ones in Boston. Reminds me that archeology might be a fun career. We ought to explore—"

"Not this trip, okay? You'll be living closer now, so we can explore some other time."

She looked like she wanted to argue, but then yawned instead. "Yeah, you're probably right. I'm just tired. Think I caught a bug on my trip back. I'll be more peppy on my next visit. We can explore then. It's going to be so great living within driving distance from you now." She shot a sheepish grin which morphed into another yawn as she added, "Seth too. He is sooo adorable, Grace."

I nodded but wondered again why her interest in Seth discomforted me. Was I afraid Seth would get hurt because of Kate's tendency toward fleeting and short-lived romances? Or was I afraid I'd get hurt if their attraction blossomed? And why did I care?

I shrugged away my concerns and looked at the contented face of my friend. "Yes, he is," I agreed. "He's very special. And so are you, Kate. I'm glad you'll be living closer, too. You'll have to get to know Adriana. The three of us can meet in D.C. It'll be so much fun. Now go, before you fall asleep in this parking lot. Get some rest. I'll meet you at home late this afternoon."

As she pulled away, I was overcome by the warmth of the friendship we shared. I'd met Kate right after moving in with my Aunt Tish and Uncle Phil in Boston, and the two of us had become fast friends. I had not only lost my mom and stepfather shortly before meeting her, but also my sister Julie. Kate helped to fill that void, and we had become inseparable. Somewhat like Adriana and I. A new feeling of missing Ade washed over me, so I punched the buttons on my cell phone to call her. It rang five times before going to voicemail. I clicked off. I was afraid that if I left a message, she wouldn't call me back. That would hurt too much.

I decided to get a cup of coffee at the *Time Out* and do a little damage control with Cassie. I missed spending time with that friend, too.

10:30 a.m. can be a lonely time at a café; the breakfast crowd had already come and gone, and the lunch crowd had not yet arrived. So, I wasn't surprised to see a mere handful of people sitting at a table in front, a group of bikers that had passed Kate and me when we'd first set foot on the canal. What did surprise me is that no one stood behind the counter.

I headed to the back, expecting to push the door open to Cassie's kitchen and office area to find her wrapped up in ledgers and paperwork.

Instead, I found her wrapped in Whit's arms.

The instant they saw me, Whit looked up with a smile, but Cassie jerked away, her demeanor changing from contentment to embarrassment in one second flat.

"Oh! I'm sorry." I turned and left the room. As I returned to the dining area, it hit me that I was *surprised* to be surprised, which smacked me as silly, of course. Cassie and Whit were both single. On their own. Both gym rats. Both sociable and—until Clay had left— Cassie had been almost as easy-going and happy as Whit.

"Hon, wait." Cassie followed me into the dining area. Her gaze darted to the table of bikers and back again. She dropped her voice to a whisper and put her hands on my shoulders, holding me close and in place, her fingers squeezing to emphasize her words. "It ain't what you think."

I shook my head. "It doesn't matter what I think."

She sighed and maneuvered me to the opposite side of the room.

The look on her face and the sound in her voice made me believe that my friend experienced deep angst about moving on after Mason, and my casual acceptance of this change in her life had plumbed a raw aspect of her healing.

"It doesn't matter," I assured her again.

She shook her head and in a broken whisper said, "It's not what it looks like."

I smiled and touched her arm. "It *looks* like you are happy."

She frowned, gestured to a table, and folded into a chair opposite me.

Whit appeared from the back, nonplussed, even whistling a peppy tune. "I'm going after those supplies," he said and headed out the door.

After he left, Cassie dropped her shoulders. "There's nothing between us. He was just comforting. That's all."

I didn't believe her but kept the thought to myself. "You're alone, he's alone. You're two consenting adults.

She rolled her eyes. "Oh, please."

"Do you love him?"

"What? No. I don't know ... This isn't going anywhere, anyway. Not while Mason's out there somewhere."

"Cassie, that's over. He's gone."

She frowned. "The night he left he said he'd be back shortly. Said he'd been asked to make some big loan. He was a banker, you know ... Anyway, the loan was for some kinda' museum and educational center. He wanted to check it out for himself. I've often wondered if any of that was true." She looked away and said in one of the saddest voices I'd ever heard, "If I just knew why he left us ..."

Her comment made me pause. I could feel her sorrow, as though it crept through the room like a slow fog, enveloping everything in its mist. Mason was dead, but she did not know that and to make matters worse, I couldn't tell her yet. I pictured her now as having spent the many years since his departure in a fruitless conjuring of rationalizations for his disappearance: a debilitating disease, another woman, a wanderlust to explore the world. Again, it hit me that Clay's departure probably compounded the hurt. I could offer her nothing ... *yet*. I had to remain quiet, so the silence stretched out uncomfortably between us.

Finally, I offered the obvious. "Mason's been gone for years, Cassie. He's not coming back."

"You don't know that," she said so quickly that it was obvious she still harbored hope, still expected him to walk through the door one day. "No one can know that. But if he does, I don't want him comin' back to find that the person he loved is with someone else now." She raised her gaze and gave me a pointed look.

I flinched and, again, didn't know what to say. I suspected her look was purposeful, that she hoped to give me a double message; that she didn't want Clay to come home and find me in Seth's arms. Was I imagining her two-fold intent?

I ignored her change in focus. "You need to move on. You can't look back." My words sounded trite, like textbook relationship advice.

She managed a weak smile. "You sound like my son."

"Clay said that?"

"He said it doesn't matter what came before because ya' can't go back. All that matters is now and the future. That it's possible to love more than once. He told me to stop stumblin' over somethin' behind me."

That quickly, I hurt like I'd been punched in the stomach. Had Clay listened to his own counsel? Had he believed his own advice?

Cassie continued. "I used to imagine how Mason would come back. I'd be fillin' a customer's mug and turn to see who had just come in the door …"

My dread turned to adrenalin, and chills rashed out on my arms. I had this conversation with her before! While sitting on the rock talking to Mason. But how?

"… and there he'd be. Bundles of presents in his arms. As though to say that he left so that he could go somewhere and make a better life for us. Or I'd open the office door and instead of the package delivery service, he would be standin' there with roses in his arms."

She paused and looked up. At the look on my face, she reached for me. "Are you okay?"

"What? Yeah … yeah, I'm fine. I just experienced déjà vu, I guess. I'm sorry, you were saying?"

"Nothin'. Just that abandonment is an illness and—

"It will kill you if you let it," I whispered.

Her brows pinched together in curiosity. "That's right." She shook her head as though to dislodge her thoughts and clear her thinking. "Well, this is doin' no one any good, so I better get back to work." She stood and turned to go, but stopped and looked back. "Hon, I'd appreciate if what you saw remained between us."

I nodded then left. I may have embraced her. I don't recall. I was too busy wrapping my thoughts around the scene I'd just lived twice.

I prayed that I wouldn't have to relive other moments twice. There'd been several since moving here that I was surprised I'd survived *once*.

CHAPTER 13

Maybe déjà vu was on my mind. Or maybe I suddenly missed my mom. Or perhaps I felt nostalgic or lonely or wistful after leaving Cassie. Whatever my thinking, it prompted me to catch a flash of light as I walked past an antique shop on my walk to the library. My gaze followed the light to the store window. Between the faded etching of the store hours and a "Help Wanted" sign, I watched a short, plump, gray-haired lady display an old mirror.

Encrusted with ivory and rubies on the handle, it looked like one my mother had owned, and which her mother—my Grandma Sadie— had given to her. My Aunt Tish had heartlessly disposed of it one afternoon while I sat in school.

Memories washed over me.

Go inside and inquire.

So I did. I didn't know if I thought or heard that chattering in my head, but my body drove on its own and headed inside before I even determined whether or not I should.

Bells tinkled as I entered the two-story building housing Hilson's Antique Emporium. It quintessentially embodied what you'd imagine an antique shop to be: an uncategorized mishmash of items, floor to ceiling, from china to tools to vintage hats, all layered in years of dust. Still, it looked quaint and smelled of vanilla candles, the overall effect welcoming, like the smile the woman offered me.

"Hello, young lady," she said as she turned from the display, leaned into her cane, and picked up a feather duster with her free hand. "Lovely day, isn't it? My gracious, I can't seem to keep the dust down in here." She inched along as she worked, as though she wore the effects of her years in her ankles.

"Nice place." I meant it. I liked it, and I liked her. Her smile was genuine, her demeanor, kind. "Are you the owner?"

"Indeed I am. I'm Hilda. And you are?"

"Grace. Wait, so your name is Hilda Hilson?"

She chuckled. "Married into that name. Had no choice. But I wouldn't have changed anything even if I could. Arthur ... that's my late husband ... he and I had over fifty years together."

She sighed as she moved her duster, her gaze directed from me to her work and back again. "It was a good life. He helped me open this shop thirty-seven years ago, after our youngest left home. We didn't need the money." She smiled and winked. "Arthur was loaded. Blue blood sort. My gracious, he indulged my fancies. Then, when I started selling on the Internet, sales got quite good. Now I'm looking for help."

"So you've been in this same location ever since you opened?" I enjoyed the small talk, this woman, and the shop. I censured my inexplicable desire to reach out and touch each item, to assess its value, to touch its history, to wonder at its travels. To think that each item had its own story and perhaps countless owners ... well, the thought titillated me. The mirror could wait a few minutes.

"That's right," she said as she continued her dusting. "I've looked out onto this street for all these years. Day and night. We live ... well ... Arthur's been gone for several years now ... so it's just me, dear. I live upstairs. So yes, I've seen all sorts of comings and goings in this town. Oh my ... accidents and chance meetings and shenanigans and all sorts of strange behavior from folks. What about you, Grace? You live in the area?"

I nodded. "Moved here over the summer. From Boston."

"Boston? I love Beantown. Our oldest child, Samuel, attended MIT, so I'm familiar with the city. He's a math professor in Dallas now. So it's just me ... well, except for my sister Lavidia Kavanaugh in Martinsburg, but she's always so busy with her grandchildren." She sighed in a way that suggested she wished things were different. "So what are you looking for today, dear?" She turned from her work and parked the feather duster, to focus on my response.

Kavanaugh? As in William Kavanaugh? What were the odds?

No, I wouldn't entertain the notion. Best to focus and move on. "That mirror. The one you just put in the window. May I see it?"

Something changed. That quickly. Something in Hilda. She straightened, paled, tilted her head, and studied me with an intense look, as though she hoped to read words on my face that would explain my life story.

"What does that mirror mean to you?" She still spoke in a slow manner, the not-untypical delivery of a much older person, but her tone had turned serious, probing.

I wasn't sure what she meant, and from anyone else, I would have thought the question impertinent, but Hilda didn't seem threatening in any way. Just curious, like she intended to solve something.

"My mom used to have one like it. She's ... dead now. It just reminded me of her."

Hilda's eyes grew big. "My gracious! You think it was hers?"

I shook my head. "That was in Massachusetts, and hers had a broken edge to it."

She thought about that.

"Oh my, this one is not broken." She sounded disappointed that it wasn't.

"So, your mother's mirror ... it was special to her?" She emphasized the word *special* as though it were a critical point to her question.

"I wouldn't say that. It just reminds me of her, that's all. Look, if there's a problem ..."

"No, no. I'm sorry, dear. I must remember my manners. I get a little too excited about solving problems ... and heartaches."

She motioned me over to the window. I followed, allowing her to set the pace. She retrieved the mirror and handed it to me.

I could feel her assessing me as I studied its details. "It's beautiful," I said. "Exactly like the one mom had, except not broken." As I held it, memories washed over me, and my hand turned into that of my mother's. A vision came to me of her picking up the mirror and giggling like a schoolgirl as she admired the reflection of the pearls that Jack had given her for their fourth wedding anniversary. I closed my eyes and swallowed the remembrance before it spilled forth on my face. I'd come to the area hoping to further heal from the loss of my family, but I got so caught up in the death here that it seemed to have shoved them into second place. And now, here they were, moving back front and center. Or was that part of the mending process? I knew that no one healed in a straight line. It was more like two steps forward and one step back.

"Grace?"

Hilda's voice brought me back to the moment as a stray tear rolled down my face. I wiped it with the back of my free hand.

She touched my shoulder. "Oh my, this may not have held special meaning to your mother, but it does for you, doesn't it?"

I scoffed. "No, it's just a memory." I began to feel uncomfortable. Was she some kind of crazy old lady who saw it as her mission in life to pair the right memento with the right person?

She leaned back and folded her hands together at her waist.

"I believe people are brought together for a reason, dear. I'm just trying to figure out what that reason is."

I waited one confused heartbeat, then two, but didn't know what to offer.

"I've had that mirror in the back for years," she said, nodding toward the rear of the store. "Something just kept telling me not to put it out yet. All this time, I've known at least two ladies in town who'd buy it in a heartbeat, but I never offered it because it just never felt right ... like it shouldn't go to them."

I swallowed, wondering where this conversation was going.

"This morning," she continued, "for the first time, a voice told me to put it out. You say the mirror wasn't that special, so I have to assume us meeting is the purpose for the mirror bringing us together."

I wanted to say, "Goodness, don't you believe in coincidences? Ever heard of chance encounters?" But I didn't. Somehow, the words rang as smart-alecky and inapplicable to Hilda. And what was that voice I heard anyway? The one that told me to enter the shop?

"Grace," her tone grew serious, yet gentle. "My guess is that we were supposed to meet. Perhaps for the job? Why don't you tell me about yourself? Is school going okay? Gracious … maybe you are still stifled, still haunted by the past?"

"No, things are fine," I stammered, growing increasingly uncomfortable. *Why had she chosen the word haunted? Was its use innocent?*

She continued studying me and peppering me with questions: "I guess you're living with your dad, now? Is there a step-mom in the picture?" From anyone else the questions could have been interpreted as disrespectful, brash, but from Hilda, the questions suggested sincere interest and concern.

Trust her, a voice said.

That voice again.

But I didn't trust the voice in my head, and I didn't trust Hilda. I just wanted to get out of there.

I handed the mirror back to her. "Thanks. I better go."

She didn't take the mirror. She studied me a moment longer before saying, "It's yours, dear. Take it with you."

"I couldn't. Look, I have money." I started fidgeting with my backpack to find my wallet.

"Gracious, no need for money." She raised her palm toward me. "It's a gift. The mirror is yours."

"But it must be worth several hundred dollars. I couldn't …" I stopped. I could see by the look on her face that I already lost the argument and that she wanted me to have it.

I met her gaze, as we took each other's measure. She was kind. Sincere. So why was I so uncomfortable?

Trust her, the voice said again.

I hesitated, but I couldn't. "Thank you … I gotta' go." I put the mirror in my backpack, turned, and headed to the door.

Before I departed, I heard Hilda call from behind me.

"Grace, be careful now. And remember, dear, I can … *discern* certain things, and I may be able to help you one day. And let me know if you change your mind about the job."

I shut the door behind me and exhaled a shaky breath. She can *discern* things? What was that supposed to mean?

And, why were there no ghosts mingling among the antiques, as there had been at Holland's house?

How many bizarre things were adding up in my life? The voices I'd been hearing. The door in the library that drifted open on its own. The shaking in Holland's house. The cop in the pawn shop. The double conversation with Cassie.

Was I losing touch with reality?

★ ★ ★

Seth met me at the Williamsport Library. During the drive back from the Civil War Medicine Museum the day before, while Kate slept, I had described my discomfort about Ms. Bealle to Seth. He offered to tag along after his morning classes to distract the librarian.

When I started to warn him about her rude demeanor, he laughed.

"She's not rude to me," he said, sporting a confident smile.

At my quizzical look, he responded, "Honest. Ask my friends. She thinks I'm kinda' cute." He winked.

He was right. At the sight of Seth, who walked in first, Ms. Bealle practically cracked her face to smile. She didn't even notice that I came into the building. While Seth schmoozed with her, I skirted off to the side, dodged behind the length of the fiction section, and headed downstairs to the computer room.

My efforts to secure a picture of Thaddeus Fleming Calhoun on the Internet proved futile. However, I learned that Braxton was right, that Calhoun did have relatives in Williamsport: a sister, Clara, and her husband, Enoch Crinshaw, had resided on the outskirts of town. With that knowledge, I searched through digitized area newspapers. In an 1874 issue of The *Williamsport Pilot*, editor George McCardell had written an editorial that described Crinshaw as a lock keeper on the C&O Canal. Because Seth had to report to work, I made a copy to read later.

The most important thing I learned from the effort was that I'd have to go to Savannah, and soon. According to the website for the Georgia Historical Society's Library and Archives in Savannah, it was open Wednesday through Friday. Today was Wednesday; if I didn't leave today or tomorrow, I'd have to wait until next week. Michael, the full moon, the equinox ... none of that could wait.

Time was not on my side.

I returned to the lobby, intending to catch Seth's eye, signal my departure, and scoot out without catching Ms. Bealle's attention. However, a grown-up male voice startled me, in that it sounded childlike in volume and delivery.

"You said pizza, Gwenie." The voice sounded panicked, pouting, like a child not getting his way. "You said pizza."

I peered around a bookcase to see a man who looked in his fifties and somewhat heavyset and—even with his hunched posture—stood at least six-foot-three. He started banging his fists on the counter, causing stacks of books to shift and fall. "You said pizza, Gwenie."

Ms. Bealle, to my surprise, flushed and darted her gaze around the room as though embarrassed by the outburst of the man. She came around the counter, shushed and pulled him away from the lobby by placing one arm on his lower back shoulder and the other around his arm. "Yes, we'll have pizza, but only if you're a good boy. And good boys are quiet in the library."

Seth stepped closer to them as Ms. Bealle steered the man away. "See you later, Benny," he said and patted the man's shoulder.

Benny didn't acknowledge Seth's comment. Instead, he repeated in a softer tone, "Pizza. You promise, Gwenie?" He clapped his hands and grinned from ear to ear.

"Yes, yes ... now, you have to go back to your book and be quiet while I finish here," she said in a soothing tone.

She steered him toward the room off to the right. With her back to me, I caught Seth's attention, and we left.

Once outside, I asked, "Who was that?"

"Who, Benny? That's Ms. Bealle's brother. He lives with her."

"She has a brother?" I had envisioned Ms. Bealle as a lonely old grouch who existed day and night in the library. The thought that she had a life separate from her work, and a family, just didn't compute in my mind.

I began to see her in a new light, a softer light that attributed her gruff demeanor to the hardships and heartaches of caring for a mentally challenged brother.

"What happened to him? Was he born that way?"

"Accident. Later in life. Story is, he was quite the man about town. A shrewd businessman. He'd started a few bistro-style restaurants. Had them in Hagerstown, Frederick, Baltimore, Ocean City. They were so successful he started to franchise. He was in San Diego, researching the possibility of opening a few in southern California when he suffered a bad car accident. He barely survived."

"How sad. How long has he been like this?"

Seth shrugged. "Ever since I've known him."

"And Ms. Bealle takes care of him, by herself?"

"She refuses to have him placed in a facility. Rumor is that her marriage fell apart after Benny moved in. Supposedly, Mr. Bealle gave her an ultimatum. Him or Benny. She chose Benny."

I had no response. I just walked silently beside Seth, chastising myself.

★ ★ ★

When Seth heard my plans to go to Savannah, he insisted on accompanying me. Despite my protests, he argued I should not travel that far alone. He said his work at the hospital was voluntary, so he could report when he wished, and he'd miss only one day of classes given that school was closed Friday for teachers' in-service. He was confident he'd get his mother's okay to make the journey, and since his dad was at a medical conference, he needed no other approval.

As for me, I needed no permission from anyone. Michael assumed the role of guardian when he moved in, but he generally looked the other way as I continued on with my life. As for Aunt Tish, her calls had tapered off to about once a week. She'd lost interest in my life after she secured more money from my estate and turned responsibility for me over to Michael.

That evening, over dinner, Kate decided she could not make the journey with me to Savannah, but I could see she was torn in her decision. Her face lit up when I told her Seth was going, and I could practically *see* the wheels spinning and plans formulating in her head, thinking about what her time together with him might produce. I began to wonder what sort of awkward triangle might result for *me* to have them both in the car, but I reasoned that Seth was just a friend, so what did I care? What's more, I didn't want to leave her alone at *Crossings* with Michael … or rather, Fergus.

Then, in the midst of our discussion, she heaved a heavy sigh, smacked her hand into her forehead and said, "No wait, I can't go. I just remembered. Roxanne called this afternoon. Woke me up. She said I needed to get my butt to Richmond to register for school." She yawned again, pushed her food away and propped her head on both hands, elbows on the table, looking as though she struggled to sit upright.

Before I could voice my concern about her driving that far, she added, "Maybe I'll leave my rental here. Take a taxi to the train tomorrow night."

"That's a good idea," I agreed.

"Then again, if I drive, I can leave earlier and stop to see my friend Mallaka at American U."

"The train sounds like a better idea," I said, hoping I wasn't sounding like a coach. "You'll be able to spend more time with Roxanne this way." *And I'm afraid you'll fall asleep on the road if you drive.*

Her face lit up. "She's a geologist, did you know? It's almost the same thing as archeologist. Just more glamorous. Archeology, I mean. You know, like *Indiana Jones*."

I bit back the urge to tell her that any archeologist and geologist would tell her that their work differed as much as that between a doctor and lawyer. Instead, I said, "Okay, well, have fun. I won't be gone long. I'll feed Tramp and Chubbs before I go, and I'll leave Michael a note about feeding them and walking—"

"I can let him know," she huffed. "Honestly, sometimes you act like you're the only adult around here."

I stifled a retort as she sulked to the couch and picked up Mr. Snuggles, the tattered teddy bear she, my "adult" friend, slept with every night. I had a feeling her visit was going to prove quite memorable.

CHAPTER 14

The next morning, Seth and I started our journey to Savannah.
He didn't act a bit surprised when I announced I wanted to take Route 81 southwest through the Shenandoah Valley, instead of Route 95, southeast, to Savannah. The fact that Clay lived down Route 81 tickled my mind, but I kept that to myself. Instead, I was ready to explain that the distance between the two routes was only about forty miles and that I wanted new scenery.

Before I could offer my rehearsed explanations, Seth said, "Good idea. We'll avoid traffic in D.C. that way."

Under a cloudless sky, we headed south, the mountains on both sides of us growing taller with each accumulated mile. At almost two hundred fifty miles in length from north to south, the Valley varies between 25 to 40 miles wide, and is bound on the east by the Blue Ridge Mountains and to the west by the Appalachian Mountains. I was glad to drive first because, other than watching traffic, the biggest challenge in riding through the Valley was deciding which mountain range to look at.

Fortunately, there never is a bad view.

At the first sign for Lexington, Virginia, my heart raced, and I tightened my grip on the steering wheel. *Clay lived there!* Seth kept busy fidgeting with the satellite radio, so I don't think he noticed.

A few miles later, I spotted another sign. This one included the name of Clay's university, Washington and Lee, at just fifteen miles ahead. Anxiety hit, and I cranked up the air conditioning.

In the corner of my eye, I saw Seth shoot me a quizzical look, as though trying to decide why I'd do such a thing on a cool day, but he never said a word.

When we reached the exit sign for Lexington and the university, I began to shake, and wondered what there was about the human heart that would make it overrule all the common sense and better judgment that my mind had just spent the last two hours formulating, as I steered my SUV off the Route 81 Interstate onto Route 60 toward Lexington.

I could feel Seth watching me.

When I passed two gas stations and several chances to use public restrooms, both of which would have explained my reason for exiting, he spoke.

"Grace, really?" That's all he said, albeit with a deep frown, which I ignored.

"I just want to see where he's living now."

His silence spoke volumes.

"That's all. I promise," I said, for good measure.

I'd memorized the map directions from my Internet search: Route 60 to Main Street, then past Preston and McDowell streets to reach White Street. Turn right, and just between Colonial and Alexander lanes, which run perpendicular to White, on the left, stood his new home at 17201. He lived there with his uncle Kent's family.

The street boasted rambling two-story houses, each architecturally different than the next. Mature trees shaded the homes, and long, manicured lawns bordered with tall, thick bushes such as boxwood and holly swept to the street. In many instances, the driveways provided the sole break in the bushes.

I spotted Clay's safari-green Land Rover parked in the driveway. Through my mind flitted memories of riding with him to Georgia, holding hands while we drove, and hours spent talking.

Despite a negative sound of frustration from Seth, I steered the car to rest in front of a neighboring house, such that I could see up the long driveway to the front and left side of his new home.

I lowered my window and studied the house.

"Nice place," Seth said.

All I could do in response was swallow and nod. I assume he saw my effort to react; I don't know because I never took my eyes off the house. My thoughts focused on Clay, wondering which window he looked out at night to see the stars, which door he exited to get to his truck, which porch swing—front or side—he might choose if he ever studied outside.

"You okay?" Seth's voice sounded gentle, patient.

I nodded again and took a deep breath.

He reached over and touched my arm. "Maybe we ought to go before he comes back out."

His words startled me, and I saw what Seth must have already seen: faint wisps of exhaust spewed from the back of Clay's truck, as though it was recently turned on for the first time that day. Fortunately, no one sat in the vehicle.

I pictured Clay sleeping a little later that morning, his first class not occurring until midday, him dashing out to the truck then discovering he forgot something, maybe a book, maybe his laptop. He'd gone back inside to get it and would return any second.

Any second!

I didn't want to be there when he came back out. I reached for the gearshift as I glanced one last time to snap a mental photograph, a keepsake, of his house.

And that's when everything changed.

The front door opened, and Clay and a woman stepped onto the porch. I recognized him instantly, every aspect of his physical make-up ingrained in my memory: from the set of his jaw to his squared shoulders to his barely recognizable stilted left leg, the latter from a wound he'd suffered in Afghanistan. Despite a leg that some would call a handicap, his whole persona suggested strength, a look that made men treat him with respect. It wasn't just his height or build; it was his confident posture and his carriage. He controlled himself and what he wanted.

The woman with him knew what she wanted too. She'd made that clear in the café a few days earlier.

Francesca.

She talked; he listened. Her smile was broad; his, flat. She rested her hand on his shoulder as though trying to move in tandem with him; he slowed his gait to accommodate her.

I'm not sure why I opened my car door. Maybe because she was there. Perhaps I was angry. Jealous. Okay, of course, I was jealous, but it could be I also wanted to hear what they said. I remember thinking that the bushes would provide enough coverage for me to remain unseen. That is if I could reach the barrier of the massive hedgerow before they saw me.

"Grace, don't do this," Seth said as I placed a foot onto the street. His tone remained calm.

They descended the steps.

My other foot touched the pavement, and I started across the street.

Then the unthinkable occurred. It happened so quickly that all I can do is share the cascading sequence of events as I remember them.

The silver streak of a car came from out of nowhere, followed by the squeal of brakes as the driver must have seen that I stood in his path.

The screeching startled both me and Clay. He looked up, and our eyes met nanoseconds before we veered our eyes to the oncoming car. I recall his head jerked back, and he mouthed, "No" before he took off running toward me.

Then, a man surfaced out of that same nowhere that had produced the car, and he leaped at me.

The next thing I remember, the stranger and I sprawled amidst the bushes, surrounded by broken limbs from the boxwoods.

As quickly as he appeared, the stranger agilely whisked to his feet … yes, *whisked* … his movement swift, smooth … as though he made no effort at all. He bent toward me, offered a hand, and smiled. Later, I'd remember his white shirt and blue jeans, a shockingly handsome face, and penetrating yellowish brown eyes that glittered like the gemstone Tiger Eye, eyes that curiously reminded me of the cop I'd seen in the pawn shop.

"Don't be afraid," he said in a deep, honeyed voice as he reached to pull me up. "You should not be here, Grace. It's not yet your time."

I've often wondered how, in that heartbeat, after what I'd just been through, I had the presence of mind to register his words.

"Not time? For what?" My voice cracked. With his help, I moved to my feet, thoughts of injury the farthest thing from my mind.

How could this stranger know my name? And, it's not yet time for what? Was he a ghost? No, he had to be alive.

"I don't understand—"

"There's a season for everything. It's not that season yet." The stranger lifted a stem of leaves from my hair and tossed it to the side. "And remember, things aren't always as they appear."

He turned into the bushes and was gone.

That's when I noticed that Seth stood beside me, and Clay was still seconds away.

Later, I would learn that Seth had not seen the stranger. Nor did Clay or Francesca mention him. I would also later wonder how it could be that time had slipped into slow motion as the stranger and I talked, because after he stepped into the bushes, Clay hadn't reached me yet although I remembered him racing toward me.

The car, the stranger, our verbal exchange, how could that have lasted mere seconds? And what did the stranger mean that things aren't always as they appear?

Needless to say, after witnessing such an event, Clay and Seth had many questions: What were you thinking? What happened? Are you okay? Is anything broken? The driver kept going; should we call the police?

When I heard "police" I came out of my fog. Seth had his arm around me, while Clay stood helpless, his gaze burrowing into me. Francesca stood four feet behind Clay, head cocked, one hand on a hip as though trying to assess the cause, and potential outcome, of this situation.

"I'm fine. Really. I'm fine." I just wanted to leave, to get away from Clay and Francesca. I shirked off Seth's arm and took a step toward my car, but Clay stopped me.

He gripped my arm and turned me to make eye contact. And there was that strong jaw and those blue-green eyes that I remembered so well, reminding me of Caribbean waters so enticing to fall into.

He measured me for a beat or two before saying, "You're not fine, Grace. You almost got killed—"

"But I didn't, did I?" I sounded angry and jerked my arm free. I wanted to say more, to tell him in the most light-hearted tone I could summon that, "*Hey, we just stopped by to say hi. Looks like things are well, so we'll just be on our way. Seth and me, that is. We're traveling together. Alone. Just the two of us. Yes, we're quite the item now.*" But the sound wouldn't come. I wanted to be rude to Clay, but he filled the street with his presence. He stood tall, strong, powerful, and looked at me with that way of his. It was all I could do just to breathe, as though he displaced all the air.

The next thing I remember was Seth gripping me by the shoulders and steering me toward the passenger side of the car. "Everything's cool. She's fine. We can all just go back to what we were doing. Yes, Grace, I'll drive from here. You just put your seatbelt on. That's it. Good. Now just relax."

He rounded back to the driver's side. I don't know if he and Clay exchanged a "look" or not because I had my eyes plastered straight ahead, seeing nothing. The open window afforded me this verbal exchange:

Clay: "She should go to the hospital." He sounded annoyed.

Seth: "I'll watch her closely." He remained calm.

Francesca: "Clay, she said she's fine." She was *definitely* annoyed.

Clay: "What are you doing here? What's going on?" He sounded undeniably confused. I pictured him running his hand over his head.

Seth: "We're headed to Savannah and needed a break. We thought we'd stop and say a quick hello. You can talk to Grace some other time about it." His hand clutched the door handle.

A pause.

Clay: "This is another ghost hunt, isn't it? If she's putting herself in danger again—"

I couldn't hear how or if Seth responded.

Another pause.

Clay: "Take care of her."

And that's when I expected the old Seth to come forth. The one who had yelled at Clay at the Williamsport carnival over the summer for being too demanding, too bossy, and too protective of me when I had clearly been there with Seth.

Just as I was now.

But the old Seth never emerged. In a tone that sounded kind and—dare I say it—comforting, as though he cared about Clay's feelings, he said, "I will. She'll be fine. Don't worry."

And the next thing I remember, my car pulled onto Route 81 again and headed south.

Seth reached over to hold my hand.

This time, I let him.

CHAPTER 15

The rest of the trip through the Shenandoah Valley unfolded as quiet and uneventful. We didn't talk much, so I withdrew into myself, curled against the window, and watched the mountains go by. I felt like I was looking up from the bottom of a bowl that had been stretched lengthwise, to its limit. I'm sure it looked beautiful, but my thoughts remained on the scene in Lexington, so its splendor was lost on me.

In South Carolina, we exited onto I-26, to start the trek east across the state. The sky darkened, and in less than an hour, a leaden gray shower pelted against the windshield. Seth declared that we should call it a night, and within minutes, we pulled into a hotel.

Lucky for us, the night attendant didn't ask for identification or proof of age. We rented two rooms, and I begged off dinner, wanting to be alone with my thoughts.

Two hours later—after spending that time lying on my bed, fighting tears, staring at the ceiling—a knock sounded at the door. I opened it to find Seth carrying a tray of food.

"You need to eat something," he said as he handed me the tray. He turned to go.

"Seth, wait."

My time alone had not brought peace with events in Lexington, but it had accorded some indifference, and I decided Seth deserved a better traveling companion.

He turned back. "You need something else?"

"No … just …" I shrugged. "Thanks. That's all."

He offered a reassuring smile. "Call if you need anything. G'night."

"Do you want to come in and talk while I eat?"

He frowned. My question appeared to throw him into doubt as to how he should answer. "Do you *want* to talk?"

"Not really. I just don't want to be rude."

He smiled again and took a step closer. "You're not rude. You're hurting." He reached out for the sides of my face and planted a kiss on my forehead as I cradled the tray. "Eat. Get some sleep. We'll talk in the morning. Breakfast at seven?"

I nodded and noted, yet again, what a good man he'd become.

"Lock your door," he said as he disappeared around the hall corner.

I closed the door determined to follow his advice, but sleep didn't come until after midnight when the rain settled into a gentle drizzle, beating a rhythmic symphony against the windows.

★ ★ ★

It's odd how a good night's sleep can usher you into a new day and a new perspective. I awoke still confused about yesterday's events, but I also looked forward to visiting Savannah, to accomplishing my mission, and, much to my surprise, to spending the day with Seth.

I found him at a table in the cramped dining area beside the lobby. He shoved an opened tourist booklet at me.

"We're an hour from Savannah. I propose we go there first," he said, pointing to a section about the Georgia Historical Society on Whitaker Street. I didn't want to squelch his enthusiasm, so I didn't tell him that the place already topped my list.

He continued, "If this Calhoun guy was as big a landowner as you say, then he probably had enough money to have his picture taken. It was pricey in those days, you know. And he may have been mentioned in a local paper for having done something. This library has copies of newspapers from the surrounding area. If that doesn't work, we'll try the courthouse, get his address, and find out about possible ancestors."

This was so far outside what I had expected Seth to say that morning, it rendered me stupid. I'd braced myself to talk about my feelings, why he shouldn't be insulted or hurt, and what I planned to do about Clay (*I didn't know*). Then I figured we'd plan where he'd be while I scoured records in search of Calhoun.

"You want to help me research?"

"Sure. Why not?" He acted surprised that I would think otherwise. "Besides, I might want to search for my biological parents someday. I may as well get some practice."

His willingness to seize the day and ignore yesterday touched me. Before I could respond, a waitperson approached our table and asked if we wanted coffee. I looked at Seth as she filled his cup and noticed for the first time how his sandy hair curled at the top in such a pleasing way.

After the woman left, I noticed him still waiting for my answer, so I said, "I like your plan. Sounds fun." Sure, it was a flimsy response, but my best effort all the same.

He smiled.

I'd done the right thing.

★ ★ ★

Every city has its uniqueness, as though it evolved from a series of cumulative events and concessions and historic social adaptations. Miami has its sizzle, Washington, DC, its intensity, and Boston, its ivory tower verve.

To my delight, Savannah's aura oozed charm and mystery.

The charm is obvious from the moment visitors enter city limits— pristine squares bordered by ornate antebellum homes and landscaped with oaks, Spanish moss, azaleas, fountains, and statues, the effect giving the city its own engaging style and distinct aromas.

As for the mystery, I thought it might just be me, as I could feel ghostly activity on just about every corner and wondered what I might see at night. But a much more objective, unknowing Seth confirmed the feeling of mystery when he said the atmosphere was different, that he expected to turn around and see men bowing or fighting a duel, or ladies lifting their skirts to ascend a curb.

The charm and mystery continued with us as we passed through the wrought iron fence in front of Hodgson Hall, the home of the Georgia Historical Society. The main floor, which houses the library, features three-story-high coffered ceilings and two balconies, vaulted arched windows and large portraits of well-known Georgians. Large mahogany doors, brass hinges, solid walnut tables and bronze railings punctuate the entire facility.

As it turned out, among the more than four million manuscripts, hundred-thousand photographs, and thousands of maps, portraits, and artifacts available for research and review, was an extensive collection of local newspapers, some dating back two centuries. It took me three hours, eight books and directories, and two employees to find a picture of Thaddeus Fleming Calhoun. Despite being old, crude, and black and white, it reproduced well enough for my use at Antietam.

When I left the side room where I'd secured a photocopy, I found Seth on the main floor, deep in conversation with an employee who spoke as if he took great pride in sharing his knowledge of the individuals shown in the large, ornately framed portraits hanging throughout the room.

I stepped outside onto a raised veranda, to the side of the library. If it hadn't been in deep shadow from the late afternoon sun, I might not have seen the soul that exited the building, to my left. His blotchy, unhealthy appearance was so grotesque, I reacted with a start and a catch in my breath. This, of course, signaled to him that I could *see* him.

He smiled, but with a curious wistfulness. "You have subtle vision?" His voice sounded low and husky.

I nodded and took a deep breath as he moved closer.

Fear prompted me to consider bolting, but I could see his look wasn't demonic, but rather diseased. His translucent aura was plagued with reddish, blotchy spots on his face and hands. Dark circles saucered his eyes, and his physique was practically skeletal.

"You have seen ghosts before?"

"Souls, yes." I hoped that by using the term, he would understand I had experience and intended respect.

"Ah … indeed." He paused, seeming unsure of how to proceed. "So your reaction was not to my presence, but rather to how I look."

"I'm sorry. I was startled that's all. It was rude of me."

"Quite alright." He smiled and spread his hands. "At least you can see what killed me."

"A disease?"

"Lupus Erythematosus," he said with a grimace, as he parked his fingers in the small besom pockets of his hounds-tooth check vest. His movements were stiff, as though his once-pained body had become conditioned to avoiding the aches that mobility produced. "An autoimmune disorder. To this day, an incurable disease. My particular affliction, discoid lupus, characterized, as you can see, by severe rash, brown scales, and pockmarks over my entire body."

"When did you ...?"

"Die? Nineteen thirty-seven. I was a research physician. Determined to find a cure for this monster that inflicts so much pain. Foolishly, I thought I'd found the elixir. But in my zeal, I accidentally exposed myself to a rather nasty concoction in my laboratory. My mixture progressed the Lupus at an alarming rate, and my body attacked itself from within. I died within forty-eight hours."

"I'm so sorry." I heard a distant trolley bell and remembered where I stood. "Why are you here? Why haven't you passed on?"

"Ah, well, my work. It's incomplete. My research journals and my laboratory notebooks are housed on a shelf in this library. They hold essential findings for the right student interested in combating this disease. I don't list the cure, of course. I never found it myself. But I got so close!" He smacked his fist against an open palm then reined himself in. "Apologies. Point is, I can help accelerate development of a cure. But it will take the right student."

"That's incredible. So there is a cure? You know that for sure?"

He chuckled and shook his head as though to suggest how naïve he found me to be. But I don't think he laughed at me as much as at the curiousness of living beings and their limited understanding of death and what death reveals about life.

"Of course, there's a cure. Lupus is just a disease, and a disease is just a part of evil ... created by the Devil himself," he said with derision in his voice. "It simply takes enough focus and guidance. Good always wins over evil eventually, Ms …?

"MacKenna. But call me Grace." I'm not sure what compelled me to be first-name friendly with this soul.

"Very well, Grace. Malcolm Prestwood, at your service. Well now, tell me about you. How are you using this gift you've been bestowed? I don't suppose you're interested in science?"

"No, I want to study history." I considered for a moment before continuing because I was still discovering the answer. "The *real* history. The truth. Not the version that's been rewritten for textbooks today."

He nodded as I spoke. "Yes, yes. I know what you mean. I have occasion to look at the textbooks," he said, motioning toward the library, "at night while the living are gone. I barely recognize our country in them. But what about your gift? Are you using it to advance people's understanding of history? The afterlife?"

His question stumped me. I'd never connected those dots before. I fumbled for an answer. I'd once wanted to open a design firm with Michael, so I was more interested in business and working for myself, than in teaching. Yet, I'd considered majoring in history education because I didn't know what else one could do with history, other than teach. I hadn't reconciled how my new interest in history meshed with business. So I answered with what I did know for sure. "I've not used it in that way yet … but I will," I said with newfound determination. "I'm still a student. But I do hope to be a historian one day so that I can help people understand … somehow. I'm helping a couple souls resolve some things right now."

"I see. Quite good." He folded his arms and nodded.

"May I ask you a question?"

"But of course."

"As my vision has improved, I've seen souls like you, helping people. Staying here with one distinct purpose before they move on."

"And you want to know why? For me, the simple answer is that the cure remains unidentified. It needs to be brought to light."

I nodded but must have looked confused.

He continued, "It's not *my* cure. But the cure does exist."

I recalled the soul I'd met at the Williamsport library, helping a young man write a song. He'd said something similar: *It's not my song … the song is already written.*

"Are you an angel?"

He smiled. "Now, if I said I—"

"Grace? Who are you talking to?"

The voice came from behind us. Malcolm and I had enough time to exchange a glance before Seth joined us.

I must have looked a little flushed or uncertain of how to respond because Seth surmised the situation instantly.

"You're talking to a ghost, aren't you? I mean a soul. Is that right? Is there one here?" He swung around so quickly, searching left, then right, he almost passed his arm through Malcolm.

Seeing that I had nothing to lose, I said, "Yes, there is."

He froze. His eyes opened wide, and he looked like he was pinned to a shooting wall by a team of executioners. "No way," he whispered. "Where? Like right beside us?"

I chuckled. Malcolm smiled, looking likewise amused. "Right here," I said, gesturing. "His name is Malcolm Prestwood. Malcolm, this is Seth."

Seth stood still, but his eyes darted back and forth, probing, searching the immediate space around us. "Hello," he said aloud, then whispered, "ask him to do something."

I shrugged at Malcolm as though to ask him to play along. He nodded.

I looked back at Seth. He was practically salivating with anticipation. "Hand him your backpack."

Seth swallowed, took a deep breath, and did as I suggested, except that he offered it in the wrong direction. Malcolm stepped left and took it. I watched as he held it against his chest, raised it up over his head, then brought it down again. I wondered what Seth thought as he watched the bag rise and fall in thin air, then hover in one spot, seemingly unsupported. I stifled a giggle when Malcolm unzipped it, removed Seth's laptop and turned it several directions, studying it.

"Incredible ... these computer devices," he said, a tinge of awe in his voice.

"Um, Grace," Seth said reaching out, trying to suspend his hands under the laptop, "tell him that cost fifteen hundred dollars."

Malcolm returned it to the backpack, zipped it shut and handed it back to Seth.

As it neared his chest, Seth received it and said, "Whoa."

"Thank you, Malcolm," I said.

"Ask him why he's here." Seth's eyes continued to dart right and left.

"He already told me. Come on, I'll explain in the car. We need to start home." I cast Malcolm a final smile of gratitude. "I enjoyed meeting you. Good luck with your quest."

He touched his forehead as though tipping a hat. I imagined the gesture to be as natural for him as breathing once had been.

"Good luck to you too, miss."

Seth hesitated, then shrugged as though to say he had no choice but to follow. We headed toward our car, but until we rounded the corner, Seth kept looking back to scan the area where Malcolm stood. Looking, searching, but seeing nothing.

CHAPTER 16

And so it was, because of that brief five-minute encounter with Malcolm Prestwood, that Seth remained keyed up enough to drive five hours straight with one bathroom break.

He had dozens of questions. I had few answers. I couldn't help him unravel the riddle of existence, despite what he hoped; however, I shared everything I'd learned about Malcolm.

We opted not to return on Route 81, and instead drove north on Route 95. Dusk settled by the time Seth pulled the car off the Interstate in southern Virginia and found a quaint restaurant. We sat outdoors in a patio dining area surrounded on three sides by brick walls and wood lattice, laced with vines. He barely spoke through most of the meal, so I suggested we pay and take a brief walk.

Once on the street, we spotted a dimly lit old-fashioned park, complete with a white gazebo-type bandstand, and headed in that direction.

"Seth, you've known about souls and these after-death experiences for quite a while now. You've experienced them yourself. So what's suddenly bothering you?"

He frowned as we climbed onto the bandstand and dropped to a bench. The moon provided enough light that I could see his face.

"Why not me?" he asked, but not in one of those pouty little boy voices. Instead, this voice came from a full-grown man, one of strength and passion, and one who wanted to share both by bettering his world. "Why couldn't I see Malcolm? Why couldn't I be the student he waits for, the one who would find the cure? I want to help people. Be part of something big like that. You have your vision, but I—"

"Seth, I had to lose my entire family before I developed this vision."

He sighed and looked away. "I know," he said, but in a tone that meant, "but I don't like it." He shook his head. "I'm sorry. I just want to understand it all."

"Maybe understanding would take you off course. It's not a blessing."

"So it's a curse?" His voice rose. "Is that what you're saying?"

I shook my head. Malcolm had made it sound like an opportunity. A *gift* he had said. Could that be true? "Blessing. Curse. I don't know. Maybe we're just supposed to look at the positive. Work with that."

"What's that mean?"

"Well, we've both learned that death isn't final. That there's more to life than our physical bodies. I've gained more peace about my parents' death. You've changed. You have a new perspective on life, and you're … well, you're just the greatest friend a person could have …"

My words faltered as I looked at him. Sitting right there. Beside me. In the moonlight. A warm breeze washing through the trees. In his eyes, I saw a yearning for connection, and I wondered if it merely mirrored back what churned inside of me.

It struck me that we both were unsure and confused. We'd both lost a significant spark that needed to be rekindled. Could we find it in each other? The look on his face resembled what brewed inside me, so much so that I wondered where one of us ended and the other began. And just like that, it clicked as so right that when Seth leaned in to kiss me, I met him in the middle.

The first quick touch of our lips must have pleased us both because we both returned for a repeat performance with a deeper, prolonged kiss.

And that's when I started to shake, as though the kiss rocked me from head to toe. Yet, as fast as it started, it ended, and all I could feel were Seth's lips on mine.

Then, as if my shaking wasn't enough to interrupt the moment, the kiss grew crowded as Clay's face popped into my mind, followed by a vision of Will standing beside me, and then Kate.

Was my conscious trying to tell me something? And why? Clay wasn't in my life now, Will was gone, and Kate's infatuations never lasted more than a week. When I decided to end the kiss, Seth pulled back.

"Wow," he said and rubbed his forehead. "I saw—"

"Kate," I said because she lingered in my mind.

"Kate?" Seth shifted on the bench. "What does that mean?"

I had no idea what it meant, but I didn't want to talk about it either. I needed to think this through before I told Seth that I'd seen Clay and Will as well. I didn't want him to misinterpret my visions because, well, I had enjoyed the kiss. A lot.

I longed to be in the car, moving, losing myself in the hum of the tires on the road and the soothing thinking time it affords. I needed to ponder this sudden attraction I had for Seth.

But he still looked at me, waiting for an answer.

"I think it's obvious," I offered with a teasing voice, trying to deflect the attention away from me. "We both know Kate took a shine to you. So she's on my mind."

He laughed. "Took a shine?"

"Mom used to say that."

"Ahh. My sisters would say that she 'has the hots' for me. I think I like that better."

I made some sort of goofy startled sound, fisted my hand, and smacked him in the shoulder playfully. He laughed, caught my fist, and brought it to his lips.

I wondered how—*and if!*—to tell him I enjoyed his company. That maybe he'd been more right than wrong about us.

He sobered and returned my hand to my lap. After he let go, he patted it as though to say it belonged there. In my lap. Not in his hand. "Sorry about the kiss," he said quietly. "I don't want to confuse you … or mislead you. I just don't know what I want anymore."

I blinked. Twice. In an instant, ours had become a different conversation, a helicopter hovering endlessly waiting to land, then blown way off course.

"I don't understand. I thought—"

"I need to figure out a lot of stuff, about me before I get involved in that way. I don't want this to come between us." He stood. "Come on, we should get moving."

"Is it Kate?"

He jerked his head back. "Are you serious? I think we all know that flirtation is nothing serious. Especially on her part."

"Maybe we should talk about this."

"No."

His response was brief and hurried, like a slap of cold water.

Robotically I stood and followed him to the car, not saying a word. I was so surprised at this reverse in our relationship that I couldn't think clearly. Did this mean he had developed feelings for Kate? Was he afraid I'd reject him?

What *were* my true feelings?

I pondered these questions for the remaining four-hour ride and never did come up with the answers.

★ ★ ★

After Seth dropped me off at *Crossings*—with a squeeze of my hand and a warm, "talk to you tomorrow," as though nothing had changed between us—I trudged past three vehicles and up the steps to the apartment, hoping I could slip into bed without waking Michael or Kate.

To my dismay, Michael met me at the door. Behind him I could see that light engulfed both the living room and the bedroom.

At the same time that I asked, "Where's Kate?" he demanded, "Where's Adriana?"

"Okay," he quipped. "Kate first. That's a quick one. The answer is, I don't know because nobody ever knows why she does what she does."

"She still ought to be here. Her car is outside. She'd have called me if she left with someone."

He thought about it. "She probably headed to her sister's," he said, surprising me with the warmth in his voice, his earlier commanding tone gone as though it had never been. "She planned to do that, right? Register for school. Ask her sister about archeology."

"What about her car?"

He shrugged. "She probably took the train. She lived in France, and you know how those Europeans love their trains." That riddle resolved he moved to the next one. "Now, where's Adriana?"

But I wasn't satisfied, and Kate's whereabouts remained unresolved in my mind. "She did mention it, but that'd be unusual, even for her." I looked around. "Her stuff is gone, but surely she'd have left a note. I wonder what she's up to ..."

Michael snorted, as though his snide demeanor had returned. "Look around, little sister," he said, a snarl creeping into this voice. He spread his arms and turned full circle. "Do you see a note?"

I could tell by his mocking gesture that there was no note and no need to look.

"Now, about Adriana?"

"What about her?" My voice sounded strained as I moved past him and plopped my backpack on the dining table. His waffling moods and his questions had caught me off-guard, and I tried to buy time by emptying the pockets of the pack. I braced for a volley of questions to rain down on me, like gunfire until I produced an answer he'd accept.

I jumped as his hand came down on top of mine, halting my effort with the backpack. "Where the blazes is she?" He said each word with slow emphasis as if he thought me too stupid to understand.

"Michael! There's no need to be so nasty."

I registered surprise on his face before he stepped back, as though he attempted to compose himself. He pumped his palms at me. "You're right, you're right." His tone softened again. "I have been trying to reach her for days. She doesn't answer her cell phone. She ignores my texts. She doesn't respond to my emails. Why? Where is she?"

He asked the latter question so softly that I looked up to meet his gaze. A glimmer of affection fought with the torment of missing her. Yet, Michael's behavior remained too volatile for me to trust that he was displaying genuine concern for someone else. I needed to proceed with caution.

"I don't know where she is ... exactly."

His gaze intensified, and it worked like a hand to push me back against the cold door of the refrigerator behind me.

"Well, exactly," he used my word and emphasized it as if mocking me, "what does that mean?"

Looking at him, scared and backing away as I was, I saw what he was becoming: a viper coiled, waiting, ready to strike. But a viper which struck out of self-protection, because that was its sole means of defense. The only hope for small ground creatures like me is to act as strong and fearless as the snake. I had to stand up to him, to make him confront the truth. Maybe that random caring that he demonstrated between the spurts of venom and those feelings he had for Adriana, maybe that would fight the devil in him. Perhaps I needed to be direct and confront him, make him acknowledge that his loss resulted from his own hands.

My courage blossomed as though Will stood beside me, reminding me again that my physical body didn't matter. That it was just a cage, a shell that held my soul. My body might take a blow from Michael, but not my soul. It was safe in God's hands.

I stepped toward him. "Michael, you did this to yourself. After you shoved her the other day, she—"

"Whoa, whoa, whoa. What are you talking about? I didn't shove her. I'd never shove a woman. You know that."

I wondered how far to take this. How much to say to make him see? To remember? Did I dare tell him he *was* that kind of guy now? The kind of brute that indeed would shove anyone in his way? And how could he not remember? Could I be wrong in thinking that possession was under way and that, instead, he suffered from some mysterious disease that had yet to be diagnosed?

"You two had an argument Sunday. In the cellar. After Seth and I left." I chose my words carefully, no mention of Greasy Jim or the altercation in the cellar. "Do you remember?"

Confusion covered his face, and he stepped back and slumped down onto a kitchen chair. His gaze searched the floor as though hoping to find something there—a memory, a comment made between them, a vision of her walking out that day.

"No," he whispered. "I don't even remember her leaving."

I remained quiet as he processed his lack of recall.

"So," he said, the blood draining from his face, and it struck me that the tone of his voice was less question than it was plea. "She says we argued? That I shoved her, and she left? And why were we in the cellar?"

"That's what she said."

Everything in me wanted to go to him, to put my arms around him, to console him. But I didn't. I'd grown so afraid of his volatile behavior that I dreaded a backlash.

He shook his head, his face growing somber. "Maybe I shouldn't know."

With that, I thought I saw yet another Michael, one that was vulnerable, uncertain, and wounded by love. "Shouldn't know what?"

"Where she is. Maybe I shouldn't know." He sounded resigned. "Maybe she's better off without me. Happier. Safer."

I don't think I'd ever heard him say something that selfless before.

He stood, dismay and confusion still written across his face. "I'm tired. I'm going to bed." As he walked toward the old house, his back to me, he mumbled to himself. "I don't understand. I really care about her. I've never met anyone like her before."

"Michael," I called out, and he hesitated. "Maybe you should see a doctor."

He nodded but never looked back. "Maybe. Maybe you're right." He switched to talking to himself again as he opened the door and stepped into the shadowy depths of the old house. "Yeah. Maybe that's what I should do. Maybe I should see a doctor."

When he closed the door behind him, I dropped into the same chair he'd used. It wouldn't be until much later—and I'm not proud to admit this—that I would think about Kate again. At that moment, my cousin filled my thoughts.

Okay, that's not true. Actually, I was thinking about myself. I looked at the stretched-out figure of Tramp lying on the floor, and I wished I could trade places. I'd cherish a little of that peacefulness. No anxiety. No stress. No ability to see souls.

What was it like to fall asleep worry-free, without fretting and waiting for what might come next?

I wondered if that day would ever come, and yet I recognized that it was going to get a lot worse before it got any better. Michael's behavior was just the calm before the storm.

CHAPTER 17

The next morning, I woke to find Michael on the couch. When I greeted him good morning, he inched into a sitting position and dragged his gaze to me, as though with dread. Like he found it alarming to be drawn back into a world where he didn't want to be.

"You okay?" I moved closer.

He hesitated and stared at me, but his gaze didn't connect. He looked like he was searching for a tall tale into which he could disappear. Then his upper body slumped and he dropped his head into his hands.

"No." He sounded weak, hoarse. "Couldn't sleep last night. Came in to watch TV. Musta' fallen asleep." He stopped to take a breath, but he looked like he gulped in more than air. His next words made me think that pride was the pill he couldn't swallow. "Will you take me to the doctor?"

Yeah, I was surprised too.

And so, that kicked off our morning. Within minutes, we headed to urgent care.

And that led to waiting. And tests.

Countless tests.

And probing questions about his lifestyle and allergies and prescriptions and drugs and travel and chemical exposure and medical history and family illnesses.

Then more tests.

And more waiting.

When it became clear we faced several more hours of waiting, Michael convinced me he wanted to stretch out on the sofa in the waiting room and nap while I drove to the *Time Out* to retrieve iced tea and sandwiches.

On the way, I called Kate's sister, Roxanne. She confirmed that Kate planned to visit and was getting a ride with her friend, Mallaka, whom she'd met in France. First, however, she planned to visit Mallaka's school, American University in Washington, DC, before traveling with her to visit Roxanne in Richmond, Virginia.

Satisfied that Kate was accounted for, I clicked off my phone, opened the door to the café, and ran into a chuckling Adriana on her way out.

With one look at me, her smile disappeared, and her gaze shot to the ground. But she stopped, and for that, I was grateful. She avoided eye contact as she answered my questions about school (it was fine) and how she faired (also fine) and why she was there (the *Perfect Rhythm* music store, where she worked during summers, was short-staffed, and she agreed to help).

Stung from the stilted conversation and sensing her desire to bolt, I asked if she'd join me for a cup of coffee while I waited for my order.

She hesitated but relented.

When Zebecca brought our coffee, she plopped into a chair beside us as though we three were old friends.

"Mind if I take my break with you guys?" she asked, not waiting for an answer. She blathered on about how busy the morning had been, how customers rudely used their cell phones, why Whit added caramel frappachinos to the menu and oh-my-gosh how fantastic they tasted, and blah, blah, blah.

Adriana and I barely said a word before Zebecca came up for air by asking a question: "Since Cassie is always gone, don't you think Whit should make the decisions around here?"

"No, it's her cafe," Adriana and I both said with attitude and in unison, for that instant sounding like the best friends we used to be.

Looking stung by our solidarity, Zebecca departed, but Adriana and I barely noticed. We'd finally made eye contact. She still didn't say a word, but her body language relaxed, she smiled, and lifted her fist sideways toward me. I mirrored the sideways fist, and we clinked them together. An unspoken acknowledgement of unity and years of friendship ahead.

She stood. "I better go. I'll call you when I'm home again."

I smiled and nodded. We weren't back to what we once had been, but she was back to what *she* used to be. And that was a good place to start.

As I headed to my car, Seth called. He talked about his morning and asked if Kate and I wanted to get together with him that evening. I agreed, but told him it would be without Kate. That she had gone to Richmond. He didn't mention the kiss from the night before. Or the strained conversation afterward. But I could sense the awkwardness between us. I'm sure he could too. It was hard to skirt around, like the proverbial elephant in the room.

Finally, I said, "Seth, what about last night?"

"What? You mean the kiss? Ummmm ... nice, wasn't it? I'd like to repeat it sometime. Soon." I could almost see him grinning through the phone.

"But what about what you said afterward?"

I heard a sigh. "Look, Grace. If I'm confusing you, I apologize. This isn't about you. It's about me. You know how I feel about you. That hasn't changed. But I need to figure out some stuff about me before I can figure out stuff about us."

I opened my mouth, but nothing came out. My brain processed several emotions, trying to zero in on the most appropriate one. Mostly, I experienced anxiety again, now back to hoping he wasn't reading too much into my feelings.

What was wrong with me? When he pulled close, I pushed him away. When he pushed away, I wanted to pull him back.

I reached my car and decided to think about it another time. I set the food on the roof and unlocked my car door. "Look Seth," I said as I retrieved the food and climbed in, "it's fine. Really it is. We're on the same page, and I'm confused too. But right now I have to go. See you tonight."

Later that day, I drove a tired and frustrated Michael back to *Crossings*. Final diagnosis: nothing wrong except too much stress at work.

I wasn't a bit surprised by their conclusion. They'd not given him the when-a-demonic-soul-takes-over-your-body test.

If they had, he would have tested positive.

CHAPTER 18

Sunday dawned warm and peaceful, at odds with the storm of anxiety swirling in my head. I had promised Braxton I would return on the night of the full moon to witness his murder.

Tonight.

There was no question of foregoing the whole ordeal. When Michael and I had returned to *Crossings* after his battery of tests the day before, he disappeared into the old house, like a druggie who'd been away from his fix too long. That evening, he swooped into the apartment long enough to interrupt the movie Seth and I were watching. He grouched and cursed at us about not keeping enough snack food in the house, and for playing the TV too loud. All the signs returned: the pale face, the sweat, the furrowed brow, the savage eyes, the clenched fists. Even his movements changed, like he stalked from place to place, rather than walked.

Michael's volatile behavior further confirmed my plan to visit Antietam that night.

To witness a hundred and fifty-year-old murder.

Seth called early Sunday, and I agreed to meet him at church. A little God talk about a strength far greater than mine sounded like the perfect way to start a day that might end with me pitted against a demonic soul. Besides, I'd grown to like Pastor Dale, and I looked forward to hearing more of his wisdom.

Turns out, church was good for my tranquility, but not my personal life because Clay saw me enter holding hands with Seth.

Unfortunately, Clay didn't witness me: (1) arriving in my own car, (2) meeting Seth in the lobby, (3) voicing discomfort that people would think I was there *with* Seth, lest people mistake us for a couple (we'd not talked about "us" at all the night before), and (4) frowning when Seth grabbed my hand and said, "Grace, we're both confused right now. I don't know what else we are, but I *do* know we are friends. Come on. No one here is supposed to judge us anyway. It doesn't matter what they think."

He was right. I didn't care what anyone in the church thought.

Until I saw Clay in the back of the room, then I cared what *he* thought.

Before I could let go of Seth's hand, Clay nodded acknowledgement, turned, and walked into the sanctuary where he sat beside Cassie. *What was he doing here?* My heart hoped he kept his distance only because of Aunt Tish's threat about a restraining order.

We followed in but sat with Seth's mother, a few rows back. Despite the logistics, I could hear people talking about Reaghan and premature labor and congratulating Cassie on becoming a grandmother again.

So that explained Clay's presence. He came home to see the babies.

I was too busy studying the back of Clay's head to hear much of the service. That is until Pastor Dale said we should avoid evil, and that those who guard their ways preserve their lives. I swear it was like I'd heard "blah, blah, blah" prior to that. Then he read Psalms 97:10. "Let those who love the Lord hate evil, for He guards the lives of His faithful ones and delivers them from the hand of the wicked."

Who wouldn't hone in on these words on the day they expected to encounter evil face-to-face? The verses poured over me like salve to a wound.

Pastor Dale said that throughout the Bible, the Devil is regarded as a real and dangerous entity, one that dare not be ignored, and that Satan and his own can disguise themselves in cloaks of righteousness, as angels of light, whose end will be according to their deeds.

Disguises. Cloaks. Their deeds. Goosebumps rashed out on my arm. *How is it that the pastor spoke to my situation?* I shook off the suspicion. No doubt everybody feels that pastors zero in on their personal trials and travails.

"If the authors of the Bible, and particularly Jesus, spent so much effort warning us about Satan," Pastor Dale continued, "then the Devil must be worthy of our attention. We have to believe he exists."

Now *that* I agreed with. I'd seen enough evil this summer *know* that someone—or something—practiced evil with fervency at *Crossings*.

He continued, this time quoting famous figures, like Edmund Burke: "The only thing necessary for the triumph of evil is for good men to do nothing." And Albert Einstein: "The world is a dangerous place, not because of those who do evil, but because of those who look on and do nothing."

So we should take a stand against evil? Each of us should do something? Was that even possible? And what were we supposed to do?

As if he read my mind, Pastor Dale read from the book of 1 Peter. "Be alert and of sober mind. Your enemy the Devil prowls around like a roaring lion looking for someone to devour."

Devour. The word chased chills down my back.

"That is evil's goal for you and your family. To devour." Pastor Dale said that word again with emphasis.

Devour.

I began to shake as the word played over and over in my mind until it consumed me like a wild animal that clamps its mouth on its prey until it's dead.

Devour.

When I tuned in again, Pastor Dale described a war that's been raging ever since the beginning. Demons vying for supremacy and power, but that God commands his angels to guard us. He said there are times when we can be called on to do the work of angels, but that we should never call on an angel for guidance or deliverance because that would open us up for spiritual deception. "Do not consult with witches and psychics and mediums who speak with the dead," Pastor Dale warned.

... who speak with the dead. The words pounded in my brain.

Disguises. Cloaks. Devours.

Was I a fool for having trusted and talked to Will? But how could that be? He left, and I remained unharmed. There hadn't been any deception ...

Had there?

And just when I wondered what I could do about it now, I heard Pastor Dale say, "... and we should only call on God."

So that was it? That's what we should do?

No, turns out there's more. He read several verses from Ephesians about donning special armor, and I heard enough to know that I needed to memorize as much of it as I could before going to Antietam that night.

Couldn't hurt, right?

As he closed, Pastor Dale reminded us that mankind's key challenge is not war as we know it, involving flesh and blood. Rather it's against the intangible forces of the dark world and the spiritual powers of evil in the heavenly realms.

Those forces, those powers, he said, will visit and attack us in many forms, using whatever means necessary to carry out their nefarious intent.

Like using the bodies of dead people? Or taking possession of my unsuspecting cousin?

When the service was over, I could tell Seth was shaken too. He looked pale, concerned. We looked at each other with silent acknowledgement of what we'd just heard. He reached out and put his arm around my shoulder. "It's okay," he whispered into my ear. "Michael will be fine."

I nodded then glanced over to where Clay had been sitting. He now stood, staring right at me. *And at Seth's comforting embrace.* He turned and followed Cassie toward the door.

When Seth and I exited the church, I scanned the church parking lot for Clay's old Land Rover Defender but didn't see it. My eyes fixated on the driveway where it met the public road, wondering how fast his departure had been, who had been with him in the car, where he was going for Sunday lunch—

"Beautiful, aren't they?"

The voice came from Pastor Dale beside me, who, moments before, had been standing at the church doors shaking hands and sharing parting words with churchgoers. I looked to my right at him, and in one glance, realized that Seth had stopped to talk to someone behind me and that Pastor Dale thought I was staring at something across the public road. I followed his gaze back to take in an unmowed field, covered in tall white and yellow flowers.

I nodded. "Yes, they are."

"The thing is," he said, never taking his eyes off the field, "they're deceptive. They look enticing. Fragrant. Like you want to pick an armful and take them home. Surround yourself with them. But, they're actually weeds and quite destructive. They cause allergies, and if allowed to thrive and reign, will destroy the crops that are meant to grow there." He paused to chuckle. "Things just aren't always as they appear, are they?"

Struck dumb, I jerked my glance from the field to Pastor Dale's face to ascertain his intent. I thought for sure he'd be looking at me in some marked fashion, perhaps pointing a finger preparing to add, "Do you get my point, Grace?" But he wasn't, and he didn't. His focus was on the field, and he showed no sign that he knew I'd heard those same words from a soul while in Lexington.

"No, I suppose not," I mumbled.

"Well ..." He snapped his posture straighter and turned to me as though he intended to change topics. "I wanted to give you this."

I looked down to see him handing me a Bible.

"A gift from the church," he added. "I wasn't sure if you had one of your own."

I did. Once. But it got lost in the move from my parents' home to that of Aunt Tish and Uncle Phil in Boston. I'd seen another in *Crossings*, but it sat in a dark corner and looked intimidating, like the house itself.

I took it from him. "Thank you. I ... I don't know ..."

He chuckled. "Don't worry. It doesn't obligate you to show up every Sunday if that's your concern. I thought you might want to do a little research ... you know ..." his eyes flicked to Seth as though he wasn't sure how much I had shared with him. "... on the things we've talked about."

I nodded again as I wrapped my hands around the smooth, cool leather cover. My fingers felt something amiss, and I looked closer to see a yellow sticky note protruding from the top. I looked back at Pastor Dale.

"Oh, I took the liberty of marking a few passages for you. In Ephesians. Never know when they might prove helpful."

Yes. You just never know.

CHAPTER 19

Will had once warned me that during a full moon, souls of the dead soldiers at Antietam Battlefield would display increased torment and agitation, with most reliving their deaths. A situation, he said, that could prove particularly dangerous for anyone with subtle vision.

Like me.

As with my visit earlier that week, I figured my best bet was to arrive, park as close as possible to the shed where Braxton died, and steal determinedly to it, not making eye contact, not scanning the horizon, not reacting to any sights or sounds or smells. To acknowledge is to reveal oneself, and that's when one becomes vulnerable. I had a plan, so I was as prepared as one could get in this situation. I'd also studied the photographs of Calhoun and Bohrman, memorizing their every facial structure, pit, scar, and dark circle under their eyes.

As it turned out, no amount of planning could have prepared me for that night.

After parking on Burnside Bridge Road on the edge of Sharpsburg, I turned off the car and sat in the dark, waiting for my eyes to adjust. The full moon provided enough light through the cloudless sky that I didn't need a flashlight.

Yet the moon, perched on a lone tall pine, looked so distant and disinterested, that I wondered if I'd be able to count on its illumination, or if it would decide to dip behind that tree when I needed it the most. I doubted that it wanted to see what I was about to experience.

As I waited, I watched a man, clad only in sweat pants, exit the rear door of a house and lug a bulging plastic bag to a container by a shed. From out of nowhere, a soul stepped beside him.

The man obviously couldn't see the soul because he carried on as normal—lifted the lid, deposited the bag and turned to go. My breath hitched when the soul flipped the container, behind the man's back. The man wheeled, looking right and left, as though wondering what had caused the can to tumble, but no doubt assuming as we all do when unusual things happen, that he had somehow precipitated it. The soul howled with laughter and staggered away.

The man may have wondered about the can, he may even have suspected something odd or sensed a cold presence, but he shrugged it off. Living where he did, beside this battlefield, he probably often wondered why his keys disappeared, his gas tank registered low, or his shed doors popped open when he'd latched them shut. The man would be fine as long as he couldn't *see*; a stark reminder that my life was in danger because I could.

Once he returned inside the house, I said a prayer, grabbed my backpack, and stepped out of the car. I brought the pack to look like a hiker as Braxton suggested. In it were the pictures of Braxton's two key suspects, and, because it made me feel better, I tucked in the Bible too.

Due to my subtle vision, the effect of stepping onto that historic and bloody combat arena at Antietam Battlefield, at night, in a full moon, was akin to passing through a wall that separates sanity from madness. I reminded myself that everything I saw belonged to history and none of it was "real" in the physical sense.

But it sure looked and threatened as real. Wreckage covered the expanse of the battlefield: downed fences, broken wagons, bloated horses, and strewn debris—haversacks, cards, Bibles, letters. Buildings nearby burned, and the sides of others looked perforated like honeycombs. Most of those served as makeshift hospitals, and from them I could hear men screaming, sobbing, praying, begging for release from their pain.

My thoughts jerked to the scripture from Ephesians that Pastor Dale marked in the Bible he gave me. The verses said to put on the full armor of God. *Full armor,* so we can take our stand against evil's schemes.

The passage also said something about wearing a belt of truth buckled around our waist, a breastplate of righteousness, a helmet of salvation and a sword of the Spirit. I didn't understand it all, but I loved the symbolism of being divinely armored with all things good and strong and reliable. I envisioned myself as prepared for some sort of supernatural battle.

I anticipated what I might *see*, but the first thing that hit me was the stench. I hadn't considered that odors would become more realistic with the full moon, too. The air smelled rancid as though it had been inhaled and exhaled by too many dying people and animals, then mixed with the odors of gunpowder, sweat, fecal matter, wet leather, and, of course, rotting flesh. My stomach lurched. Revulsion accumulated in my throat like the rancid aftertaste of a rotten meal. My gag reflex kicking in, I whipped back to the car and braced myself against the putrid effect, one hand over my mouth, determined not to proceed until I overcame the urge to vomit.

With my stomach stabilizing and my gaze turned away from the unfolding horror behind me, my sense of sound took over—the screams, gunfire, cannons booming, swords clashing, hoofs thudding, wagons hurrying to and fro, men yelling attack commands, the wounded begging for medical help. The sounds sliced into me, stealing my energy and replacing it with anxiety and gloom.

The noise surprised me because the actual fighting had ended by nightfall all those years ago in 1862. That knowledge made me more anxious, because I placed too much assurance on the familiar, on logic, on the routine of life. This was death. *Paranormal.* It functioned in a different realm than my own and had its own isolated cubicle of time.

So far, I wasn't doing so well. My legs dragged as though nightmare-heavy, my heart raced, and my greatest desire was to climb back into the car and flee. I fought the feeling that I'd been flung into a horror story.

"Get a grip on yourself."

Yeah, I think I said that out loud. Then, because it made me feel better to hear my own voice, I kept talking. My mind flitted back to the days when I'd first moved to West Virginia, before I'd learned to trust and rely on faith. In those days, I'd chant my fears away. I began again: *Only your mind can produce fear. Fear makes the wolf bigger than he is.*

I turned and moved like an automaton toward the shed, looking down, chanting to myself, concentrating on getting to the building, seeing what I needed to see, and getting out of there.

About forty yards from the shed, visibility got worse. I looked up to see a pall of smoke. It had to have come from the thousands of guns and cannons, like a fog descending on the area, its swirling elements barely recognizable in the limited lighting.

The soul of a soldier about thirty yards away caught my eye, and what's worse, he saw me *seeing* him. He disappeared, then frumped down at my feet, like a cat pouncing to toy with a mouse. He was *that* agile, as though composed of part man, part animal. Cackling at high volume, he put a hand at his stomach as though holding more laughter in.

I reeled to the side and kept walking, picking up pace, determined to reach the shed, thinking of the man by the garbage can whom I decided would be fine *as long as he couldn't see.*

Frump.

The soul dropped in front of me again wearing that same leer. This time his skin rashed out in pockmarks that oozed a glowing substance, and his pustuled face glared at me ... *from his three eyes!*

My heart pounded as if I was about to step off a cliff, but I spoke with preternatural calm. "Yea though I walk through the valley of the shadow of death, I will fear no evil, for Thou art with me."

The soul stretched taller, howled, and spat a horrible liquid at me, or so I thought, for when I gasped and touched my shirt, it was dry. Just when the panic began to swell again, the soul stiffened and looked down on himself. A liquid of a different shade leaked over his lower lip. I followed his gaze to his stomach and watched as he peeled away layers of what looked to be cornhusks. Will had said bandages were in short supply, so the men used the leaves of crops to cover their wounds. From his gut, poured the same liquid that oozed from his mouth.

Blood.

The soul made an odd gesture of resignation, then stretched out a shaky hand toward me.

My breath caught. I couldn't move.

He drew closer.

When his fingers reached within inches of my face, he collapsed to his knees, racked with sobs that wrenched his body as though he released a lifetime of fury and hopelessness. As I stood frozen, watching, he fell to the side, issued a final guttural moan, and grew silent.

Had I just witnessed his long-ago death? I tried to steady my breathing and staggered to the stability of a fence pole a few yards away, reminding myself to act nonchalant ... as though I were out for a stroll.

I peered into the darkness, careful to look but not *see*.

It was impossible to do. I couldn't help but *see*, and I quivered at the carnage I saw off to my right, toward the battlefield. Bodies everywhere, some piled on top of others. In layers! Seth's comments about matrixing flashed in my mind, the notion that our brains are wired to recognize shapes and patterns in the frightening, inexplicable things we see. It had to be nonsense because why would my brain form such horrible images as protection?

Just as quickly, it struck me that the fighting had ended, and there were no more cannons or thuds of soldiers combatting. Instead, an eerie quiet descended, reminding me again that time prevailed as distorted in this realm. There was no logic, no normalcy. Instead of fighting, I saw torches glittering through the darkness where thousands of men lay dead or mutilated or in agony. Ragged soldiers, dazed and bereft, walked, hobbled, and crawled aimlessly, some calling for missing friends, mothers, sweethearts. Still others attempted to haul away the wounded. Some scavenged dead bodies.

I remembered Will saying that more than twenty-three thousand men died or became casualties that day in 1862, the pastoral fields turned into a massive graveyard.

I moved on, continuing until I reached the shed and stepped onto the porch. A sliver of lamplight cast dim illumination through the open door onto the empty porch. Swallowing the boulder of fear that lodged in my throat, I took a deep breath and shoved the door open, attempting to look nonplussed, as though I merely sought some light to spill outside. I prayed the souls wouldn't process the thought that I could see the light produced by their lamps.

It's amazing what the human eye can take in, in the span of a heartbeat. The interior of the shed looked much as it did before when I was here earlier in the summer—two lamplights, wounded men sprawled on feed bags around the edges of the shed, two makeshift operating tables fashioned from doors, two surgeons at work, and blood everywhere—on the walls, ceiling, and floor where it puddled. Blood connected every person and element in the room. And, of course, I spotted that horrid pyramid just outside the wide-open back door that I'd seen on an earlier visit: the pile of amputated arms and legs.

I turned away from it. Despite horror crawling over me, I tried to continue the charade. Cupping my hands to my mouth, I looked left into the darkness and yelled, "You guys go on ahead. I need to rest. I'll catch up with you." I was too out of sorts to feel foolish.

I made a small commotion of dropping my backpack to the porch floor before dropping down beside it, angling my body such that I could see both inside the shed and the steps to the tiny porch. Feeling anxious and anything but nonchalant, I removed one of my sneakers and picked at it, hoping that I looked like a hiker who'd stopped to give her aching feet a rest and remove stones from her shoes.

Each second passed like hours as I sat there, trying to look oblivious to the otherworldly carnage around me, and no doubt failing at it. I couldn't help but take in the scene inside. Braxton leaned over the table to the left, crude saw in hand, facing away from the back door. He looked worse than I'd ever seen him, which startled me because I thought a dead being most always looked the same. Instead, he looked exhausted, disheveled, battered, as though he'd been physically and violently battered and hurled against a wall. His glasses sat askew on his nose and a smudge of blood ran from the corner of one lens to the scar on his right cheek. Never had anyone looked more worn by battle's horror than he did at that instant. He didn't look up from his work, and I wondered if he even registered my presence. What's more, did *this* Braxton even register that I was scheduled to be there that night?

The other surgeon—the man I surmised to be Lorentz Bohrman—was as pale as a sheet and mirrored Braxton's look of exhaustion. Sweat formed on his brow as he focused on his patient, and he often lifted his right arm to pat the sweat onto his bloodied, rolled-up shirt-sleeve. Around the walls of the building, wounded soldiers waited in agony.

I don't know how long I sat there. Ten minutes? Twenty? I watched the same scenes unfold that I'd seen during my earlier visit, when I had been seeking information for Will.

But, I saw new movement too, such as the two souls that entered the shed, passing so close, they breezed through my backpack and my right foot. After the taller of the two deposited his injured comrade on the floor and eased him against the wall, he patted the man's shoulder twice, muttered a hoarse, "God be with you, Mick," and exited, his bare feet making slurping sounds with each step on the blood-saturated, earthen floor of the shed.

Other souls staggered in and out, delivering new bodies and carrying out the dead as I perched there, just waiting for the murders to unfold.

Then it happened, and I was reminded that if you push hard enough against any extreme, you will end up at its opposite. The drama unfolded with such haste that it ended up displaying itself in slow motion, such that I experienced *every* horrid detail.

A man stepped into the archway of the open back door, a pistol in each hand. He looked deranged, driven by a mission of gargantuan evil proportion. In an instant, I recognized him … not from the photos I carried in my backpack, but rather from one I first saw in the old house.

A face that had recurred in my nightmares.

The soul I believed to be methodically taking over my cousin's body and soul.

The one who killed Will and drove his wife to end her life on the railroad tracks.

Fergus!

Dressed in tattered buckskins, he looked stocky, yet agile and physically fit. His eyes, revealed a savage gleam, like those of a carnivore. He looked half-mad, almost conscienceless, as though he intended to exact revenge or make someone in the shed pay the price for his anger, for the vile makeup of his heart.

I watched as he carried out the murders, shot by cold-hearted shot.

So fast ...

He raised a pistol to the back of Braxton's head and pulled the trigger before I could prepare for the blast. Blood spurted before Braxton crumpled onto the surgery bed, then slumped to the floor.

Bohrman shrieked a fearful exclamation, and Fergus pointed the same pistol, shooting him in the gut. Bohrman's knees buckled and, as he dropped, his head thwacked into the edge of the makeshift hospital bed.

... in slow motion.

Fergus eyed the two patients on the tables and, as though he decided they would die anyway, he moved on. He hastened three paces, scanning the edges of the room, assessing.

So fast ...

One by one, he stepped toward each wounded man—before they could move or argue or plead—and shot each one in the head, using first one pistol and then the other.

... in slow motion.

It was easy to keep from reacting and making noise because my whole body was stunned. Paralyzed.

When he finished killing, he turned and hurried toward the back door, but stopped beside Braxton, crouched down, and placed one of the pistols in Braxton's hand. He jerked to his feet, assessed his work, then turned, as if he planned to exit through the same back door in which he had entered.

Meanwhile, I sat there stone-cold, like a seated statue. The horror of what he'd done cut through me, and I couldn't process my own pleading, internal command to look away, such that when Fergus turned, our gazes met ... *in slow motion* ... and he halted and cocked his head, but never broke his gaze. He raised his gun and pointed it at me. I gasped as he pulled the trigger.

I anticipated a blow like I'd heard when he shot the others. When it didn't come, I made the mistake of looking down at my chest and saw nothing. I looked back at Fergus to see that he looked startled too. His stare pierced into me as he walked through the length of the shed ... *so fast* ... and stepped onto the porch toward me ... *in slow motion* ... never once breaking eye contact.

Renewed terror surged through me, but I couldn't move or speak. He drew closer.

Closer.

I don't remember breathing or blinking.

So fast ...

When he reached within two feet of me, he stopped and bent to assess me, his eyes transfixed, studying me as I sat rigid as a crouched rabbit before the wolf's attack.

A diabolical gleam flickered in his eyes, and his hand moved toward my face.

... in slow motion.

My breathing hitched, signaling to him that I was both aware and afraid of his intent. In that instant, he grew angrier and bent his fingers, curling them like a claw as though he meant to rip my face apart. His hand inched lower, and I assumed he intended to grab my throat, to strangle me.

In that fast moment, stuck in the slow motion of time, I trembled on the edge of hysteria.

When his hand touched my neck, an alien sensation coursed through me. It had an unearthly quality that sent chills crawling down my spine, but without pain. Just as quickly, a soothing warmth washed over me, squelching the chills, as though my neck was fortified from his touch.

Thin blue streaks emanated from my neck and washed over Fergus's hand, connecting us. With a slow crawl, the streaks snaked up his arm and spread to cover his body. For an instant, it enveloped and paralyzed him.

His hand fell through me back to his thigh, and the streaks disappeared. I recalled Mason's comment that the dead have limited mobility, and Braxton's assurance that Fergus would be here as a residual. A fragile spark of hope surfaced remembering that Fergus stood before me in partial form only because he had not died here. His center, his energy, his power resided at *Crossings*.

Surprise registered on his face when I remained undamaged. He brought his hand back to his face, looking at it as though he didn't understand. Standing erect, he puffed his chest and pointed a finger at me.

In bizarre, exaggerated slow motion, his words— "We're not finished"—spewed forth, but came out slow and snarly, like, "Weeeeee'rrrrreeeee nnnnnooootttttt fffffiiiiinnnnnnnniiiiiisssssshhhhhheeeeeeddddddddddd," reverberating as though they'd come up from the very depths of hell giving them an extra ring of truth.

A threat and a promise.

I registered the warning; that as assuredly that the sun would come up in a few hours, Fergus determined to exact revenge on me for meddling.

He whirled, faced into the darkness and howled an unearthly sound, as though trying to send a message to the Devil himself. With one last murderous look at me, he turned and raced into and through the shed, then exited out the back door into the night, much as he must have done more than a hundred and fifty years ago.

I had no time to relax before the souls in the shed rose from their bodies.

Bohrman's soul emerged first, looking disoriented, then startled as he assessed his surroundings. In a tick of time, his transparent form separated from his body and rose until he vanished.

Then, one by one, the souls of the other victims rose from their bodies and departed the shed. Three looked peaceful, bearing countenances of happiness and anticipation. With the other two, I read looks of terror and torment on their faces.

After the others left, I watched Braxton's chest heave one final sigh and cease movement. His soul rose but came to a stop beside his body. He scanned the shed, taking it all in before glancing toward the door. When we made eye contact, he walked—no, it was more like he floated in that odd way that nonliving beings do—toward me, and I climbed to my feet.

My throat tightened as he drew near. I wasn't afraid of Braxton anymore, but watching someone approach that you watched being murdered ... well, it proved a daunting sensation, and I sounded near hysteria when I spoke. "Fergus killed you! I saw it with my own eyes. Fergus! I can't believe it." I rambled on like a crazed person, not taking a breath.

I'm not sure what I expected of Braxton. Perhaps that he looked shocked, or even a little indignant. I definitely thought I'd see anger or sadness. Instead, stoic, brooding Braxton responded, "Now we know. I suggest starting with the root cellar at *Crossings*. It's back over the hill, going northwest. Then the tunnels. You may find something there. I will await your results." With that he turned to leave.

"Wait!" *That was it?* I needed to say something kind to this man whom I'd just seen be murdered in a most heinous way, but all I could offer was, "I ... I'm sorry ..."

He wrinkled his brow, and in that instant, the truth hit me. The physiognomy of his face was not the result of scowls and sneers; instead, every slight, every harsh word from his men, every loathsome thing he'd witnessed in the war had signed its name on his face, serving as a chronicle of his life's despair and tragedy.

I lowered my voice. "I mean about your ... death. You didn't deserve this."

"Ms. MacKenna, no one *deserves* to be murdered." He turned again to go.

"But ... I mean *this*," I said as I gestured with a sweeping hand, "all of this. You didn't deserve any of it. The murder, the war, the way the men treated you ... you tried to help them. Someday ... somehow, I'll do whatever I can to clear your name."

He turned back and stared at me, but said nothing.

I continued. "I always thought you were … well, you know, maybe a little aloof, but I've come to learn that you just numbed yourself to all this horror." I shrugged. "I just want you to know I'm sorry. That I judged you and was afraid of you."

He lifted his chin. When I thought he might say a kind word and step out of character, he proved me wrong again. With no inflection or emotion, he said, "The men had good cause to be afraid of me. I was a surgeon. A butcher. I removed their last hopes of returning to a normal life. They would rather have surrendered themselves to the enemy than to me."

As he spoke, I saw the whole dreadful war experience reflected in his eyes. As if I were an invisible presence beside him in his tent, in the makeshift hospitals, and as he moved from patient to patient. I saw his loneliness, the ostracism from the other men, the shunning, the scathing fear and anger directed at him from beleaguered soldiers, the solitary nights lying on his bedroll, no one to talk to except perhaps Bohrman, a man he hadn't trusted or respected. I saw Braxton longing for Eva, the one person who offered him love and a respite from the horror and mayhem.

He clenched his hands as he continued: "For survival, I grew indifferent. I grew numb to everything but necessity. If I seem gruff, it's because I spent the latter years of my life fighting the Devil face-to-face."

A pause fell, and I could think of nothing to offer before he continued, his gaze drifting as if he studied something in his mind.

"It tends to sour you for the pleasantries in life … although, I do look forward to experiencing them in my next life. And I know I will. It's not until you die that you understand God's mercy. That it's always there. That men have free will to be as happy as they choose to be, even when evil intervenes. That we allow our own hopes to be destroyed. It's all so unnecessary."

He paused and pulled his shoulders back. "I will await what you learn. Thank you, and good night, Ms. MacKenna." His tone, back to being curt and scornful, signaled he was through.

Feeling dismissed, I decided to leave.

"Eva's in the tunnels."

The words had come out of my mouth, even as they crystallized in my mind as true. With one voice, one sentence, the answer loomed.

I'd said it myself, hadn't I? *Eva's in the tunnels.*

Oddly, the assurance had formulated in my chest and worked its way to my throat, then up to my mouth before my brain even processed it. I heard the words, "... the tunnels," and knew with the same certainty that night follows day that's where I'd find her.

Braxton stared at me, his assessment intense, then brushed a hand over his head and nodded, as though he'd read some truth on my face that I wasn't even aware was there.

"Yes, yes, of course. Fergus killed her there. It makes sense now." He spoke to himself or the air, I wasn't sure which, but the next words were directed at me. "Go to her. I'll await her in the dimension. Set her free." He paused and stiffened before adding, "Please."

I nodded. By "dimension" he referred to that space between this life and eternity. I learned that from Will. There was no need to say more, so I left. I didn't need Braxton to say "thank you." *Who wouldn't be grateful, after having existed in torment for the past hundred and fifty years?*

I wasn't afraid as I returned to my car; instead, my blood coursed with a mission: to tackle the next domino of locating Eva and asking her about Fergus.

But I added a new domino too: reuniting her and Braxton.

CHAPTER 20

During the drive home over the long, dark stretches of road, I wrestled with thoughts of the voice I heard at the shed.

Braxton said that once I identified who killed him, I would have a good idea of what happened to Eva and that, in turn, would help to solve the riddle of what Fergus sought.

Eva's whereabouts would have been the next step in this convoluted riddle. Prior to hearing the voice, I thought that she could be anywhere. The options overwhelmed me, beginning with anywhere along the extended passage of the Underground Railroad to the entire United States or Canada.

I felt better having a specific step to take next.

However, one daunting problem remained: Fergus's demonic soul dwelled in the tunnels, too.

★ ★ ★

My cell phone read one-twenty in the morning when I pulled into my driveway. I cut the lights so as not to wake Michael.

However, I looked up from the lawn to see the light spilling through the windows, and there he was, pacing like a caged animal. A ripple of unease coursed through me so I crept up the steps to the attached apartment, hoping to avoid alerting him to my presence. I peered through the window and studied him.

I could tell it wasn't *my* Michael waiting for me. It was Fergus *in* Michael, just as it must have been when Adriana heard a different voice coming from his mouth. He looked restless, agitated, a man beyond human dimension. Glasses removed, black shadows rimming glaring eyes and a scowl—all just a reflection of what festered in Fergus's vile heart. The rage boiled so hot in him, he appeared consumed by it. His chest puffed out in diabolical haughtiness, as though he would destroy anything in his way, and his agitated pacing convinced me that he would pounce on me if I entered.

As he neared the back of the room, he stepped *onto* the wall and walked up it as if he were a puppet dangled sideways by strings!

I swirled from the window and backed deep into the shadows, covering my mouth to keep my fear from voicing itself. Possession was developing so quickly, despite the Equinox still being almost a week away. *Now* was the time to go into the tunnels.

Right now.

No time to rest and recharge.

No time to reflect or plan.

Fergus dwelled here, in my apartment, so I couldn't go inside anyway. Not after the encounter I had with him at the battlefield.

To find and converse with Eva, I would need to search when her energy was strongest—at night. I already memorized the map of the tunnels. More time would not help anyway, and I couldn't ignore this or shrug it off. I couldn't outmaneuver or outrun or outthink this.

I had to go *now*.

I took a deep breath, crept back down the steps, retrieved a flashlight from my car, and headed to the entry to the root cellar and the icy black tunnels at the far side of the lawns.

★ ★ ★

While living at Crossings, I learned the greatest fear is not knowing what to fear. I mean, if you are fearful that a murderous lunatic will break into your home, you at least have a rough idea of how a lunatic acts and how he may go about his nefarious deed. But when you deal with ghosts and their otherworldly powers, your fear of the unknown is vast and consuming, and it sometimes infuses you with inexplicable instincts and adrenaline that you never before experienced.

It was with those driving forces that, within seconds, I raced across the expansive grounds between the house and the root cellar, ignored the dark trees that smothered and ogled me, heaved open the wooden door that I heretofore had never been able to wedge, and entered the yawning void of darkness which earlier had terrified me.

Once inside, I stopped and breathed the stale air, in and out ... in and out ... hoping to slow my pounding heart and adjust to the creepy isolation. The inky blackness around me felt heavy, threatening. Was it due to my imagination or vestiges of Fergus's wanderings left behind? Or, had fears lingered from the slaves who passed through here, fully aware that getting caught meant torture or death?

I forged ahead, directing the flashlight's beam around the moldy-smelling passage. It reflected back an endless monotone of brown: hollowed-out hillside walls, dirt and stone floor, and aged hand-hewn support beams. Here and there, tree roots broke through the ceiling.

Off to the right, things scampered; I didn't care what they were or where they went. As long as they weren't Fergus, I could tolerate them.

My vision zeroed in on what the narrow cone of the flashlight revealed, making it hard to assess the vastness of the tunnels; however, I could see enough to know that Holland's map had been accurate; crude, torn, representative of how it had looked two hundred years ago, but still, accurate.

After about a dozen steps, the passageway split in two directions. I turned right. The tunnels resembled a maze; so it didn't seem to make much difference which direction I chose. With time and luck, I would proceed through, circle around and end up coming out the left side anyway.

That is, if Fergus didn't enter from the opposite end via the house's cellar.

Enveloped in total blackness, I shivered and played the flashlight beam around the dark walls and floor, and into each of the chambers, the light jerking at my command—up, down, right, left, to the front and side—my feeble attempt to comprehend and dilute the unknown before passing through. I prayed nothing unexpected would pop up in the beam. And yes, I shined it behind me, too. I didn't want a repeat of the horror movies I saw on TV where the victim is too dumb to pay attention to what approaches her backside.

The deeper I progressed into the tunnels, the heavier the air became, bringing with it stagnant odors of mud and decay, as though I descended into the center of the earth. Despite the tunnels' substantial height, at least seven feet, occasional wisps of a web or a plant root brushed my face, alarming me.

At times, I heard a squeak or scratching but continued on anyway.

Step by step.

Turning right.

Shining the light.

Wondering: What if an earthquake struck? Or a storm? Could there be quicksand or a deep chasm or fissure down here? What if a pouring rain swept through the area? Would the tunnels flood? Would I drown?

Turning left.

Worrying: Who cares about an earthquake when a demonic being might find me first? Would I be destroyed here and never found? Would I be relegated to haunting these same passages until someone came along and set me free?

Turning right again.

Wallowing: What if I'm wrong? What if Eva isn't here? What if someone else is? What if no one is?

Another right.

Watching: What did I expect to find? A soul? A skeleton? A grave? All of those?

Heart pounding, palms sweating, I kept going, scouring with the flashlight.

Step by determined step.

When I reached what I believed to be the final chamber before the last tunnel that would lead to the door connecting to the cellar of *Crossings*, I heard something. Footsteps? I froze, pulling the beam tight against me. Was I hearing things? Could it be someone coming through the cellar toward the tunnels?

I jerked around to return from the direction I came. My foot stuck to a soggy spot, and I lost my balance. The flashlight and I tumbled in different directions. When the light met the floor, it shut off, leaving me in blackness. Frantic, I scooched to my knees, sweeping and smacking the ground, desperate to find it. Mud and gunk stuck to my hands, but adrenaline drove me, defeating the fear of touching anything untoward in the blackness.

I located the light and climbed to my feet, tapping the flashlight's heel to force it to work again. When it came on, its beam shined half as bright as before. I panicked, thinking the light might die and leave me in complete darkness in an underground maze, cognizant that no one—save Fergus—would be the wiser that I was there.

I held my breath and listened.

No sound. Perhaps my mind played tricks on me in the darkness.

I flashed the weakened light around. Due to my fall, I was disoriented and each direction looked the same, so I had no idea from where I'd come.

The noise came again, and it sounded like swooshing and faint echoes reverberating off the walls. That should have made my decision easy: retreat in the opposite direction. However, the acoustics in the passages made it impossible to tell from where the noise came. That old strangling dread, that fear of helplessness, washed over me.

The sound drew closer, the pace hurried.

Closer.

But I couldn't move. I couldn't even will my fingers to turn off the flashlight or hide the beam against my body. What good would that have done anyway? Souls can see in the dark.

I thought I was incapable of absorbing any more fear, but in the next instant, I learned otherwise. A heavy, powerful blanket of air wrapped around my upper torso, covered my mouth and dragged me backward. It was solid, cold, lifeless, as though a monstrous mass of particles supplied the power, even as it conformed to the shape of my body.

I smelled something floral. A rosy scent. I startled when a voice, soft and feminine, whispered in my ear. "Trust me."

The presence pulled me into a chamber, beyond an old wooden door that closed on its own, then released me.

I whirled, jerking the light's dim beam into the room, hoping to see my captor. Despite knowing it—or something—was there, I gasped when the light revealed the soul of a woman. At least a foot shorter than me, frail and gaunt, she wore a long, ragged dress, dirty boots, and layers of a tattered shawl around her shoulders and arms. The light revealed skin a light mahogany in color. She stood still, looking at me with expectation, as though giving me time to adjust to her.

I managed a weak, "You're—"

She placed her index finger over her lips, an age-old sign to be quiet.

Then, I understood why, as footsteps approached and paused, just outside the door.

As I hitched my breath and clamped my lips, I smashed the light into my side to hide the weak beam. As we waited, we locked gazes, two strangers, two different types of beings, two inhabitants born centuries apart, finding common ground.

I was too afraid to look away. She looked semi-transparent like all the souls I'd met, but beautiful, almost angelic looking, with long locks of tightly curled black hair that brushed the sides of her face and down her back to her waist.

After what seemed hours, the footsteps moved away. I exhaled but waited for her to speak.

She smiled. "You are brave." Three little words. Yet, I heard so much, her voice soft, almost melodious. I detected kindness, gentleness, and heard a Southern accent with an educated distinction to each word.

The accent. Her age. The mahogany skin. The smell of roses.

"Eva?"

She nodded.

"I'm Grace MacKenna," I whispered. "I—"

"I know who you are." She gestured toward me. "You are related to William and the young man named Michael. The one Fergus is attempting to inhabit."

Inhabit? So there it was: confirmation. A cold premonition unfurled from my stomach. "But how could you—"

"I listen, in the lower reaches of the house. I have been hiding here, from Fergus, since my death."

I hugged myself; suppressed a shiver. "But ... but that's more than a hundred and fifty years. How could you hide that long?"

"I am careful. I limit myself to the western side of the tunnels because this is where Fergus killed me," she said as pragmatically as though she'd said, "your shoe is untied." She continued. "He favors the eastern side. But sometimes, when I know he has gone into *Crossings*, I follow from a distance."

"That's amazing. To live ..." *Ugh, I needed to watch my choice of words* "... to exist like that for so long. I can't imagine—"

"We do not have time for that now, Miss Grace. Fergus is fully incited this night. You must leave while you can." She gestured to the door in an obvious attempt to coax me to follow.

"I just came from Braxton," I blurted.

"Braxton!" She threw a hand to her heart and reached out with the other to place it on my arm. Her reaction reminded me that even souls can show emotion, albeit through conditioning. In that moment, I saw the depths of her love and her grief at its loss. "Where?"

"Antietam. He died there."

She nodded. "Fergus killed him."

"You knew?"

"Fergus said as much. Before killing me."

This was when I turned selfish. I thought if I told her that Braxton now waited for her in the dimension, she might move on to be with him. Surely, having been locked in these tunnels for so long must have been akin to having existed in a coffin, and I marveled at her determination to remain behind either to find Braxton or to see justice done. Yet, I suspected that once she learned Braxton had moved on, she would depart too.

But I needed answers!

So I withheld information and, instead, asked her to tell me what had transpired at *Crossings*, so many years ago that led to her death.

She directed me deeper into the chamber, away from the door, and gestured toward the ground. I flashed the light there, saw a log, and dropped to it. She sat beside me, saying, "We must keep our voices low."

As she told her story, I could see it all in my mind as she had witnessed it, as though I stood by her side through it all.

"After killing my brother, Moses," Eva said, "Thaddeus Calhoun followed Braxton and me for weeks, all the way from South Carolina to Maryland. It was hot. Summer. I was with child, and so tired and worn from the journey. Braxton took pity on me, such that when we encountered Fergus outside of Williamsport, Braxton paid him in gold to hide me.

"When he thought Fergus wasn't looking, he slipped the rest of the gold to me, imploring me to be cautious. To use it to achieve freedom. We agreed to meet again one day in Toronto. And I told my beloved good-bye."

When she paused, I touched her hand and said, "I'm so sorry."

"After many tears and a painful good-bye, and knowing we might never see one another again, Braxton returned to his command, and Fergus took me to *Crossings*."

"Was anyone else there at the time?"

"Braxton's brother Aaron and his wife Savilla, both abolitionists. They welcomed me into the safety of *Crossings*. Within three weeks, I gave birth to a daughter. All that time, I watched, and I sensed Fergus knew about the gold. That he was biding his time, formulating a plan to get the rest of it."

From there, the sequence jumbled together as Eva spoke of several disjointed events, but I saw it all. To secure silence regarding the gold, Fergus hurried to Antietam, found Braxton, and killed him, knowing the death would be assumed to be more of the carnage from the battle. Fergus later returned to *Crossings* with more escaped slaves he claimed to want to help. Aaron and Savilla left for a short while to help prepare the way ahead via the Underground Railroad.

"While they were gone, Fergus demanded I turn over the gold. That's when he told me he'd killed Braxton. I refused to cooperate. I knew I needed that gold for our child, to take her to freedom. Fergus dragged me away from the others and into the tunnels. In a fit of rage, he killed me, failing to secure the gold first."

I put my hand over my mouth to stifle voicing pity, rage, for what he'd done to her.

She continued. "I was unconscious for a while before dying. By the time my body succumbed to the destruction, and my soul rose, I overheard Fergus tell the other slaves that I left *Crossings* of my own accord and that I was too ashamed to keep my child. A young Negro couple, Sally and Isaac, took her and cared for her as their own."

"Will saw your child in Pennsylvania after escaping from prison in Ohio! I'm sure of it." I remembered him telling me about his escape, how he and Fergus came upon a farm family that hid two slaves in their cellar, and how the slave woman tried to hide the child from view but that he had seen the child's light-colored skin.

She nodded. "After dying, I hid here and watched Fergus search day and night. Before he could find the gold, Union soldiers arrived, captured him and sent him to prison. The same prison where Will had been incarcerated. The soldiers believed Fergus to be a traitor because Calhoun used his brother-in-law, a northern sympathizer who lived locally, to convince the soldiers."

"Enoch Crinshaw!" My stomach tightened.

Eva nodded. "Later, when Fergus returned from prison with Will, I watched as Fergus murdered him too. After scouring the house and the tunnels and coming up empty-handed, he retrieved a pistol from behind some books on the shelves in the parlor. I guess he'd hid it there long ago. Then, he pulled some papers from his vest and put them where the pistol had been, like he was marking the spot. That evening, he rode away. I don't know why. Provisions … food perhaps. About a week later, he returned as a prisoner of Calhoun and Crinshaw."

Through Eva's eyes, I saw still more death.

She continued. "Once Fergus died, Crinshaw turned the gun on Calhoun and shot him. Crinshaw searched like a wild man for the gold, but he too left without it. He did not leave alone, however. He took

Calhoun's dying body, I assume to dispose of it elsewhere, so there would be no evidence pointing to him."

When she finished her story, I slumped backward, exhausted, overwhelmed. "That's incredible. So Fergus saw his killer. He's not remaining here to resolve his murder. He has stayed behind for another reason."

Eva nodded. "The gold."

"But he's dead. What good is it to him now? He can't buy his way out of eternal damnation ... can he? This makes no sense."

"Evil never rests, Miss Grace. And it doesn't forget. Yes, Fergus is assigned to eternal damnation. His deeds will punish him through eternity. But he is seeking favors, believing it will ease his suffering."

I exhaled a ludicrous noise. "Braxton implied that same thing. You're saying he's made a pact with the Devil?"

"He believes his time will be less torturous if he can get the gold into evil hands. Hands of the living with evil intent. Hands he can use. If it is discovered before he finds it, his purpose for being at *Crossings* will be destroyed. He'd be taken. He'd have no choice."

"Taken? By whom?" My heart lurched at my next thought. "Or what?"

She stood. "I can't answer that question. It's not my place. And it wouldn't help you with your cousin anyway."

"What?" I scrambled to my feet and reached to grab her arm but my hand fell through and served to compound my fear. She could leave at any second. "But you have to help me! My cousin's life depends on it."

"No, your cousin's life depends on you and the arsenal you use."

"My ... my arsenal?"

She stepped closer, and her demeanor softened. "You already know the answer to that. I am sorry. I cannot tell you more."

I shook my head, trying to think, adrenaline coursing through my veins. *What did I need to know from her to solve this?* "What about Crinshaw? Why didn't he ever come back?"

"He tried, several times, but could not get near. Will's soul protected the house from intruders, and Fergus's soul guarded the tunnels."

"But Crinshaw was a horrible person as well. Why didn't Fergus use him? Lead *him* to the gold? It sounds like Crinshaw would have carried out evil intent anyway."

"Fergus would never help the man who killed him. Years later, when Crinshaw's descendants tried to gain access, they too could not get near."

"His descendants?"

She continued, ignoring my question. "Besides, Fergus had to find the gold before he could lead anyone to it."

"He still doesn't know where it is? But he's been down here a hundred and fifty years. Surely in that time—"

"He cannot search and dig and uncover material things, Miss Grace. He is a soul. He needs to inhabit a living form in order to do that."

"Which is why he's after Michael."

She nodded.

"But where is the gold? Tell me, and I'll get it now, so that I can remove his purpose for being here. Then Michael will be safe again."

"I do not know."

"But it was *your* gold—" I sounded angry, so I took a deep breath and began again in a calmer voice. "It was your gold, Eva. Why don't you know?"

"Aaron and Savilla hid it for me. As I said, they didn't trust Fergus."

Aaron and Savilla hid the gold, and they're long dead. I backed to the wall and slid down to a catcher's position, defeat overcoming me. I lowered the light to the dirt beside me and dropped my head into my hands. Everyone who knew the whereabouts of the gold was long gone. What would I do now? "So there's no hope."

"There's always hope," she said from beside me. I looked up to see her crouching at my side. "Savilla sewed a guide ... a map of sorts. More like a tapestry. If you can find that, you may be able to figure out where the gold is. At the top of the tapestry is a depiction of a building and three—"

"Crosses," I said, my heart beating wildly and my hopes soaring that she'd say yes.

She cocked her head and studied my face. "Yes ... and beneath that is—"

"A hill and a yellow fence with a gate. And under that is some sort of a pasture, and the colors weave into a ... maze or a series of channels ... tunnels. These tunnels!"

She kept nodding as I talked, her smile growing. "You have it?"

"No, but I know where it is." I stood up. "The library. On a wall in a conference room."

In one fluid movement that souls make, she stood beside me again. "Study that to find your answers. Now come, you must leave while you can."

She turned and motioned for me to follow. As we maneuvered through the underground, my mind raced, trying to think if anything remained that she could tell me.

We reached the weathered door exiting the tunnels before I could think of what I might need to know.

She smiled and turned to go. "God speed, Miss Grace."

Guilt surged through me. "Eva, wait. Braxton is in the dimension ... waiting for you."

If a soul could gasp, then I'd say that's what she did. Her hand flew to her heart again.

"My Braxton?" her voice broke. "After all these years? He is waiting for me?"

My adrenaline fizzled, my determination faltered, and my eyes glazed. The sheer happiness and hope she revealed on her face overwhelmed me.

"I'm sorry." I wiped a lone tear. "I didn't tell you earlier because I needed to know so many things, and I was afraid, and I just—"

"Miss Grace," she said, touching my arm again. "It's alright. You're telling me now."

"Thank you, Eva. I wish we could have known one another. Then, I mean."

"As do I."

"Would you tell Will when you see him, that I ..." I shrugged. "That

I miss him."

She smiled. "Why don't you tell him?"

I thought she meant that I should talk out loud in some absurd manner such that Will might hear me from beyond. I anticipated her next comments—the part about beings with bodies and beings without bodies dwelling in the same space, just on different realms. And that heaven isn't in the sky, it's in an invisible dimension all around us.

But when I looked at her, I could see she intended a different meaning. "What are you saying?"

She smiled. "He's with you. Never left. He intended to because he believed he thwarted your path and purpose. But then he became tied to you in an earthly way, and you became more of his unfinished business. He'll be there when you need him."

She was wrong. We'd said good-bye. I saw him go. A sudden inexplicable doubt passed through my mind about the veracity of everything else Eva told me. *Who was she really? Could she be trusted? Was this Fergus in disguise again, toying with me?* But that notion registered as crazy. She wouldn't lie ... would she? Her responses were too genuine. I must have misunderstood something.

Before I could quiz her, she continued. "Good-bye, Miss Grace. Thank you for bringing Braxton back to me."

With that, she turned and faded away from the living world.

Her departure emphasized my aloneness, and I hurried from the underground back to *Crossings*. As I thought, the apartment was empty. With Fergus in the tunnels, Michael had fallen asleep on the couch again. I sneaked into my room, pets at my side, and fell asleep trying to imagine what a reunion must be like between two lovers who'd been separated for a century and a half.

CHAPTER 21

Late the next morning, with Michael off to work, I drove to the local waffle diner for a combination of breakfast/lunch and WiFi. Despite the chaos and threats and *weirdness* in my life, I tried to cling to normalcy. I forced myself to start online homeschooling classes, lest I jeopardize graduating from high school in the spring. Aunt Tish didn't pay much attention to me these days, but if I failed to graduate on time, she'd move me back to Boston to eliminate further embarrassment.

After I finished schoolwork, I drove into the heart of Williamsport. First stop: the bank. After that, and far more important, I planned to visit the library where I intended to study the tapestry.

The ATM machine at the First Potomac Bank and Trust wasn't working, so I parked in the side lot and walked around the building to the front door. For the first time, I noticed that Hilson's Antique Emporium sat across Canal Street from the bank. *Directly* across. Hilda was right; she *did* have a good view of a large portion of Williamsport. I wondered if she ever saw the bank being robbed or someone kicking the ATM. Was she watching me at that moment?

Before I could look back to the bank's sidewalk, something caught my eye. Two doors away from the Emporium, outside a barber shop, stood a soul, leaning against the shop's trade red and white striped pole. He wore heavy-looking, dirty-tan boots and a uniform of some kind, and seemed to be unaware of my presence, his eyes scanning the street.

Before I could pinpoint my motive, I turned and headed for him, crossing the street and stepping onto the tree-lined sidewalk. I'd been too preoccupied to talk with the whittling ghost I saw by the canal, but I decided to take the time to talk to this one. I kept him in my vision, but he still had not spotted me. I was so busy trying to figure out what my opening line with him should be, that it took me a few seconds to realize he was backing into the shadows of the building, head back and eyes wide as though startled. Whatever he was staring at was hidden from my view by a huge oak tree.

His facial expression frightened me enough that I tucked against the tree, certain that some sort of inexplicable demon was going to pass us at any instant. I waited, two seconds, then five, but all that stormed by was a brisk-paced Ms. Bealle heading in the direction of the library. She didn't see me, and for that I was grateful. I chuckled as a crazy notion flittered through my mind: that the soul was a good judge of character and inadvertently had saved me from an encounter with the grouchy woman. But I shrugged off that idea. She was just an overbearing person, not a demon.

Concerned that something else may still be coming, I inched my head around to take a look, but saw nothing. Whatever alarmed him was now gone.

That's when the soul and I made eye contact. He had moved back to his position against the barber's pole and watched me approach.

As always, I was conscious of guarding against appearing to passersby as though I'd lost my sanity and was talking to the air, so I looked around before rattling: "Hi. I'm Grace. Yes, I can see you. I'm sorry, I don't have time for pleasantries. May I ask why you are waiting here? Why you haven't moved on?"

His head jerked as though taken aback at my abruptness, but then smiled as though he understood my situation. He was about my height, all muscles and reminded me of a linebacker with no neck. His blond hair was shaved close to his head and made his ears and nose stand out all the more.

He shrugged in that conditioned way that souls do. "I was a fireman. Died in a blaze here ... years ago. Nineteen sixty-two. I was only twenty-eight but never fulfilled my goal to save a life. For me, things were left unfinished. I don't know if you can understand that."

I nodded. "So you've determined to do that? To save a life before you move on?"

He smiled.

"But how? I mean, if someone needs your help, your strength, they're going to either see you help them or if you remain unseen, they'll assume that something bizarre or miraculous happened. People will want an explanation. They always do and—"

"And they'll get one. Ever heard of super-human strength? There's a reason for the term."

I hitched in my breath, daunted by his explanation. "Are ... are you an angel?"

He grinned, and I noted a gentleman nearing me from my right that studied me with a concerned look, brows pulled together, eyes intent. I opened my mouth to urge the soul to answer my question but clamped it shut as the feeling washed over me that I wouldn't get an answer anyway.

Exasperated and determined to seek out this soul again one day, I turned and headed back to the bank.

After withdrawing cash at the counter, I turned to see Nidhi Michelson, the branch manager, standing at her office door, smiling at me. I'd met her weeks before when I first moved to the area.

Nidhi, a short, dark-skinned woman of about 45 or 50, waved me over with a huge smile and exaggerated gesture. She moved her plump body into the office ahead of me and sat behind her desk.

"So Grace, how are you? Are you enjoying the area?"

I offered her a couple socially acceptable impressions of Williamsport.

"You know," she said, "I never did meet your aunt. But I hear your cousin is now your guardian. Is that right?"

I nodded, but she didn't even notice.

"How's that working out?"

Well, he's been possessed by a demon, and I fall asleep each night wondering if he'll murder me. "Fine. He and I are close."

"So, are you and Cassie still such good friends?"

Where did that question come from? Had I missed the transition?

As though she read my mind, she chuckled and grimaced at the same time, then shrugged. "The last time I saw you, Cassie helped you sign for an account here."

"Oh, yeah." My turn to shrug. "Yes, we're close friends."

"Good, good, good," she murmured to herself. "She seems to be doing well. With the café, I mean."

I nodded, not sure what to say, what to offer in exchange.

"Such a shame about Mason. I still find that whole thing so hard to believe." Her eyes grew big and she thumped her hands on her desk. "You know about that, right?"

In that moment, I didn't sense meddling or an ulterior motive from her. Nidhi struck me as the friendly sort, the kind that liked to find common ground with people where possible. The link between us was Cassie, so she chose to use that to get to know me.

When I nodded my familiarity with Mason's disappearance, she sighed. "Such a wonderful man. I worked with him, you know."

"No, I didn't know."

"I think I was the last person to see him before he disappeared."

Ahhh, no wonder she still wanted to talk about it. My heart raced, my desire to see the tapestry on hold. "What do you mean? What did he say to you? Did you get any hint of what was going on in his life?"

If she thought me too nosey, she ignored it. Instead, she toyed with a pen on her desk, lost in memories as she talked.

"It's all a matter of public record," she said, as though to rationalize sharing the information. "When he left, he told Clyde ... that's Clyde Drury, another bank employee ... anyway, Mason told him he planned to visit one of our customers. Clyde mentioned Mason's activity later, to Gina ... that's Gina Montcrief ... a teller, but we don't know much more than that the man wanted a loan for some sort of controversial museum. Then Clyde said Mason planned to take the contents of a safety deposit box to wealthy old man Mint ... an eccentric old coot. A millionaire many times over. He'd signed paperwork giving Mason permission to do that. He even gave Mason the key to his box."

I listened to her talk but honed in on the word "controversial." I mean, *who wouldn't?* Cassie had mentioned a museum too, but she hadn't called it controversial. And, when Nidhi mentioned "wealthy" and "contents of a safety deposit box," those terms raced up my curiosity radar quicker and higher than the controversial museum. "A millionaire? What was his real name?"

She flushed. "Oh, I can't give you names. Confidentiality, you know. Mint wasn't his real name. Folks just said he was worth a mint and the name stuck. He's dead now, but still, I can't divulge his estate like that."

"Was Mason accused of stealing the contents of the box?"

She looked indignant, flustered that I dared to ask such a thing but answered nonetheless. "Nobody ever knew. As I said, the man was an eccentric, so he didn't even remember what he asked Mason to bring." She offered a tentative smile. "'Course, you know how urban legends go. Rumor said there was a lot of money in the box. That Mason took it all, but I don't believe that."

"Neither do I."

"I'm rather sure the old coot could have vouched for Mason's innocence, but then he died that same night. Heart attack. And—"

"That same night?"

Nidhi nodded and leaned in. "And so did Clyde! That very night. Poor man. God rest his soul. Killed in a sledding accident. Up on Chocton Bluff. Such a sad time that was."

Two other people died the night that Mason was murdered? What were the odds of that? Even though two of the three didn't sound controversial, it seemed odd. I tried to process what she said, wondering what to ask and what she would answer. Before I could decide, she continued.

"The police investigated, of course, and determined that Mason never showed up at either place. As I said, I don't believe any of the rumors. I worked with him for six years. He was a delightful man and loved his family. I don't believe he stole any money. But then, I would never have thought he'd take off the way he did."

I bit my lip and offered a lame response, "I guess we never really know people."

She stiffened. "I don't know about that. I think I'm a good judge of character. Helps with my work, here." She motioned at the bank. "Mason was just true blue. Salt of the earth. You know the kind?" She shrugged. "There are a lot of dishonest people in Williamsport that I don't care to do business with. The Cauldecorts. The Shenkmans. The Crinshaws—" As if she realized she'd insulted several key clients in town, her faced reddened. "Well anyway, I can usually judge people well."

I didn't care about that. But I did care about one thing she said. I tried to act disinterested, even removed a fleck of fake lint from my shirt. "You mentioned the Crinshaws. I've heard that name before."

"Of course. I've seen you around town with Seth. I'm sure you've heard him mention his birth—" She broke off, her reaction telling me that once again her mouth had engaged before her brain.

I felt the blood drain from my face. Could it be true? Seth's mother or father was a Crinshaw? *The* Crinshaws? As in descendants of the diabolical Enoch Crinshaw? The man who murdered Fergus and Calhoun?

"Oh, sure ... he's mentioned being a Crinshaw." I tapped my forehead as though to poke fun at myself. "I just can't place the first name at the moment." I held my breath as I willed her to answer.

A knock sounded at Nidhi's office door. One of the cashiers stood there. "Your appointment is here."

Nidhi stood. "Oh, I must go, Grace. Now you take care and do stop by again."

Once on the street, I took several deep breaths as questions tumbled together in my mind: Should I go to Mason now? Ask him to explain what Nidhi said? And what about Seth, could it be true? Is he a Crinshaw? And what should I do with the information? Dare I tell him what I learned? Dare I *not* tell him?

"Grace?"

That voice! I turned to see Clay standing a few feet away.

Right there. Big and beautiful as life. All six-foot-splendid-two of him.

He scanned the area before stepping closer, reminding me again of the restraining order that was supposed to keep us apart. "Are you alright?"

No, I'm not alright. I just found out Seth's heritage, and he doesn't even know it yet. And, I miss you terribly. And I'm angry that you're waltzing around with Francesca. And I just learned tidbits about your father that I can't share with you. And my cousin is being overtaken by a demented demon, and you're not even around to help me! And don't you know I love you? And have you stopped loving me already? And why are we acting like strangers?

"I ... yeah ... I'm fine." I hesitated, swallowed, tried to look composed. "What about you?"

He opened his mouth to speak, stopped, nodded. "Yes ... no ... I—" He looked away, up and down the street again, then took my arm at the elbow and started leading me toward the alley. "Let's move over here where we can talk. I shouldn't even be here, but Reaghan went into early labor. I don't want to jeopardize what we agreed—"

"But it's okay," I said, allowing him to lead me. *Heck I'd let him lead me anywhere, wouldn't I?* "Aunt Tish is gone. Back to Boston. Michael is my guardian now." We came to a stop between the bank and a drug store, but still in view of the street. "I'm free to do whatever I want, with whomever I want. He wouldn't mind if we—"

"But I would." His voice was rough, his delivery quick. He pulled his shoulders back, and I watched his jaw twitch such that when he spoke again, his voice was gentle. "I would mind, Grace."

What was that supposed to mean? He didn't want to communicate with me?

"I see." I pulled my arm back and looked away. I didn't want him to see the disappointment on my face. We stood side by side, but emotional distance pressed between us like a wall.

"No, I don't think you do." His voice sounded sad, defeated. "You said you could do whatever, with whomever. That's why all the trips and outings with Seth?"

"What? No. Seth means nothing to me. We're just friends." As the words came out of my mouth, I cringed with the knowledge that they weren't true. Seth did mean more to me than friendship. He'd become an amazing, caring guy. But this was Clay! The man I loved.

Didn't I?

And, who was he to ask me about the company I kept?

"What about you and Francesca?" *Ugh, I sounded childish.*

His head jerked back. "What about her?"

"She seems to be special to you."

"Grace, she's an acquaintance. A friend. The daughter of my mom's new employee ... or boyfriend ..." He rolled his eyes and flailed his hands. "... whatever Whit is. I was as surprised as you to see her in Lexington."

Things aren't always as they appear. The soul that saved me from the speeding car had said that. Pastor Dale, too ...

"Then why don't you want to see me? I thought we had something special."

He rubbed his hand across his head and made a face that suggested confusion, frustration, some combination. "I made a promise to your aunt and the police that I wouldn't come near you until you turn eighteen. I intend to keep that promise if possible."

"But why? You don't have to. Don't you see?" I reined myself in when I heard pleading in my voice. "I miss you ..."

His shoulders dropped as he exhaled a weary sigh. He reached to touch my cheek. "You are so beautiful. I hope you mean that. But, Grace, it's a matter of honor. Of keeping my word."

"Things have changed. That promise doesn't matter anymore."

He gripped my arms. "It does matter. To me. Don't you get that? Maybe that's the difference between us. I want to do this right. I'm not going to sneak around like some juvenile. And I'm not going to do anything to jeopardize your ability to stay in the area. I don't want you moving back to Boston."

"This isn't sneaking. We're standing here in broad daylight. And don't you think I should be the one who decides what's best for me?"

"You take too many risks," he said in a reprimanding tone. "Like our trek to Georgia. And that trip to Savannah with Seth. Both times you were almost killed. This ghost sleuthing has to stop. I know it's real to you. It was real to me too at those railroad tracks in Georgia. But maybe it's a reality you should not be a part of. What good will it do anyway? What do you hope to prove?"

He never broke his gaze, his own face inches away. We both breathed heavy and heaved with frustration. His gaze dropped to my lips and my traitorous heart skipped a beat. He slipped his fingers up to my hair, moaned, and rained kisses on my eyelids and cheeks before moving his lips to meet mine.

"Grace, you're only seventeen years old," he said as he continued the pleasurable assault on my face. "You haven't been around much to know what you want." He planted more kisses. "You need to be sure." His lips hovered at my ear. "Is it true ... you haven't developed feelings for Seth?"

He took my face in his hands, and our gazes locked. I was amazed at the sudden importance he placed on my reply. I could see it in his eyes.

I hesitated, trying to decide how to answer. Uncertainty must have reflected on my face.

He let go of me. "I see."

I panicked. "It's not what you think. He's changed and, yes, he's special to me. But that's all. He's been there for me. I owe him time and attention in return. No, I don't mean I *owe* him ... I mean I care about him. He's a good man. Like you. But that doesn't change how I feel about you."

I could hear my own turmoil, and I could see it wash over him like a tidal wave of destruction, diluting any hope that dwelled in his heart.

Tears welled in my eyes. "I'm sorry. I know I'm not making sense. Seth needs me right now, and there are things I need to do for him. And, he's been helping me with ... something ... but that has nothing to do with us, Clay!"

He rubbed his forehead and backed away. "I need to get to the hospital and play uncle."

"No! Clay, please don't leave like this." I reached for him but stopped when I saw the rigid lines of his jaw and his fisted hands.

"I need to go. Think about what you want. Not just right now, but for the rest of your life. When you finally zero in on the long-range future, rather than just momentary gratification, then we'll talk."

"What's that supposed to mean? I am focused on my future. Don't treat me like I'm a child. You know I have no choice about my subtle vision."

"You do have a choice. Choose to ignore it and stay safe."

"You don't understand what's going on at my house and with Michael and—"

"Grace, I have to go." He took a deep breath. "Before I say something I'll regret." He diverted his gaze to the street again, shifting it one direction, then the other. "Or before someone reports seeing us together." He turned, but hesitated and looked back. "Be careful. Please. Do that for me. Just be careful. You're dealing with something very dangerous."

He walked away.

I stood there for another minute trying to figure out what had happened, and I swear my peripheral vision caught a shadow moving from the window in Hilson's Antique Emporium.

CHAPTER 22

A t the library, Seth wasn't available this time to distract Ms. Bealle. Instead, Holland Greer provided the buffer.

To my relief, neither of them saw me enter. They huddled together in a room behind the circulation desk, door wide open, intent in conversation. I wasn't surprised that Ms. Bealle may have hurried to the library to see Holland, but I wasn't expecting to see angry faces—flushed skin, furrowed brows, jerky movements.

I scooted behind one of the floor-to-ceiling bookcases and hesitated.

Part of me wanted to sneak closer and listen to their conversation. I imagined Ms. Bealle now as a lonely divorcee taking care of a handicapped brother, wishing her life differed, and trying desperately to impress Holland Greer in the hopes that he might bring her companionship and a brighter future. No doubt the fireman ghost had merely reacted to the aura of frustration and defeat that surrounded the poor woman.

As for Holland, an image flashed through my head of him as an evil Snidely Whiplash, the archenemy and antithesis of the cartoon character Dudley Do-Right of the Royal Canadian Mounties. In those old cartoons, Snidely was the archetype of evil and would tie little Nell Fenwick to the railroad tracks. I imagined Greer sacrificing Gwendolyn Bealle to the same fate.

Another part of me wondered what they would do if they saw me. Ask me to leave? Embarrass me? I'd suffered worse things than that. Still, I prayed I could get out without another confrontation with Holland. With time as my enemy, I proceeded toward the basement by winding around the long way to the stairs.

The room I wanted sat empty. I entered and shut the door. The tapestry perched a little too high to study in detail, so I pushed a chair closer, climbed up on the table, and assessed the needlework.

It was exquisite, each stitch matching in length with the one before it. I imagined Savilla diligently working at it and finding pleasure in helping someone achieve freedom. Perhaps she even sewed it right under Fergus's nose, without him ever being aware of what she created.

I studied the piece with the notion of it being a map. The layout depicted modeled the map I'd gotten from Holland. The channels in the pasture beneath the crosses and the gate could be mistaken for ditches or rows for crops, until one pondered why the rows would intersect. Only one channel didn't connect at both ends; instead, it ran in an odd angle to the right, into a portion of the tapestry that had frayed through the years. I ignored it since I wanted to assess the routes that took me into its depth, not out of it. Yes, the passages had to be a maze or tunnels. Each passage bore little brown splotches of fabric which, from a distance, looked like stones. Up close, I could see that not all of the stones were brown. In one tunnel on the left, near the center, appeared a small splotch of cream-colored stone edged with fine gold thread. That *had* to be where the gold was buried! None of the other tunnels bore distinguishing colors or marks.

Convinced that I had a rough idea where to find the coins, I snapped a picture with my cell phone, climbed off the table, crept out of the library, and headed to the local hardware store to buy a shovel, a hurricane lantern, and matches. If I had to spend more time in the tunnels, I didn't want to rely on a fickle flashlight for illumination, and Michael had absconded with my other lanterns for his bedroom in the old parlor.

★ ★ ★

When I pulled into *Crossings*, my cell phone rang. It was Roxanne, asking if I'd heard from Kate.

I tensed. "What! No, I thought she was with you. Took the train to Richmond. You haven't heard from her either?" I know, a dumb question on my part, because otherwise she wouldn't have asked first, but I had to hear her answer.

"Train? No, she was packing her car when I talked to her last. I'm getting worried," Roxanne said. "She doesn't answer her cell phone."

"Her car's here, but she's not. What about her friend at American U? Kate said she might go there."

"Mallaka hasn't heard from her since seeing her in Paris. If Kate doesn't call by morning, I'm calling the police."

We agreed to communicate if either one of us heard from her.

I ended the call but ramped up the concern, and I confess it, my annoyance. Kate was one of my best friends, but she had a history of being irresponsible.

Where had she gone?

With her foremost on my mind, I couldn't help but unload my thoughts when I opened the apartment door and saw Michael. Chubbs laid beside Tramp, a couple yards away, looking relaxed. My tell-tale sign that Michael was himself ... for now.

"Have you heard from Kate?" I parked my backpack on the table, beside where he sat reading a magazine and eating a sandwich, and dropped into a chair, exhausted.

"Kate?" He pulled his eyebrows together in confusion as he chomped with his mouth open and flipped to a new page. "Last time I saw her she was heading over that hill behind the house." He smirked and looked up. "Now she thinks she's going to be an archeologist."

"Michael!" I jumped from my chair. "Why didn't you tell me this earlier?"

"You heard her say she wanted to study archeology."

"About her heading over the hill."

He splayed his hands. "You didn't ask."

"Yes! I did. You stood right there," I pointed to the side of the room, "and told me you knew nothing about where she'd gone. You even challenged me to look for a note because you said there was none."

Michael eyed me like I'd gone mad. "Are you okay? You must have dreamed that conversation." He sighed, exasperated. "Look, she packed her car to leave, then said she wasn't feeling well. That she might take a taxi instead. After lying down ... I don't know, a half-hour or so, I guess ... she said she needed fresh air and was going for a walk. There you have it. You must have dreamed the other exchange."

His words scorched into me. He looked so genuine, so earnest, that for a harrowing heartbeat I wondered if it could it be true. Had I dreamed it? I'd experienced so many dreams and voices and souls and odd occurrences in the past week that I wondered what was real and what wasn't.

Either way, I wouldn't get a different answer from Michael now anyway. Best to back off and approach him later. I turned and headed to my bedroom.

Behind me, Michael added, "She must have taken a taxi to the train. I'm kinda' sure I saw her do that. Before she left, I mean."

I plopped on the bed, exhausted. I should have thought about Kate and why she would leave *Crossings* without her car, or returning to the tunnels to search for the gold, or solving Mason's murder, or talking to Seth about his birth family.

But no, all I could think about was Clay.

I was honest with him regarding my feelings about Seth. But I wasn't honest about the depth of my feelings for *him*. He'd made me mad, doubting my maturity, questioning my decision-making, and it reminded me of when I first moved into *Crossings*. I'd been hiding things then. I wondered now if I was still hiding. Hiding behind feelings that I couldn't quite describe or define. Maybe I just hadn't used the right words or said the right things.

I closed my eyes to block the harsh light and replay our conversation in my mind.

Four hours passed before I opened my eyes again.

I hadn't meant to fall asleep. I awoke with a start and looked at the clock. *Eleven thirty!* Scrambling off the bed, I donned Grandma Sadie's cross necklace on top of the gold coin and snuck out of the house. Despite Michael's half-believable, half-normal behavior tonight, I had to move forward with my plans to save him from Fergus.

As I headed to my car to retrieve the lantern and the shovel, I faced northeast toward Williamsport. The moon reflected off the slow moving river. Outdoor pole lights dotted the landscape. The town slept, and I wished I could too. I'd loved to have stayed in bed instead of facing the task ahead.

CHAPTER 23

Minutes later, I stood inside the door to the root cellar, lantern in one hand, shovel in the other. I heard nothing but the sound of my pounding heart.

As before, the limited lighting daunted me. When your vision is impaired, your other senses take over. The smell and feel of the dank earth wrapped around me, making me feel as though I was *in* the earth, like a grave. This time, I didn't know Fergus's whereabouts. Michael was asleep when I left the apartment. I'd heard him snoring. *Could demonic souls continue possession while their victims slept?* For the first time, I hoped so.

At the point where the tunnel broke off in two directions, I turned left, intent on getting to that centermost tunnel where I believed the gold might be hidden. I had to find and remove it before Fergus could claim it.

Perhaps my imagination ran wild, or dread enveloped me at the thought that Fergus had inhabited this side of the tunnels for the past century, but the air smelled fouler than the other side. Dizziness hit me.

I stopped and leaned into a wall, trying to compose myself, hoping to keep my wits about me. If I encountered Fergus, then what? What protection did I have? I dipped back in my memory to the words from Ephesians about preparing to battle with evil. Why hadn't I taken the time to pray and bone up with a refresher before I headed here tonight?

Mason's advice about ghosts having limited mobility came to mind, as did Pastor Dale's comment that ghosts can't kill. Their powers are limited to haunting and harming. It was the harm part that worried me now.

Unfortunately, he'd also said that because ghosts have already been killed, they can't be killed again.

So what would I do if I met up with Fergus? I was alone here; Eva was gone.

The icy comprehension of what lie ahead spread through me and my body locked in fear. "God, help me," I cried, into the darkness, into the coldness, into the bleak nothingness that faced me.

As if in response, my whole body shook. It started at my head and reverberated down my entire core. Thoughts of an earthquake flitted through my mind, but as soon as I formed the thought, the shaking stopped.

The next thing I remember, I moved with speed and strength through the tunnels. Like something had taken hold of my body, and my movements were not my own.

Ignoring the rooms along the way, I stole through the tunnels.

Right. Running.

Left. Running.

Then right again, and reached the center area in less than a minute.

I'd memorized the tapestry location of the cream-colored stone, so I sprinted to where I believed that spot to be and set the lantern on the ground.

Like a crazed woman, I began digging, no concern of what was behind or around me.

All I focused on was digging.

I never experienced such strength before. Even as I dug, I marveled that under different circumstances, I would have taken two breaks by the time I dug as much as I had.

Was this what the fireman ghost referred to as "super-human strength"?

Or, was it pure panic-driven adrenaline kicking in?

It didn't matter. I just kept digging.

Tossing the dirt.

Digging.

Tossing more dirt.

Digging.

Heaving. Sweating. Sighing. Switching hands on the shovel.

Digging.

Hitting something!

I threw the shovel to the side and fell to my knees, clawing and scraping the dirt with my hands.

Until I reached something different than earth. A cloth! Burlap? A bag?

I yanked at it, but it wouldn't come loose. I needed to know what the object was before I spent more time attempting to free it, so I worked my fingers through the folds, found an opening, cringed, and plunged my fingers into the unknown.

Hard, round, thin cylinders. It had to be the gold coins!

I heard myself laughing and crying nonsensical sounds.

"Well now, there ya' go. I knew you'd been lyin.'"

Startled, I screamed and whirled around so fast I fell from my knees onto my butt. My heart thumped like a drum.

I looked up to see Greasy Jim holding a flashlight and switchblade over me. He licked his yellow teeth as a sneer crossed his face.

I barely had time to register his intent before another figure came up behind him.

Fergus!

Oblivious to the soul sneering at him, Greasy Jim continued. "You done good. I was getting tired of waitin' on that hill but figured it was just a matter of time. Now just keep digging and get the rest—"

Before he could finish his command, Fergus reached out with a hand that morphed into a huge claw. He crushed and lifted Greasy Jim, then hurled him against the beams in the corner of the ceiling.

I saw pain and horror on Greasy Jim's face before he soared through the air like a rag doll slammed against concrete. As you might expect a doll to fall, so did he, into a misshapen lump, his right leg and arm both bent in the wrong direction, his neck cocked at a worrisome angle.

Fergus didn't even look in the direction of where he'd tossed Greasy Jim.

Instead, his gaze burned into me.

"Some idiots never learn, do they, Ms. MacKenna?" I knew he was referring to both his earlier encounter with Greasy Jim as Michael, and to *me*. "Now, as that idiot was saying, well done."

Fergus's eyes transfixed me, and I sat there as vulnerable as a ground creature before the snake's strike. Terror entered every cell of my body.

He grinned, and a diabolical sparkle flickered in his eyes. Joy at my precarious status showed on his face. "Just when I was getting quite tired and may I say bored with you, you change course and make my work easier." He laughed. It was sinister, threatening. "Or should I say, you've made your dear cousin's work easier."

I don't know from where my strength—or perhaps stupidity—originated, but I found myself responding, my voice steady. "You're not going to use Michael anymore. This gold isn't yours. It's mine now."

He startled for a moment, before throwing back his head and laughing, a diabolical series of sounds. Then he screamed. Or howled. I couldn't tell which. It was unholy and unearthly, his rage fierce. "You are a fool to challenge me. You are not leaving these tunnels alive."

"No!" I shuddered at what spewed out of my mouth. "You can't kill me. You can't harm me either." *Where had these words come from, given that I believed him quite capable of hurting me?* As though my body functioned under a different set of commands other than my own, I scrambled to my feet, never losing eye contact. "You're just a pathetic excuse for a man."

Why was I saying these things?

I stepped closer to Fergus.

What made me do that?

"The little boy from New Orleans. Son of a poor scrubwoman. Rejected by his father, and then, Josiah. Full of self-pity. Grew up to make people pay for his misfortunes. Lying. Deceiving. Stealing what he couldn't earn. Even another man's wife."

How could I know all that?

In that moment, several expressions flashed across Fergus's face. He looked shocked. Curious. Fearful. Furious.

Was I reading him correctly? Where had my words come from, and why did he step back as though leery of me?

He puffed out his chest and said, "William. We meet again."

CHAPTER 24

As I started to swing around to see what he was talking about, I felt a sensation and instinctively threw my hand to my upper chest and neck, inadvertently covering the coin and cross necklaces in my effort. My skin prickled, and my body reverberated and, I don't know how else to explain this, but out of me stepped Will.

Right. Out. Of. My. Body.

I gasped and stumbled back from the strain that his departure caused.

Will! Just as I remembered him. Handsome. Shoulder-length hair. Beard stubble. Green eyes. Lean, strong face. Tattered Southern uniform.

"Will!" I gasped. "But how?"

In my elation, I forgot about Fergus and reached for Will, but he stretched out an arm and shoved me behind him, never saying a word or taking his gaze off Fergus.

"Ahhhh, such a pleasant reunion." Fergus's voice dripped sarcasm. "You're never at the meeting site, comrade, so I thought you'd moved on. How many times must I get rid of you?"

"Once is all you get ... comrade," he said the last word with disgust. "You and I both know that your strength is no match, so it's you that will be leaving. And might I say, I pity you for what's ahead."

As Will talked, I remembered my cross necklace that hung overlapping with my gold coin, and removed the former from my neck. From behind him, I thrust it toward Fergus the way that Will had taught me to do when we'd combated his dead wife, Naomi, in Georgia.

Fergus laughed, one of those disgusting, demonic, guttural laughs. "Your little girlfriend wants to help. Even she doubts your abilities.

What a fool you are, Ms. MacKenna. Don't you know that only works on vampires?"

"She's right," Will said. "That, and the right plea will bring all the assistance we need to destroy you forever."

Fergus sobered and looked at me. "You're a fool to trust—"

"Stop!" Will ordered. "It's over for you now, Fergus. This is your end. You have failed, and Lucifer knows it."

Fergus's look turned to fear, and his hand shot out toward me.

Will interceded and batted Fergus away, then grabbed the lantern. He yelled something, but all that registered with me at the time was "command" and "glory" and "proceed" and "Hell." Then he shattered the lantern glass, reached into the flame and somehow pulled out what looked like a rope of fire, but without the rope! It was almost three or four yards long. Will flung it like a bullwhip at Fergus, and when it reached its target, it coiled around him several times.

Will grabbed me and threw me to the ground, wrapping himself around me, shielding me like an airbag.

When the rope of fire tethered Fergus, he stumbled back and howled in agony, then issued a series of blasphemous curses. "You fool," he wailed, and I could tell he glared at me. "You stupid, ignorant little girl. You think this ends it? It's only begun. You have no idea what you've done."

Before our eyes, Fergus changed, slowly, grotesquely. His body spotted over, then turned sickly yellow, then skeletal. His frame began to hunch, and his face melted. His eyes emptied to mere sockets, and his teeth disappeared.

His bony structure howled out a final despairing scream as of someone falling into a bottomless pit. I flung my hands across my ears to block the hideous wail as it gorged through the tunnels. Despite the brutal heat from the fire, shivers coursed through my body.

Before the wail ended, dark cloaked figures swirled into the room. They looked ghastly, with hollowed faces, no eyes, no mouth, and moved in on Fergus like they intended to devour him.

Will thrust us both to our feet and said, "Trust me!" He bent and swept the gold into his hands and looked as though he was going to step into me again.

"Will, no! What about him?" I pointed to Greasy Jim.

Will cursed, hesitated, as though not wanting to leave the gold unattended. But then he tossed it aside and stepped into me again.

As one, we raced to Greasy Jim, picked him up and threw him over my shoulder. He felt no heavier than a blanket or a shawl I might have draped on.

Next, we grabbed a lantern and ran. Faster than I'd ever moved before. As I reached the end of the next tunnel, an explosion rocked the entire hillside. I looked back to see a red and orange glow, as flickers of light burst into hellish, scary flames. Then the smell hit me. The fire and smoke had nowhere to go but toward us.

I began to cough. My eyes burned and teared up, but I couldn't rub them because I held Greasy Jim in my arms. If Will hadn't been using me to move, I think I might have fallen and died right there.

Using his strength, I kept moving, but I felt my face burn and my hair singe.

Things fluttered over my feet and from the sound I determined it was rats! Dozens of them racing away from the smoke. Then bats. Everywhere. Vying with us to get out as fast as possible.

As we reached the tunnel door, another figure stepped in front of us, out of nowhere, flashlight in hand, and a sack of something on his shoulder. He kicked at the door. In the light of the fire that raced our way, I could see his features.

Clay!

In that instant, he registered my presence too, and his gaze dropped to take in the man on my shoulder. His gaze cut back to me, shocked. Black soot covered his face and shoulders, but I could still make out his expression. He turned and kicked again, shoving the door the rest of the way open and hurried outside.

I followed.

Once the fresh air hit me, I continued a few yards, dropped to my knees and lowered Greasy Jim on the ground. I watched as Clay limped a few yards, fell to his knees and emptied his arms too. Just beyond him, I saw a figure watching us. I was about to look away, not caring who stood there, when the light of the flames illuminated a man.

Holland Greer.

Too exhausted to care, I gulped for air, trying to empty my lungs of the smoke. I collapsed and the world darkened.

In that foggy blackness, Will came to me. We hugged and talked, the exchange occurring something like this:

Me: "Will! You came back! But how? You said it was impossible!"

Will: "I never left, Grace. I was with you all this time."

And in his words I heard the same voice I'd heard in Holland's house and when discussing the tunnels with Braxton. I assumed without him telling me, that he had centered his energy in the gold coin that I wore, and had left my body to drift open the basement door in the library and to shake the secret room at Holland's house. He'd been there when Seth kissed me at the bandstand in Virginia, and when Fergus reached for my neck at the shed in Antietam.

Me: "So you saw Braxton? And Eva? Together?"

Will: "You helped them. You showed much courage. Jack and your mother were proud too."

Me: "Jack? Mom? I miss them so much. But I have Michael now. What about him? Will he be okay now? And what about Fergus? If you never left, then maybe he's still here too and—"

Will: "No, Grace, he's gone. Forever. You saw the demons yourself. You saw how they—"

Me: "Devoured him. That's what happened, isn't it?"

Will: "Yes. He won't bother you anymore."

Me: "Then Michael will be okay?"

Will: "I don't know. Fergus had already taken such hold of him. It was quite destructive on Michael's body when Fergus left. There may not have been enough of Michael left to fight his way back."

Me: "But he has to be okay! All this can't have been for nothing."

Will: "It's not in our hands. There will be time to focus on that later after we've secured the gold. For now, you need to wake up and deal with something more pressing."

He left, replaced by the chaos around me. My eyes opened, closed, then opened again.

A commotion of voices came from my left, sirens from the right. Flashing lights competed with the flames to illuminate the hillside.

I pulled to a sitting position and looked back toward the tunnels. Lit from their bowels, they turned the black sky a yellowish orange.

Silhouetted against the flames, firefighters hustled about, attacking the fire. Dozens of them. They yelled, and scrambled hoses here and there. From what I could hear, the firefighters didn't know how, or what, to fight. Confusion reigned as to *what* was on fire and what prompted it since the tunnels were mostly composed of dirt. They were hesitant to fight a force they couldn't see, and I understood that so well.

Later, I would learn that the explosion rocked nearby Williamsport, which, of course, prompted investigation. That led to residents spotting a huge conflagration across the Potomac River. Within minutes, Williamsport fire and rescue personnel responded as well as half of Martinsburg's units, from the south.

When I could sit without falling over, I looked at Clay. EMTs hovered over him as he sat on the ground, elbows on bent knees, hands splayed through his hair.

Will had said I needed to wake to deal with something more pressing. Panicked that Clay was hurt, I yelled his name as I staggered to my feet and raced the distance between us.

He heard me and stood as I reached him.

"Thank God you're okay." I flung myself into him and cried as I patted his chest, arms and face, making sure he wasn't burned or bruised. As I searched him, I kept crying. "You're okay. You're okay."

But when I met his gaze, he still looked stricken. He shook me tenderly as though to bring me out of my stupor.

"Grace, listen to me."

I saw grief in his eyes the instant before it hit me that the EMTs hadn't been working on him at all, but rather at what— *or whom!*—he'd placed on the ground. I tried to break free.

"No, Grace, wait!" Clay yelled above the noise and tried to secure a hold on my arms.

I jerked loose and dropped to my knees.

A body! Covered by a sheet, head to toe.

I grabbed the sheet and jerked it back.

Kate!

A sob rippled at my throat and built its way to a full-fledged wail.

"No, no, no," I cried as Clay dropped to his knees and pulled me into his arms.

I don't know how long we knelt there. I just know that he held me for as long as it took to exchange horror and sorrow.

We said nothing. There *were* no words. What could be said anyway?

Nothing would change the fact that Kate was dead.

CHAPTER 25

Several hours later, I sat in a hallway at the City Hospital in Martinsburg. Kate's body was taken to the morgue awaiting autopsy, although I'd already learned the coroner determined time of death as about seven or eight hours earlier. Greasy Jim lay in surgery. Clay was being examined in the emergency room. Michael—whom firefighters found passed out on the lawn between the house and the tunnel—lay in a coma in ICU, to my right.

Someone handed me hot tea.

Someone else plopped a pillow behind my back.

Detective Somebody-or-Other peppered me with questions. He wanted answers that made sense. Explanations that proved conclusive. Pieces to a puzzle he was instructed to complete.

I had little of that to offer him.

He said it seemed odd that I'd be in the tunnels, and I wanted to respond that it seemed odd he called himself a detective since he didn't *detect* any of this in advance. He showed up now, *after* the damage, and tried to piece things together. Why didn't he detect that Kate needed help? Why didn't he detect all this earlier and save us hurt and pain?

But I didn't say that. None of it was his fault.

Instead, I just kept repeating the truth: "I don't really know what happened."

Because I didn't.

Not *really*.

I didn't know why Pastor Dale said demons cannot kill people.

Or why Holland Greer was there, or Greasy Jim. Why tonight?

Or what brought Clay to the tunnels.

Or why Fergus mentioned a meeting site to Will or screamed that this merely began—not *ended*—things.

Or why the fire spread or what the tunnels looked like now, or why the tapestry had depicted a tunnel that ran off to the side that I had earlier chosen to ignore.

Or what remained of my home.

Or why Kate was in the tunnels.

Or why she had to die.

Of course, I didn't tell the detective any of that.

"That's it for now," he said, rising from the chair beside me and studying his tablet. "I've talked with Clay Baxter. I'll have to wait to talk with Michael Rosenburg and James Bender. Assuming, they survive."

I flinched as much at hearing Greasy Jim's surname as I did the detective's calloused words, *if they survive*. It made Greasy Jim human, rather than the criminal and ogre that he was. As for Michael, I couldn't fathom life without him.

Seeing my reaction, the detective said, "Yeah, eh, sorry. Forgot Rosenburg was related to you. Anyway, the deceased's—"

"She has a name."

He checked his notes. "Uh, yeah, Kate Fletcher's family has been notified. I suggest you find somewhere to stay for a while. Your apartment suffered extensive damage. The fire inspector won't want you around until he's done." He shook his head in wonder. "Amazes me that old house survived."

Doesn't surprise me a bit.

"And don't leave town. We have a dead woman ... err, Ms. Fletcher ... downstairs," he yanked a thumb over his shoulder toward the stairwell, as though I wasn't painfully aware of where Kate was, "and we need to figure out why. I have your cell number. I advise you to answer my calls. And, you call me," he said, tucking a business card in my hand, "if you think of anything."

He turned and left.

Sometime later, I don't know how long, I looked up to see Seth approach from my left, at the same time that Clay arrived via the stairwell to my right.

DL KOONTZ

I looked at them both and felt nothing. Just numb. Before either could say a word, I looked away and spoke in the steadiest voice I could manage. "I'm not going anywhere until I know Michael will be alright. I don't have answers for you. And I want to be alone. Please."

Seth nodded. He'd known Kate, spent time with her, entertained her flirtation. So I wasn't surprised he didn't say anything. He looked stricken.

Clay looked beleaguered too. He had never met Kate, but he'd found and tried to save her. Still, he forged on, despite our collective stupor, to add some sanity and practicality: "Stay as long as you need to."

He fished two twenty-dollar bills from his wallet and handed them to me. "For food. Mom's giving me a ride to my truck, at your place. I'll take Tramp and Chubbs to her house."

My pets! I'd forgotten about them in the commotion. The detective said the apartment suffered damage. What if they—

Clay read my expression and pumped a palm. "They're fine. I got there ahead of the fire department, so I ran to the apartment first, looking for you. When no one answered, I went inside and grabbed them. Put them in my truck."

He hesitated. In a hoarse voice, he added, "Then I searched for you outside. I heard commotion near the root cellar. I had no idea what I'd find." He swallowed. "Your friend? In the dark of the tunnel, I thought at first it was you."

He looked away before clearing his throat and gazing back. "Mom has empty rooms. You can stay there."

I nodded. Then, not because I necessarily meant it—because I didn't feel *anything* at the moment—but rather because it was the polite thing to do, I said, "Thanks."

"I'm sorry." He turned to leave.

At my neck, the gold coin vibrated, as though Will asked to be remembered, to have Clay take him home.

"Wait!" I hurried off the chair and moved to Clay, pulling the two necklaces from my neck. "When you get to *Crossings*," I said, placing the coin in his palm, "please put this ... in the piano bench ... since the house seems to be okay." I tried to keep my voice steady, positive. "For safe keeping, of course. It's very special. And take this too." I handed him the cross. "But give it to Cassie to return to me, please."

He looked confused, his gaze darting from the necklaces to my face. I figured he remembered, during our trip to Georgia earlier that summer that Will placed his center in that coin. When he opened his mouth to speak, I pulled him into an embrace and whispered in his ear.

The hug was brief and methodical, and when I pulled back, I saw understanding mixed with concern on his face. He studied me a moment, nodded, then exited down the stairwell.

I stumbled back to the chair and sat. Seth remained in the same spot, not saying a word, as though he were cemented to the floor and didn't know what to do about it.

Our eyes met, and he extended a hand. I clasped it, squeezed it, treasured its warmth and strength, but I didn't utter a word.

He mumbled, "I'll call you," then released my hand, touched my cheek, and left.

I sat there alone.

Waiting to hear about Michael.

Thinking about Kate.

And, *reliving* the last several hours and adding a few more unknowns to my list of unanswered questions: Why hadn't Will come out of hiding in the gold coin in time to help Michael and Kate? Why was he going to rescue the gold before helping Greasy Jim, a human being? Why, when I needed help the most for my own safety—at the pawn shop and on the street in Lexington—had another being assisted me, but not Will?

Yet, he had intervened each time it helped draw me closer to the gold—my conversation with Braxton about the tunnels, the drifting library door, the secret room at Holland's house, my neck when Fergus reached for it at Antietam. All of these instances helped to hurry along my effort to find the gold, as though Will was driven by that, rather than my well-being or that of others.

And what had Will meant when he said Fergus was rejected by

Josiah? The only Josiah I ever heard about was Josiah Sawyer, the suspected occultist who built the original *Crossings*. Could that be to whom Will referred? How would Will know the extent of such rejection?

Then again, was it Will who had prompted me to go into Hilson's Emporium, and interrupted my kiss with Seth, and announced Eva's location to Braxton? None of those incidences seemed to have selfish, ulterior motives. Or had they all been prompted by my intuition? Or God?

With the gold coin returned to *Crossings*, I'd have time to think undisturbed about these questions, although that wasn't my reason for sending it with Clay. The truth was that I didn't want to take it into Cassie's house and place her in jeopardy.

I'd sent the cross with Clay to protect him from what I now suspected dwelled in the coin.

And when I whispered in Clay's ear, I asked him to put the coin at Will's tombstone in the cemetery over the ridge, near where we first kissed, rather than in the piano bench inside the house.

Why? Just in case my budding hunch was correct, that Pastor Dale had been right on two counts: (1) I never should have talked to the dead, and (2) My beloved Will was a cunning, charming, and dangerous demon in disguise, masquerading himself in a convincing cloak of righteousness.

And, I had fallen right into his elaborate trap.

The End ... for now.

Escaping from the Abyss

Book III in The Crossings Trilogy

by D.L. Koontz

When you look into the abyss, the abyss also looks into you.

—Friedrich Nietzsche

Brimstone
Fiction

$\mathcal{P}rologue$

M y mother once told me the past can steal your future if you're not careful. It's true. I allowed it to rob me of my seventeenth year.

But what do you do when the past won't stay behind you? How do you move on when memories and even ghosts literally step into your present and demand attention?

Last year, I escaped Boston to move alone into *Crossings*, the estate I inherited from my stepfather in the remote mountains of West Virginia. As imparted in two previous memoirs, I encountered souls from the past haunting my house, and my "subtle vision" matured, enabling me to interact with them, too.

The second memoir proved hardest to pen because my cousin, Michael, suffered at the grip of a demonic soul, part of my estate burned in a fiery explosion, and worst of all, my friend, Kate Fletcher, died.

At first, I attributed her death to paranormal activity since ghosts were part of the backdrop of my life, and her body had been found at the time of the fire. However, the detective investigating her death called two days later and dispelled that concern.

"Uh, yeah," he said as though paying little attention to the conversation he initiated. The sounds of crinkling tinfoil came across the line. "We, uh, we got the coroner's report back on the deceased."

The back of my neck prickled at his word choice. "You mean Kate Fletcher."

"Umm, yar der—"

"Excuse me?"

The sounds of swallowing and a whoosh of liquid came over the line.

"Sorry ... eating ... ton o' calls to make. The deceased ... that is, Ms. Fletcher died from a meningococcal infection."

"A what?"

"She died from meningitis."

Meningitis? How could that be? I wrapped my free arm across my front, suppressing a shiver as a whisper of shame unfurled in my stomach. I'd thought her death was all about me, but it was all about *her*. Why hadn't I detected she was ill? She had endured achiness, fatigue, chills, and headaches in the week leading to her death.

"Hello?" His voice roused me from my thoughts, but the queasy sensation in my stomach remained.

"I'm here."

"Thought I lost you. Coroner said meningitis is a bacterial infection. Attacks the brain and spinal cord. Acts like the flu but can kill within 24 hours. Talked to her mother already. Mrs. Fletcher will be picking up her things."

"Kate's things?"

"In the trunk of her car. At your house. Clothes, toiletries, passport, stuff like that. You said she talked about visiting her sister in Richmond. Her sister confirmed those plans. Figure she must have packed for a visit, but decided to explore the grounds before leaving. For whatever reason, probably pure curiosity, she went into the tunnels, but never made it out."

"And nothing prevented her from coming back out?" I cringed at my own question, but I needed to know.

"She didn't die of smoke inhalation if that's what you're wondering. No signs of force anywhere. She simply collapsed and died before anyone found her. Coroner said she'da been dead no matter where she dropped."

I gripped the phone in a vice grip and tried to remain calm at his callousness. "Thank you. I appreciate the call."

"Sure, sure. She's being laid to rest tomorrow, I understand. Now you can attend, relax, and enjoy yourself, knowing that no one intentionally harmed her."

Heat prickled along my cheekbones. "It's a funeral, not a party."

"Yeah, well, in my line of work you'd be surprised how often suspects don't separate the two."

"Suspect? Are you saying I'm suspected of something?" The fire chief had closed the case on the fire since there was no sign of arson and no insurance money involved. Why would I be suspected of anything?

"I'm saying things aren't resolved at the house, and I think you know it. I'm going to share my files with the local sheriff. But I'll be keeping my eyes on all this."

When I clicked off the call, I vowed to keep as low a profile as possible.

I should have been relieved that paranormal activity was not involved in Kate's death, but I was left desolate, hollowed out in ways I wondered if I'd ever settle, and thus began a year of mourning and self-imposed seclusion. For six months, September through March, I grieved and blamed myself for not recognizing her symptoms as dire. Guilt plagued me. I had been distracted during her visit by supernatural activity. I wandered through the tunnels after she went missing, but the labyrinth was so expansive and inky black, I passed her body without realizing she laid there.

After the fire, Michael and I fled *Crossings*. He recovered and relocated closer to work, forty-five minutes from me while I moved into my friend Cassie's garage apartment across the river in Williamsport, Maryland. The new locale soothed me like aloe on a burn as the diversions of town life wafted to my windows, reminding me that life moved on: the rich aroma of coffee brewing at the café next door, music pounding from passing vehicles, and the laughter of children passing as they scampered to school. Those reminders of life sustained me, even as my own life went stagnant.

I haven't much to report about my period of mourning. I spent little time with my friend, Adriana, and even less with Clay and Seth, both local young men I'd grown to love. My history and romantic feelings for them were sweet *and* bittersweet. And confusing.

I plodded through homeschool classes online but otherwise excused myself from social functions, avoided commitments, eschewed dates with Seth, and ignored my promise to Clay's dead father's ghost to resolve his murder.

After six months of this hermit-like life, on a cold day in March, Michael and my friends—Cassie, Adriana and her family, Seth, and Pastor Dale—staged an intervention and demanded I return to the pulse of life. In an attempt to appease them and keep them at bay, I made an effort (although, if pushed, I couldn't name much I did) and agreed to move back to *Crossings* when I turned eighteen, six long months away. It struck me as a safe pledge to make at the time.

These promises and half-hearted undertakings also resulted in me working part-time at Hilson's Antique Emporium. I first met Hilda Hilson the week before the fire when I discovered her shop in Williamsport, although I had bee-lined it out of there after she demonstrated an unusual interest in me.

Let me begin my story at this half-hearted step out of my seclusion, shortly after the intervention and when I returned to Hilda's shop. A chance encounter that day proved to stick with me, even brewed in me, for months until my eighteenth birthday when I finally was thrust back into life and endured my final showdown against certain souls—these rulers of darkness and spiritual forces of evil, plaguing my estate and my life.

www.ingramcontent.com/pod-product-compliance
Lightning Source LLC
Chambersburg PA
CBHW031947170626
46807CB00006B/2390